Ber

# American Contributions to Chemistry

Anatiposi

**Benjamin Silliman**

# American Contributions to Chemistry

Reprint of the original, first published in 1874.

1st Edition 2023 | ISBN: 978-3-38250-206-5

Anatiposi Verlag is an imprint of Outlook Verlagsgesellschaft mbH.

Verlag (Publisher): Outlook Verlag GmbH, Zeilweg 44, 60439 Frankfurt, Deutschland
Vertretungsberechtigt (Authorized to represent): E. Roepke, Zeilweg 44, 60439 Frankfurt, Deutschland
Druck (Print): Books on Demand GmbH, In de Tarpen 42, 22848 Norderstedt, Deutschland

# AMERICAN CONTRIBUTIONS TO CHEMISTRY.

## AN ADDRESS

DELIVERED ON THE OCCASION OF THE

CELEBRATION OF THE CENTENNIAL OF CHEMISTRY,

AT NORTHUMBERLAND, PA.,

August 1, 1874.

BY
BENJAMIN SILLIMAN,
OF YALE COLLEGE.

[Reprinted from the American Chemist for August-September and December, 1874.]

PHILADELPHIA:
COLLINS, PRINTER, 705 JAYNE STREET.
1874.

# AMERICAN CONTRIBUTIONS TO CHEMISTRY.*

---

*Introduction.*—The history of modern chemistry, commencing with Priestley's immortal discovery of oxygen, or dephlogisticated air as he called it, on the 1st of August, 1774, by a memorable coincidence is almost identical in date with the evolution of the United States of America out of their colonial pupilage by the declaration of their independence of the mother country. The emancipation of our science from the dominion of phlogiston, with its seductive but false philosophy, may be likened to the overthrow of aristocratic traditions, and monarchical supremacy, under which our ancestors were held, and the building up of the American system of self-government in their place. We note with satisfaction that the scientific revolution was a little in advance of the political revolution; and it would not be a difficult task to show, were it pertinent to our present purpose to do so, how closely and logically the rapid march of human society, the world over, during the century whose close we celebrate to-day, has kept pace with and waited upon the advance of the pioneers of scientific discovery. How Franklin and Black, Rumford and Cavendish, Priestley and Lavoisier, Galvani and Volta, Scheele and Berzelius, Dalton and Davy, Ampère and Faraday, Hare and Henry, Oersted and the Herschels, Liebig, Agassiz, and a multitude more of the noble army of martyrs to science, who have devoted their lives to the search for truth for the truth's sake, have, by the discovery and

* In attempting to comply with the invitation of the committee in charge of the Chemical Centennial at Northumberland, to prepare an "Essay upon American Contributions to Chemistry" as an address to be delivered on that occasion, I found the "Essay" insensibly and almost unavoidably assuming the historical form, and taking a wider range than may seem consistent with a strict rendering of its title. But such as it became it is now presented as a slight contribution toward a more elaborate historical discourse which yet remains to be prepared. B. S.

elucidation of principles before unknown or but dimly discerned, opened the way for the yet greater army of inventors and projectors, who have followed in their lead; with steam engines, railways, steamships, mechanical spinning and weaving, voltaic casting of metals, bleaching and other chemical arts without number, electric telegraphs, illumination by gas, photography, improved agriculture, artificial heat and artificial cold; using and applying in endless forms for human advancement, the public wealth, and private enjoyment the labors of those who have toiled to reveal the hidden truths of God in nature, too often unrequited for their self-sacrificing devotion in the good things of this world, but content to work that others might enter into their labors.

Among the greatest discoveries of modern times, comparable to the discovery of the law of gravitation itself in the previous century, was the discovery of oxygen by Priestley, August 1, 1774, which we are here to honor this day. What Newton's discovery did for celestial mechanics, in bringing order out of confusion, and co-ordinating things before beyond our reach, has Priestley's discovery done for the former chaotic confusion of facts in chemistry inherited from alchemy and the iatro-chemists, but impotent to explain the constitution of the universe of matter, for the want of the philosophy to which a knowledge of oxygen was the key.

In attempting to review the contributions to our science at the hands of American investigators during the century we celebrate to-day, it is proper in bar of criticism to say that I was called at a very late hour to the task in hand, and have become more sensible as the work opened before me of the disproportion between the brief time at command and the extent of the task assigned me. If important omissions are detected—and that there are such can hardly be doubted—the speaker must beg of his fellow workers in the common field some indulgence, as is due to human frailty; and while he is conscious of a desire to do full justice to the labors of all, he has also the knowledge that all among living laborers have not responded to his call for co-operation.

If an apparently undue proportion of space has been given to some portions of the historical part of our essay, it may be said in fairness that it is far easier and more just to write history than to anticipate it, and we who live in this latter end of the first century of modern chemistry must see to it that we leave such footprints in the sands of our time, that the future historian of the science cannot fail to do us justice.

In considering the contributions to chemistry made in the United States, the subject naturally divides itself under two subdivisions—the historical and the contemporaneous contributions.

Under the first division we may consider very briefly the scientific societies, public seminaries of learning, and channels of communication which were open to the investigators and students of science during the latter part of the last and the commencement of the present century. In doing this it will be convenient and in order to consider to some extent the work done in those times of which records exist. If some of it seems to us not very important, we must remember that such was then the case the world over, with a few brilliant exceptions, and of such exceptions I think it will appear that we have our full share.

*Learned Societies.*—Of societies devoted to scientific purposes, and which have left us any published memoirs or transactions, we find very few prior to the close of the last century.

In New England there was "The American Academy of Arts and Sciences," at Boston, instituted in 1780. "The Connecticut Academy of Arts and Sciences," established at New Haven in 1799, and, oldest of all, we find in Philadelphia "The American Philosophical Society," established by Benjamin Franklin in 1743, and recognized by provincial charter in 1769. This completes the brief list of learned societies instituted prior to the close of the last century which have published anything. The Literary and Philosophical Society of New York, which published a single volume in the early part of this century, had but a brief existence, and its volume of memoirs contains only one paper on chemistry.

*Some of the Men Prominent in Early Scientific History in the United States.*—In the history of science during the latter half of the last century we find prominent the names of Franklin, Rumford, and Priestley; the first two Americans by birth and education, the latter by sympathy and adoption. In the evening of his peaceful and philosophic life Priestley was a refugee from a strange intolerance and persecution which has left a stain upon the good name of England.

FRANKLIN was the founder of the American Philosophical Society in 1743, the oldest of all the scientific societies of America; he was also the originator of the University of Pennsylvania, and of the Public Library in Philadelphia. He was the president of the Philosophical Society after its charter in 1769 until his death in 1790. His own scientific researches were chiefly physical, and his labors as an investigator had mainly ceased prior to the dawn of our chemical century. But his tastes and well-grounded love of all knowledge and of all investigation into the laws of nature, made him to the last a devoted student and the zealous patron of all departments of science. He died just before Priestley's arrival in America, but in London, many years before, they had been associated in electrical investigations, and Priestley's History of Electricity was undertaken by the advice of Franklin, to whom the manuscript was submitted for criticism.

RUMFORD, whose scientific reputation is sure to grow with the passage of time, as it has done indeed constantly since his death, after imbibing from Dr. Williams, his instructor, a love for mathematics and the exact sciences, while yet a boy; and from the lectures of Dr. Winthrop, at Harvard, his early love for physical and chemical research was, by the force of circumstances over which he had no control, in a sense expatriated and forced into a position of disloyalty to the Republican cause. His life reads like a romance. We find him, after a term of service as a British officer, passing into the position of confidential adviser of the King of Bavaria, and in full charge of matters military, administrative, and philanthropic, with a field of usefulness and a rôle of honor seldom awarded to a humble born citizen of a foreign land. Yet amid all his great official cares and preoccupations, and his honors, social, military, and political, he was ever loyal to scientific research; embracing every occasion to glean new facts in the experience of daily life even when most oppressed with heavy public duties. This is everywhere evident in his memoirs. Thus, in the opening paragraph of the memoir which is undoubtedly on the whole his most important contribution to molecular physics, the research which first established on experimental grounds the relations of heat to motion,* he says, in his opening address to the Royal Society, in whose Transactions this remarkable paper first appeared: "It frequently happens that in the ordinary affairs and occupations of

* An Enquiry Concerning the Source of Heat which is Excited by Friction. Complete works, I. p. 471. Am. Academy edition.

life, opportunities present themselves of contemplating some of the most curious operations of nature. * * * I have frequently made this observation, and am persuaded that a habit of keeping the eyes open to everything that is going on in the ordinary business of life has often led, as it were by accident in the playful excursions of the imagination, put into action by contemplating the most common appearances, to useful doubts and sensible schemes for investigation and improvement, than all the more intense meditations of philosophers in the hours expressly set apart for study."

We claim Rumford as an American, and we look with the greatest satisfaction upon his scientific career and upon the character of his work, which in its method and expression is a model of elegance which will ever render his writings a classic in the literature of science. Let any young student who wishes to learn how physical and chemical truths are evolved by inductive research take up the study of almost any one of Rumford's memoirs—for example, that upon "the propagation of heat in fluids," in which, among other important data, the maximum density of water was first determined and the law of its unequal movements under equal variations of temperature first fixed by experiment—and he will find with what largeness of grasp and accuracy of detail the mind of this master marches upon the area of the unknown to take captive the facts of observation and marshal them in order to science. No writer of his time has left a nobler record of original power in physical science than Rumford. None in his time and for succeeding times has done more, and so well, to solve some of the toughest problems of social science than he.

Joseph Priestley's name is immortal in the annals of our century of chemistry. We are proud to claim him as an American by adoption, and are quite willing to adopt with him all his discoveries. A distinguished French Academician of this century once said, on presenting for the first time to the Academy of Sciences in Paris a memoir on the Law of Ohm, respecting electric conduction (long before accepted and familiar in Germany, but then first made known in France), "Truly, Mr. President, this is not a French discovery, but it is worthy to be made such!" So say we of Priestley and the discovery of oxygen: if it was not an American discovery, it is worthy to be made such. Whom England cast out with obloquy, we accepted with cordial hospitality. His heinous sins of republican ideas and hostility to an established church became virtues here, while his pure and blameless life, devoted during his later years, as in all his earlier career, to the cause of humanity and all truth, is his best defence against the charge of heresy which served as one poor factor in the indictment under which his house was destroyed by a mob, his apparatus, manuscripts, and library, the fruits of diligent years of research, consumed and scattered in the disgraceful riot at Birmingham in 1791, while he and his family fled for life to safer retreats. It is not part of my duty, agreeable as it might otherwise be, to draw the life and memorialize the scientific discoveries of Priestley. On this occasion that pleasing task falls to other and abler hands.

After his removal to the United States Dr. Priestley, re-established in the philosophic repose of his delightful home, here on the banks of the Susquehanna, again resumed his scientific studies. Here he completed his discovery of çarbonous oxide, and here he composed his later papers which are recorded in the early volumes of the American Philosophical Society's Transactions; and in Dr. Mitchill's Medical Repository. These contributions were largely devoted to sustaining the phlogistic theory, of which he remained to the last an ardent defender, notwithstanding his own researches, and especially the discovery of oxygen, had supplied the weapons with which the antiphlogistians triumphed. There are few more remarkable examples than his in the range of philosophy, of the power of a grand idea to maintain itself against the inevitable logic of facts—of the subtle power of a plausible but untenable hypothesis to lead captive the imagination and pervert the reasoning powers. Even the absurdity of taking refuge behind an assumed principle of *specific levity*, to which the disciples of Stahl were driven to avoid the unquestionable testimony of experiment, seemed not to stagger the faith of Priestley, who has shown himself the master of a powerful logic when dealing in the polemics of statesmanship and the church. But while we may wonder almost if the defender of phlogiston at Northumberland can be the same man who is the author of some of the most remarkable researches in chemistry in his time, we cannot but admire the charming spirit in which he conducted his controversies with Woodhouse, Green, McNevin, and Dr. Mitchill, a controversy which, begun as strangers personally, led to a warm and lasting friendship, especially with the latter chemist.

In his paper, read December 20, 1799, before the Philosophical Society at Philadelphia, entitled "Experiments on the change of place in different forms of air through several interposing substances," he recognizes distinctly, for the first time, the phenomena of gaseous diffusion, and demonstrates the facts by original and ingenious experiments. He did not, however, carry the research far enough to reach the *law* governing the phenomena, a generalization reserved for Graham in our time.

We have quoted from one of Prof. Dove's lectures the anecdote illustrating the spirit of the French Academician in his willingness to gallicize a German discovery. We all remember the recent controversy excited by the opening sentence in Ad. Wurtz's *Discours Préliminaire* prefixed to his Dictionary of Chemistry (1868): "*La chimie est une science française.*" While with certain qualifications it is true that modern chemistry has its starting-point with Lavoisier and his colleagues, still we cannot fail to recognize in this sweeping declaration the same spirit of appropriation, nor wonder at the animosity it excited in Kolbe and other German and English writers.

*Early Scientific Foundations.*—Of foundations for exclusively scientific purposes made in the latter part of the last century, we enumerate but four:—

1. That of Rumford to the American Academy in Boston.
2. The foundation of the Rumford Professorship out of the residue of Rumford's estate at Cambridge.
3. The Magellan foundation, given to the American Philosophical Society in Philadelphia.
4. The Erving Chemical Foundation at Cambridge.

In the year 1796, Benjamin Thompson, Count Rumford, made to the American Academy, at Boston, a donation of five thousand dollars three per cent. stock in the funds of the United States, the income of which was for the award of two medals every second year for original researches and a published memoir in any part of America, upon heat and light. (*Memoirs Am. Acad.*, II., 141, 1804.)

The history of this foundation is recorded in Dr. Ellis's charming Memoir of Rumford, lately published by the American Academy, pp. 250–268. It appears that the Academy, in discharge of its trust, caused, in 1799, advertisements to be published in all the principal cities of the United States, giving notice that they were prepared to award this honorable distinction to any worthy claimant who might be entitled to receive it. But it was not until the year 1839 that an occasion was found which was deemed by the Academy worthy of this honor; and it must ever be a source of just pride to the chemists of America, that in the year mentioned the Academy gave from the interest of the Rumford fund the sum of six hundred dollars to Dr. ROBERT HARE, of Philadelphia, in consideration of his invention of the compound blowpipe, and his improvements in the voltaic pile.

It may seem to some rather surprising that the Academy did not make the award to RUMFORD himself, in his lifetime, for his various discoveries respecting light and heat. They were probably restrained from doing so by a scrupulous regard for the literal terms of the trust; seeing, while Rumford was an American, he was not, during the time of his principal researches, resident in "any part of the continent of America."

This consideration need not restrain us, however, from doing honor to the American who demonstrated that heat was a mode of motion, more than a generation before the time of the modern philosophers to whom this discovery is often awarded.

In 1870 the Rumford Medal Fund had accumulated to upwards of thirty-seven thousand dollars, and by a decree of the Supreme Court, made under authority of the Massachusetts Legislature, the Academy was authorized to award Rumford medals annually; to add to such award a pecuniary grant for scientific work, not more than three hundred dollars in any one year, and to expend such further sums as in their discretion may seem best calculated to facilitate the making of discoveries and improvements which may merit the premiums to be by them awarded, etc. (*Life of Rumford*, p. 266.)

The "Life of Rumford" and "The Complete Works of Rumford," published by the American Academy of Arts and Sciences, now in progress, will probably fill five or six 8vo. volumes, of which Dr. Ellis's Life of Rumford is one. This and three volumes of the "Complete Works" are already published by the Academy. No American, since "Franklin's Life and Works" were printed, has received a more enduring scientific commemoration than this.

THE ERVING FOUNDATION of £1000, in 1791, for the endowment of the chemical chair in Harvard University, was, I believe, the earliest foundation of its kind in America. It is further noticed under the name of Aaron Dexter.

The Rumford Professorship at Harvard was, by the will of Rumford, declared to be founded "to teach by regular courses of academical and public lectures, accompanied by proper experiments, the utility of the physical and mathematical sciences, for the improvement of the useful arts, and for the extension of the industry, prosperity, happiness, and well-being of society." The "Rumford Fund" for this professorship amounted, in the books of the college treasurer in 1870, to $52,848. On this foundation, there have been four appointments, viz.:—

| | | |
|---|---|---|
| Dr. Jacob Bigelow, | from | 1816 to 1827. |
| Prof. Daniel Treadwell, | " | 1834 to 1845. |
| Prof. Eben N. Horsford, | " | 1847 to 1863. |
| D. Wolcott Gibbs, | " | 1863 to 1874. |

While chemistry was not a subject specified in the will of Rumford, it was so plainly congenial to his purposes, that the Rumford professor was in charge of the chemical work of the Lawrence Scientific School from 1847 until, quite recently, its incumbent, under the new *regime* at Harvard, has been remanded to the specific work of the foundation, and the chemical work has been placed under the direction of the Erving chemical chair.

The Rumford foundation has contributed to our American scientific literature, aside from the separate memoirs of its distinguished incumbents, some of which will have our attention hereafter among our chemical contributions, a volume entitled "Elements of Technology" (Boston, 1829), containing the lectures of Dr. Bigelow, delivered during his ten years of service on that foundation.

The Magellan Fund.—In January, 1786, Mr. J. H. de Magellan, of London (not to be confounded with the navigator Magalhaens, b. 1474, d. 1521, and after whom the Magellan Straits are named), gave to the American Philosophical Society the sum of two hundred guineas, to be vested in a permanent fund, the income of which was to awarded in medals of gold, with a specific inscription, in reward for original observations "in navigation or natural philosophy, mere natural history alone excepted." I have not found any award of this medal for researches in chemistry.

These are all the foundations of which I have observed any notice, for the encouragement of chemical and physical research, prior to the close of the eighteenth century, in this country.

*Chemistry in America prior to the Commencement of the present Century.*—Of public seminaries of learning, other than medical institutions, where chemistry was taught from a separate chair, and as a distinct branch of the college curriculum of instruction, prior to A. D. 1800, we find but one, and this distinction belongs to Nassau Hall, in Princeton, N. J. On the 1st of October, 1795, the day after the annual commencement in that year, the trustees of that institution elected Dr. JOHN MACLEAN Professor of Chemistry. He was a young chemist of Scotland, fresh from the instruction of Black and Hope and of the French School. But it is only just to add that Dr. Maclean, on the death of his colleague in the Chair of Mathematics and Natural Philosophy, assumed these duties in addition to those of chemistry. Dr. Maclean ever deserves honorable mention as one of the earliest and most successful teachers of our science in this country. Prof. Silliman in his reminiscences gratefully recognizes his obligations to Dr. Maclean and to Princeton. He says (vol. 1, p. 100, Fisher's Life), "I regard him as my earliest master in chemistry, and Princeton as my first starting-point in that pursuit." Dr. Maclean in 1812 accepted the chemical chair in William and Mary College in Virginia. In Paris Dr. Maclean had learned to admire the antiphlogistic theory, as the "new chemistry" of Lavoisier was then called, and which he taught and defended at Princeton.

In 1797 he published "Two Lectures on Combustion, supplementary to a Course of Lectures on Chemistry; read at Nassau Hall, containing an examination of Dr. Priestley's considerations on the Doctrine of Phlogiston and the Decomposition of Water." These lectures display both ability and learning, and form an interesting chapter in the history of the phlogistic discussion.

Dr. Maclean contributed several articles to the *N. Y. Medical Repository*, and his name is associated with that of Prof. Silliman in editing the first American edition of Henry's Chemistry in 1808.

Lectures on chemistry were given in connection with the Chairs of Physics or Natural Philosophy, and in the medical departments of several colleges at an earlier date than at Princeton.

*At William and Mary* the Right Rev. James Madison was Professor of Chemistry and Natural Philosophy as early as 1774.

*At the University of Pennsylvania* we find Dr. John Ewing filling the Chair of Natural Philosophy and Chemistry from 1779 to 1801.

*At Yale* a chemical chair was instituted in 1798, but no professor was appointed until 1803.

*At Columbia* it was resolved in 1800 that chemical instruction should be separately given as a condition for the bachelor's degree, but no professor was appointed until 1802.

In the other academic colleges we find that chemical instruction was commenced at Bowdoin in 1805 by Parker Cleaveland, who held the office to 1858; in South Carolina College in 1811; in Dickinson College in 1811, and at Brown University in the same year; at Dartmouth in 1820; in Rutgers in 1830, and in Williams in 1830.

In the medical colleges we find chemistry early recognized as a branch of the curriculum of medical study, but at first in connection with materia medica. Thus in—

| | |
|---|---|
| The University of Pennsylvania | in 1768. |
| King's (Columbia) College | " 1767. |
| Harvard College, Mass., | " 1782. |
| Dartmouth College, N H., | " 1798. |
| College of Medicine, Md., | " 1808. |

What kind of chemistry it was which was taught prior to the discovery of oxygen, it is easy to understand. and yet we must not suffer ourselves to undervalue the knowledge of those days. But of one thing we may be sure—we shall find little to detain us in examining the contributions to chemistry made in those early times. A few names of chemists stand out in bold relief on that distant background, but we find on examining the record that they shine rather by the brightness of their performances in other departments of knowledge than in chemistry. This is true of that eminent man, Dr. JOHN WINTHROP OF HARVARD, already named. Of the chemical work of his successors, Williams and Webber, if they did any, we have no record, and the same is true of AARON DEXTER, Prof. of Chemistry and Materia Medica at Cambridge from 1783 to 1806. But of the eminent abilities of JOHN GORHAM, who succeeded Dexter, we shall speak among the men of this century.

So in Philadelphia we find that eminent man, Dr. Benjamin Rush, elected to the chemical chair in the University of Pennsylvania, August 1, 1769, but we discover no record of his chemical work. He had been a student at Edinburgh, under the instruction of Dr. Joseph Black, and was an able expositor of the doctrines taught by the renowned Scotch teacher to whom belongs the honor of inaugurating the quantitative methods in chemistry, first set forth in his research into the difference between the so-called mild and caustic alkalies, in his well-known essay "De Magnesia Alba," in which he distinctly recognizes the function of carbonic acid, under the name of "fixed air." Dr. Rush was undoubtedly the first professor of chemistry in America, and as such his name must ever be entertained with respect, while he owes his well-earned reputation to his labors in other departments.

Dr. James Hutchinson, who succeeded Dr. Rush, had finished his studies in London, under the renowned Dr. John Fothergill, and that he had attained notable proficiency in the science of chemistry we must believe, from the fact that in the year 1774, the trustees of the Philadelphia College presented him with a gold medal "for his superior knowledge in chemistry," inscribed "Jacobus Hutchinson, 1774," and on the reverse, "Naturæ Artisque Arcana Retexi." After his death in 1793, the chair of chemistry was filled by the appointment of Dr. James Woodhouse, of whom more particular mention is made below.

I have been unable to find any original contributions by Dr. Hutchinson to our science. He lived amid the troubles of the American Revolution, and took an active part in the direction and organization of the medical department of the army under Washington, as well as in the local politics of Pennsylvania.

James Woodhouse was the Professor of Chemistry in the medical department of the University of Pennsylvania from 1795 to his death in 1809, succeeding Dr. Hutchinson; Dr. Priestley having declined the chair, to which he had been unanimously elected. Dr. Woodhouse was a frequent contributor to the *Medical Repository* of Dr. Mitchill, the *Medical Museum* of Dr. Coxe, and the American Philosophical Society, but his original investigations were few. His paper in answer to Dr. Priestley's arguments on the doctrine of phlogiston, which will be found in the *Am. Phil. Trans.* for 1794, p. 452, was sustained by well-devised experiments. He also, while in England in 1802, communicated to *Nicholson's Journal* (vol. ii.), "Experiments and observations on the vegetation of plants, to show that the common opinion of the amelioration of the atmosphere by vegetation in solar light is ill-founded." This paper was reproduced in the *Ann. de Ch. et Phys.*, xliii. 1802, p. 194, and in the same journal he published "An account of an experiment in which potash calcined with charcoal took fire on the addition of water, and ammoniacal gas was produced" (*Nicholson's Journal*, xxi. 1808, pp. 290, 291). He was, I think, the first to demonstrate, by several comparative experiments, "the superiority of the anthracite coal from the River Lehigh, in Northampton County, Pennsylvania, over the bituminous coals of Virginia, for intensity and regularity of heating power," an interesting historical fact.

Dr. Woodhouse in 1807 edited an edition of *Cheptal's Elements of Chemistry*, in two volumes, with many notes and additions, besides editing an edition of *Parkinson's Chemical Pocket Book*, 1802, with an appendix containing the principal objections to the phlogistic theory of chemistry, and a plate of his working laboratory. Professor Silliman attended the lectures of Dr. Woodhouse in 1802–3, and has drawn his portrait in his personal reminiscences. (See *Life of Silliman*, by Fisher, 1865, i. 100.)

Aaron Dexter, Professor of Chemistry and Materia Medica at Harvard College for thirty-eight years, from 1783 to 1816, was neither a man of research nor a successful teacher, if we may trust the memories of some of his pupils, who still survive, but we owe him thanks in that his influence (says Quincy, in his History of Harvard University) probably availed to induce Major William Erving to endow the chemical chair in Harvard College by a bequest of one thousand pounds in 1791, which chair has since been called after the founder.

In New York, where the learned Dr. Samuel Bard early instituted a medical school, which was united with King's (now Columbia) College, and which conferred its first medical degrees in 1769, we find but little to require our notice in chemistry prior to the appointment of Dr. Samuel Latham Mitchill, who was elected in 1792 "Professor of Chemistry and Natural History," in Columbia College. Few names in the early annals of American science are more worthy of our respectful regard than that of Dr. Mitchill. He was the first professor of chemistry in the United States who introduced a knowledge of the Lavoisierian nomenclature, preceding Dr. Maclean in this by two years. Very soon after his appointment we find him in 1794 publishing an essay on the "Nomenclature of the New Chemistry," and involved in a friendly controversy with Dr. Priestley on phlogiston, to which allusion has already been made. In 1797 he published in *Nicholson's Journal* (i. 481–487) "An attempt to accommodate the disputes among the chemists concerning phlogiston." Dr. Mitchill was a man of wide grasp and varied learning, keenly alive to the importance of all knowledge, and an earnest worker in many lines of research. He established in 1798 the *New York Medical Repository*, etc., the first journal which was devoted to general as well as medical science in the United States. In 1796 he made "A mineralogical exploration of the banks of the Hudson River," which was the earliest attempt in America in this line of research, and in 1804 he published in the *New York Medical Reporter* "A sketch of the mineralogical history of the State of New York." In 1809 he also published in *Tilloch's Magazine* (xxxiv. 125) a "Discourse on Mineralogy." Of chemical papers he published, besides many minor notices in his own journal, in *Tilloch's Magazine*, in 1800, "On the non-action of nitric acid on silver, copper, and tin" (vii. pp. 83–85), and again in *Tilloch* (xx. 1800, 97), he communicates "Some interesting particulars on the history of the muriate of soda." In 1802 he presented a memoir to the American Philosophical Society, entitled "Observations on soda, magnesia, and lime, in the water of the ocean, and how the water of the ocean may be rendered fit for washing without the aid of soap." (*Trans.*, v. pp. 139–147.) In 1801 Dr. Mitchill published his "Synopsis of Chemical Nomenclature and Arrangement."

While Dr. Mitchell's chief contributions to science were in zoölogy and general science, we see by this sketch that he was one of the earliest contributors to our chemical literature, and the first author in the United States, whose name appears in the list of writers upon chemical philosophy.

*Of journals and periodicals devoted to science* in the last and the early part of the present century, there were very few or none, aside from the Transactions before referred to, in which science, properly so called, found any recognition, and such as there were were generally medical journals prior to the end of the last century.

*The Medical Repository*, conducted by Dr. Samuel L. Mitchill and others, in New York, commenced in 1798, and was continued with various editorial changes until 1824. It was the vehicle for a number of chemical contributions, and especially did Dr. Joseph Priestley near the close of his life publish in it several letters devoted chiefly to the defence of the phlogistic theory. It counted among its contributors also Dr. James Woodhouse, who was the antagonist of Dr. Priestley in the phlogistic controversy, Dr. McNevin, Dr. Griscom, and others.

*The Philadelphia Medical Journal* was the resort of Dr. Robert Hare, as well as of the authors before named; Coxe's "Medical Museum," in Philadelphia, the Baltimore Medical Journal, the New York Medical and Physical Journal, by Dr. Hosack and others; and the Boston Journal of Philosophy and the Arts need not detain us, as their objects were mainly medical, and chemistry was only incidental to them.

The chemical student of to-day will find little to reward him in his search in these border lands of our science.

In January, 1810, appeared in New York the first number of *The American Mineralogical Journal*, conducted by Dr. ARCHIBALD BRUCE, Professor of Materia Medica and Mineralogy, etc. This was the first journal entirely devoted to science, and supported exclusively by original American contributions, which appeared in the United States. It ceased with the appearance of its fourth number in 1814, and in all covers only 270 pages. It received the support of many of the working men of the times in its own departments, and contains the original record of many interesting observations in both mineralogy and chemistry, to some of which more particular reference will be made.

In 1817 appeared the first volume of the *Journal of the Academy of Natural Sciences of Philadelphia*, aided by the well sustained liberality of William Maclure, a name never to be forgotten in the history of American science. This journal, although essentially devoted to natural history, was also the vehicle for some early chemical contributions. We find among its contributors the names of Keating, Vanuxem, Morton, Troost, Bowen, H. Seybert, and others of the older chemists and mineralogists.

In July, 1818, appeared the first number of the *American Journal of Science*, conducted by BENJAMIN

SILLIMAN, of Yale College. A perusal of the "Introductory Remarks" by the editor at the opening of the first number, reveals the spirit in which this undertaking was commenced. After paying a deserved tribute of respect and affection to Dr. Archibald Bruce, whose death had just then put an end to his journal, Prof. Silliman remarks: "Most of the periodical works of our country have been short-lived. *This* also *may* perish in its infancy; and if any degree of confidence is cherished that it will attain a maturer age, it is derived from the obvious and intrinsic importance of its undertaking; from its being built upon permanent and momentous national interests; and from the evidence of a decided approbation of the design on the part of men of the first experience, obtained in the progress of an extensive correspondence." The founder lived to see the completion of the first series of fifty volumes, and thirty-eight volumes of the second series in 1864, which closed the first century of volumes in 1870. This journal belongs, then, to both the historical and contemporaneous divisions of our subject, and in its successive indexes will be found the titles and authors of the larger number of the most important American contributions to chemistry.

It is not requisite to our purpose now to consume valuable time in enumerating the titles of the various journals, proceedings, and transactions which have appeared in constantly increasing numbers since 1818. They are familiar to all students of science, and few of them are specially devoted to chemistry. We should not fail, however, to name—

*The Franklin Journal* (now the *Journal of the Franklin Institute*), commenced by Dr. Thomas Jones, of Philadelphia, in January, 1826, under the auspices and as the organ of the Franklin Institute of Philadelphia. It has been continued monthly ever since, under various editorial changes, and has now just completed the sixty-eighth volume of its third series, which has lately passed under the editorship of Prof. George F. Barker, of the University of Pennsylvania, making, with thirty volumes in the first two series, ninety-eight volumes in all. This journal, although avowedly and largely mechanical, has always been, to some degree, and especially of late years, a vehicle for original communications in physics and chemistry. Its life commenced with the opening of the semi-centennial of the century we celebrate.

*The American Chemist*, New York, is a monthly journal devoted exclusively to chemical subjects, under the editorship of Professors CHAS. F. CHANDLER and WM. H. CHANDLER. It was commenced in 1870, and has concentrated and called out an amount of original work and authorship in chemistry, which is the best evidence of the large number of working chemists now engaged in our science in the United States. In its pages appear, as in no other American journal, the full record of such occasions as this which we now celebrate, with full abstracts of foreign chemical papers in all languages.

Of the *Boston Journal of Chemistry*, and other more purely special or technical journals, of which each department of chemical art now counts one or more, we can speak only in the most general terms. Among these, however, we should by no means pass without special mention the *American Journal of Pharmacy*, which, from its commencement in 1825 to the present time, has been the repository of all that is most valuable in this branch of chemistry. In it are recorded the labors of Daniel B. Smith, R. E. Griffith, Geo. B. Wood, Bache, Carson, Hodgson, Durand, Parrish, Bridges, Bullock, Maisch, Mayer, and above all of W. Procter, Jr., whose untimely death still leaves him with a record the bare enumeration of which fills seven closely printed columns, comprising the titles of over six hundred articles, of which a large number are original. A general index to forty-two volumes of this journal was compiled in 1873, by H. M. Wilder—8vo. pp. 314. Philadelphia.

*Transactions of Learned Societies.*—In these we find the only record often of the early work of American chemists, and we will next consider some of the more important of these.

"*The American Academy of Arts and Sciences,*" at Boston, was established by a charter of incorporation granted May 4th, 1780, and its first volume of *Memoirs*, to the end of 1783, appeared in 1785, in 568 pages, 4to. Of the fifty-four memoirs printed in this volume, the most numerous and important are the astronomical and mathematical papers, among which we cannot notice without interest at this time the observation of the transit of Mercury over the sun November 12th, 1782, by Rev. Philips Payson and James Winthrop, Esq.; nor can we fail to observe the very marked difference between the quality of the science developed in the astronomical papers, as compared to the meagre attempts to discuss chemical subjects. The volume contains only two papers which can be called in any wise chemical, viz., "*Observations upon the Art of Making Steel.* By the Reverend DANIEL LITTLE, F.A. A.," in which the author states it as the opinion of writers of the time "that the principal difference between iron and steel consists in this: that the latter is combined with a greater quantity of phlogiston than the former. Phlogiston exists in all inflammable substances, and in some that are not inflammable." And hence in cementation we must use a substance like charcoal, the coal of bones, etc., to form a "cement which contains the greatest quantity of phlogiston." The author's experimental addition to the art of making steel was in the use of the marine plant known as rock-weed to form the cementing material, which he found to produce a superior quality of steel. The second chemical paper is a memoir entitled, "*Experiments on the Waters of Boston.*" By J. FERON, a Surgeon-major in the French fleet then stationed near Boston, printed both in French and English. This appears to be the earliest attempt at the chemical examination of water in this country. In the sea-water taken at the head of the "*Long Wharf,*" he finds on evaporation 472 grains of solid residue in an English quart, which, dissolved in distilled water, left on the filter 6 grains of "calcareous earth" (probably gypsum). The filtered solution being evaporated, left 400 grains of "sea salt, with an alkaline basis" (sodium chloride), "from 40 to 47 grains of sea salt with the terene basis, or *sal. cathart. amar.*" (meaning magnesium sulphate), "and a small quantity of oil" (meaning probably magnesium chloride). He also examined the pump-water in common use at that time, and finds it near the sea contaminated with marine salts. That from Beacon Hill, Charter street, and New Boston, was nearly free from impurities. He tested their hardness by soap, determined their specific gravity and temperature, and "by the alkaline lixivium used for making Prussian blue" (yellow cyanide of potassium) he proved the absence of "any metallic principle" (*e. g.*, iron), and then compared the pump-water with distilled water, in forming tinctorial infusions in vials of equal size, using as his test equal quantities of pulverized rhubarb exposed to the same degree of heat, and also repeating the trial with cochineal, logwood, and beet juice, detecting in each case the difference of color due to the presence of alkaline salts. He also used nutgalls with "the fixed alkali" (potassium carbonate, probably), "which turned it to a deep green." He inferred from these tests the presence of earthy and alkaline salts, "with some marks of the marine acid." He used silver nitrate and solution of mercury, and obtained the appropriate insoluble chlorides. By a solution of fixed alkali he obtained also a white precipitate of about six grains to the quart, "which dissolved in acid with effervescence" (calcic and magnesian carbonates). Left at rest in bottles, some of these waters gave off "a quantity of air, rising in bubbles to the surface," and let fall a small sediment. "Lime-water dropped into these waters formed a white cloud, and detached a precipitate of the same color." The water of *Beacon Hill* and *Charter street* gave no such precipitate with the alkalies nor with lime-water. He asks if the reaction with lime-water and the escape of air-bubbles does not indicate an earth, suspended by means of a superabundance of air (meaning carbonic acid). He then proceeds to determine the solid residue by evaporation, and with considerable skill to estimate the chief constituents of the saline mass, using the methods of analysis then known. His paper, translated into modern chemical terms, would not be esteemed an unworthy contribution to-day; and considering the fact that there was then hardly one seat of learning in America where chemistry was recognized even by name in the curriculum of study, nor was there then an operative laboratory, we must regard with respect this early contribution to the science. It certainly exhibits a truly scientific spirit, reflected, no doubt, from the French schools, in which the author was probably trained. Dr. Feron communicated to the Academy a "Second Essay on the Boston Pump Waters," which is contained in vol. ii. p. 170 of the *Memoirs of the Academy*, 1790–93.

Dr. Samuel Tenney, surgeon to one of the Massachusetts regiments during the Revolutionary war, being stationed near Saratoga, sent to the Academy at Boston in Sept. 1, 1783, "An account of a number of medicinal springs at Saratoga, in the State of New York." This, I believe, is the earliest record we have of these now renowned mineral springs, which had been first observed by the surveyors only thirteen years before; and prior to Dr. Tenney's visit and description they had been frequented only by a few poor people from the immediate neighborhood. Dr. Tenney very accurately estimates and foretells the importance of these saline waters. He gives a clear and intelligent account of the mode of their occurrence, and shows his sagacity by his experiments made on the spot with only such agents as his medical chest afforded to determine the chemical character of the waters. He distinctly recognizes their alkaline character. One he finds to be a chalybeate, and in all he finds "fixed air" to be the agent holding the "calcareous earth" and iron in solution. He says, "It is obvious these waters are essentially the same with the acidulæ of Pyrmont, Seltzer, etc., which have been so famous in Europe." From the great accumulation of calcareous deposits left by these waters he concludes that the flow of water must have been formerly much greater than at the time of his observations, and he reasons hence that these springs have all the appearance of being in a state of decay. His speculations as to the cause of the fault or break in the rocks along the line of which the springs are situated are curious. He finds the elastic power of "fixed air" set free from the lime rocks, by the "vitriolic acid" which "abounds in the subterranean regions, an adequate cause to produce such an explosion as would burst asunder the most solid rocks, leaving reservoirs to be filled with water charged with carbonic acid, forming a proper menstruum for dissolving the calcareous earth or iron ore which it might meet in its passage." He cites many cases of the medicinal value of the waters administered under his own directions to the men of his regiment.

Dr. Tenney's account of the Saratoga waters did much to bring these springs into general notice. It is curious to compare his chemical results with the recent analyses of the same waters by our colleague, Dr. C. F. Chandler, in evidence of the difference afforded in this comparison of the state of the art of analysis at the two periods, nearly a century apart.

With the exception of two technical papers on the manufacture of solar salt at Cape Cod, and on the manufacture of potashes, the latter by Aaron Dexter, of Harvard, there are no further chemical papers in the volumes of the American Academy for a long course of years.

*The Connecticut Academy, and the Weston Meteor, Professors Silliman and Kingsley.*—The Connecticut Academy of Arts and Sciences was incorporated by the Legislature of that State in the year 1799. In the first volume of its memoirs, published in 1810, will be found

"An account of the meteor which burst over Weston, in Connecticut, in December 1807. By Professors Silliman and Kingsley" (pp. 141-163). No scientific paper had before appeared in the United States which excited so much attention and comment as this. Owing to the extraordinary nature of the phenomena described, and, no doubt, also, to the fairness and vigor of its description, this paper was very generally reproduced. It was read, March 4, 1808, before the American Philosophical Society, and appeared in the Transactions of that Society (vi. pp. 423-443, 1809). Contrary to a standing rule, to take no notice of matters appearing in the public prints, this paper was also read, at the time, before the Royal Society at London, and the French Academy at Paris. Thomas Jefferson, then president of the American Philosophical Society, is reported to have said on this occasion, in the well-known language of David Hume regarding miracles, "that it was easier to believe that two Yankee Professors could lie than to admit that stones could fall from heaven"—a remarkable evidence of the limited knowledge of such subjects then prevailing in this country, even in the minds of the most cultivated people. But it is chiefly with the chemical side of this paper we are now concerned. It contains, under a separate heading, a "Chemical examination of the stones which fell at Weston (Connecticut), December 14, 1807. By B. Silliman, Professor of Chemistry in Yale College." This examination extends to each of the constituent parts of the stone, viz: 1. Of the stone at large. 2. Of the pyrites. 3. Of the malleable iron. 4. Of the black irregular mass. 5. Of the crust. 6. Of the globular bodies. The chemical portion of this memoir is the earliest research of the kind of which we have any account in this country. There was not at that time a laboratory fitted with the appliances needful for accurate analytical research. The weighings were made on a common pharmaceutical balance, with weights of only ordinary accuracy. There was then no book or treatise on analytical chemistry accessible here, beyond the special work of former investigators, given in their memoirs. Prof. Silliman appears to have followed in this case the memoirs of Vaquelin and Howard, in their analyses of the meteoric stone of Benares, and beyond this to have been guided by his own sagacity.

*The Oxyhydrogen Blowpipe of Dr. Hare*, 1802.—Probably no chemical discovery made in this country has been more generally cited or less generally understood in its scientific significance, than the oxyhydrogen blowpipe of Dr. Hare; or, as it was called by his colleague, Prof. Silliman, "Hare's Compound Blowpipe." Having some knowledge of the facts, I propose to review them briefly, and to show that this was in reality a memorable scientific event.

No one can read the original memoir by Dr. Hare in *Tilloch's Philosophical Magazine* (xiv. 1802, pp. 238–245 and 298–308), without perceiving in it the evidence of a truly philosophical mind, proceeding by successive steps in a most natural order of induction from a simple attempt to improve the ordinary hydrostatic blowpipe to the discovery of a philosophical principle far in advance of the science of the time. Dr. Hare's paper was entitled "Memoir on the Supply and Application of the Blowpipe. By Mr. Robert Hare, Jr., member of the Chemical Society of Philadelphia." ("Published by order of the Society.") The author was at that time about twenty years of age. The Chemical Society of Philadelphia appears not to have been a publishing society, and Dr. Hare's original memoir, although separately published as a pamphlet in Philadelphia in 1802, was never, so far as I can discover, reproduced in any American scientific journal or transactions. It is reproduced as an "Extract" from M. P. Aadet in the *Annales de Chemie*, 30 *Pluviose, an.* xi. (tome xlv. 113–138). A second paper by Dr. Hare, supplementary to his first, appeared in the Transactions of the American Philosophical Society at Philadelphia, in 1804, under the title "Account of the fusion of Strontites and volatilization of Platinum, and also a new arrangement of apparatus" (vi. pp. 99–105). This paper was read June 17th, 1803. In it he reaffirms his former results given in his first memoir, adding those on the fusion of strontia and the volatilization of platinum, and describes the form of apparatus executed by Prof. Silliman at Yale College, in which the gases were confined within the pneumatic trough. In this paper, with characteristic generosity, he recognizes his obligations to Prof. Silliman, his associate in conducting these experiments. The term "Compound Blowpipe" was first given to Hare's apparatus by Prof. Silliman, who also in 1812 describes his form of the apparatus more at length in the *Memoirs of the Connecticut Academy*. This paper of Prof. Silliman, "On the powers of the Compound Blowpipe," was reproduced in Bruce's *American Mineralogical Journal*, p. 199.

In the Transactions of the American Philosophical Society, Philadelphia (vol. III, pp. 328–399), is a paper read May 7th, 1812, entitled "Experiments on the Fusion of various refractory Bodies by the Compound Blowpipe of Dr. Hare. By Benjamin Silliman, Professor of Chemistry and Mineralogy in Yale College." This paper is prefaced by "A section of the Pneumatic Cistern of Yale College, with the Compound Blowpipe of Mr. Hare burning hydrogen and oxygen gas." This arrangement of the oxyhydrogen blowpipe by Prof. Silliman was extensively reproduced in other laboratories, and was adopted substantially by Dr. Hare. The double platinum jet with converging ducts forming the continuation of two solid silver tubes, and uniting in a common passage, somewhat larger just before their exit, at the common orifice below, joined by screws to avoid solder, were Mr. Silliman's mode of construction, and it was with this jet he conducted the "experiments on the fusion of various refractory bodies," as detailed in this paper, which relates the results of experiments upon more than thirty of the most refractory bodies known, many of which had never before been fused. This paper was republished in *Tilloch's Magazine*.

In the third edition of Henry's Elements of Chemistry (1814), edited by Prof. Silliman, the Pneumatic Cistern of Yale College is figured on the frontispiece with the inscription "Showing the compound blowpipe for oxygen and hydrogen from the original constructed by Prof. Silliman, and invented by him and Dr. Hare."

In September, 1816, Dr. E. D. Clarke, the well-known traveller, and then Professor of Mineralogy in the University of Cambridge (England), published simultaneously in the *Quarterly Journal of the Royal Institution* (London), vol. ii. p. 104, and in the *Ann. de Ch. et Phys.*, tome iii. p. 39, his "account of some *experiments made with Newman's Blowpipe, by inflaming a highly condensed mixture of the gaseous constituents of water*," etc. Newman, the well-known instrument-maker in London, had, a few months before (April, 1816), described in the *Journal of the Royal Institution* (vol. i. p. 65), his blowpipe, in which air was compressed by a syringe. He does not appear to have contemplated the use of any gas but common air. Dr. Clarke, in a foot-note to his paper above cited, refers to Dr. Hare's paper of 1802, but he makes no reference to Prof. Silliman's very full statements of his results on the fusion of refractory bodies made in 1811, and published in 1812. That he had not seen this paper, is certainly possible. A comparison of the results obtained by these two observers shows, however, a singular identity in most of the details not easily accounted for. Prof. Silliman, after the publication of Dr. Clarke's paper, made a reclamation, which was published in the *Journal de Physique* at Paris, for January 1818, and is reproduced with comments in the first volume of *Silliman's Journal*, p. 97. Dr. Clarke subsequently published a book entitled "On the Gas Blowpipe" (1819), which at once called out from Dr. Hare his "Strictures," etc., which appeared in the second volume of *Silliman's Journal* for 1820 (pp. 281–302). This is a good example of the vigor and thoroughness with which Dr. Hare was wont to deal with those who encroached on his rights No explanation was ever offered by Dr. Clarke for his clear trespass upon the researches of his American contemporaries, although the whole case was fairly laid before him.*

We have already mentioned that the American Academy at Boston selected the oxyhydrogen blowpipe of Dr. Hare for the honor of the first award ever made by them from the Rumford medal fund, which had been accumulating on their hands for more than forty years. It was fit that an American discovery which had been almost coeval with the institution of the Rumford medals, should have been selected for this decoration. It might seem ungracious in us to ask why it was so long delayed, seeing it was at length so worthily bestowed.

We have dwelt somewhat at length upon the historical portion of Dr. Hare's discovery; we now return to say a few words of its merits as a discovery.

That Dr. Hare deserved the title of a discoverer. and not merely the lesser distinction of an inventor, will appear, if we remember that he had the sagacity to recognize, in his original memoir, the fact overlooked by Lavoisier and other experimenters in the same field, that in order to obtain the maximum possible effects of heat, the body to be heated must be sustained *in an atmosphere of burning gas*, and that charcoal, impinged upon by a jet of oxygen, did not fulfil this condition. Hence Hare, after discussing the fundamental defects of Lavoisier's methods, says, with great sagacity,

* A perfectly fair and impartial statement of the facts respecting the blowpipe of Dr. Hare will be found in the *Ann. de Ch. et Phys.*, 1820 tome xiv. p. 302, by Gay-Lussac: "Sur *la Fusion de divers corps refractaires avec le Chalumeau de* HARE." This statement is translated in vol. iii. of Silliman's Journal, p. 87, 1821.

"To avoid these evils, it was thought desirable that means might be discovered of clothing the upper surface of any body which might be subjected to this species of operation with some burning matter, of which the heat might be equal to that of the incandescent carbon with which the lower surface might be in contact; or by which bodies might be exposed on solid supports to a temperature equal or superior to that of the porous charcoal uniting with oxygen."

"It soon occurred that these desiderata might be attained *by means of flame*, supported by the hydrogen and oxygen gases; for it was conceived that, according to the admirable theory of the French chemists, more caloric ought to be extricated by this than by any other condition. * * * * *

"Such was the reasoning which originated the desire of employing the flame of the hydrogen and oxygen gases. But before this could be accomplished, it was necessary to overcome the difficulty of igniting a mixture of these aeriform substances without the danger of an explosion."

These are remarkable words to have been written in 1802. They show their author to have possessed equally the higher powers needed to seek for and discover a great principle, and the lesser power to devise the means to apply it in a mechanical combination. The discovery precedes the invention—the discoverer is master to the inventor. Rarely, as in Hare's case, do we find the two sets of powers combined. Every real discovery is the fertile parent of many inventions. Rumford's paper on the "Source of the Heat excited by Friction," which had been communicated in substance to the Royal Society in 1798, was not published in their Transactions until 1800, and could hardly have been known to Hare in 1801, when he made his discovery. Indeed the philosophical conclusions flowing from Rumford's researches on heat were slow in making their way, and the step was a long one from the phenomena of heat as connected with motion, to the fundamental idea developed by Hare—such a long step as to leave the entire originality of Hare in this case beyond question.

Properly considered, the fundamental principle which led Hare to the invention of the oxyhydrogen blowpipe has also led Siemens in our time to the invention of the regenerative gas furnace, by which, as Hare says in the memoir already quoted, "To avoid these evils" (viz., the contact of solid fuel and the loss of heat consequent on its conversion into gas), it was thought desirable that means might be discovered of clothing the upper surface of any body" to be heated "with some burning matter," . . . . "or by which bodies might be exposed on solid supports to a temperature equal or superior to that of the porous charcoal uniting with oxygen." "It soon occurred that these desiderata might be attained by means of flame supported by the hydrogen and oxygen gases."

In the Siemens furnace the objects to be heated are sustained on a solid support in an atmosphere of burning gas, the oxygen of the atmosphere arriving by one inlet, and the combustible gases by another, and the two uniting in a true Hare's blowpipe flame to do their work. The accessory contrivances for the alternation of the flow of gas and air through the regenerative cellular flues of fire-brick, are evidences of a high degree of inventive skill, applied to the solution of a problem which, in its essential features, was clearly set forth by the American philosopher, ROBERT HARE, in 1802, in his memoir which we have just been considering.

*Of Hare's other Contributions to Science.*—It is well in this connection to refer briefly to the labors of Dr. Hare in other departments of chemical and physical research.

It will be remembered that the award to him by the American Academy, in 1839, from the Rumford Medal Fund, was equally for his "improvements in galvanic apparatus" as for his blowpipe.

In 1819 Dr. Hare published his memoir entitled, "A New Theory of Galvanism, supported by some experiments and observations made by means of the calorimoter, a new galvanic instrument" (*Silliman's Journal*, i. p. 413). In view of our present notions in molecular physics, we may perhaps smile at the statement by which the author opens his paper. "I have," he says, "for some time been of opinion that the principle extricated by the voltaic pile is a compound of caloric and electricity, both being original and collateral products of galvanic action." Yet we cannot fail to observe that this statement, if clothed in the language of modern science, is a distinct recognition of what we call the correlation of forces. In Hare's calorimeter we have a form of apparatus which is admirably adapted to develop a large quantitative flow, and one which has now a wide use for this purpose, the substitution of plates of carbon for copper and of amalgamated zinc for the unprotected metal, being the only changes which modern art has introduced into Hare's original instrument, long forgotten, and perhaps before unknown to the existing generation, but now revived again, and permanently installed in the laboratory of the physicist.

In 1821 Dr. Hare published his memoir entitled, "A Memoir on some New Modifications of Galvanic Apparatus, with Observations in support of his New Theory of Galvanism" (*Silliman's Journal*, iii. p. 105; also, in the *Phila. Med. Journal*). In this memoir he describes his "deflagrator," which may be considered as a mobilized voltaic pile, capable of instantaneous immersion in the exciting fluid, and of equally instant suspension. In place of the laborious process of filling by hand the troughs of Cruickshank or Wollaston, Hare supplied the means of bringing any number of voltaic couples into immediate action, without the loss of an instant of time, and thus, for the first time, secured a maximum effect, which, in the previously existing instruments, was impossible.

It happened, as a consequence of the general adoption here of Hare's form of the voltaic pile, that powerful deflagrators were in common use in America long before any apparatus of equal power was known in Europe; for it was not until 1836 that Daniell discovered the double-cell battery, and a little earlier that Kempt had shown that amalgamated zinc would resist the local action, which, prior to that observation, prevented the construction of sustained, or so-called constant batteries. In the absence of these two important discoveries, Hare's forms of voltaic apparatus were the best possible, and well deserved the reward they received at the hands of the American Academy. Faraday, in his Experimental Researches, very honorably conceded to Dr. Hare all that his warmest friends could ask. After recounting the steps by which he had himself been led to the same mode of construction, he adds: "On examining, however, what had been done before, I found that the new trough was, in all essential respects, the same as that invented and described by Dr. Hare, Professor in the University of Pennsylvania, to whom I have great pleasure in referring it." (vol. i. p. 345. § 1123, *Experimental Researches*, June, 1835.)

The perusal of Dr. Hare's papers, above referred to, as well as his numerous controversial and other discussions with other authors, will clearly show that he always held his qualities as an inventor quite subordinate to his theoretical views, and that the latter were ever prompting him to new researches. His discussion with Faraday on Induction (*Expt. Res.*, ii. 251, 1839–40), and his letters to Berzelius and to Liebig, on Theoretical Chemistry, are in point. The general index to the first series of *Silliman's Journal* contains the titles of no less than 150 papers by Dr. Hare, upon a great variety of chemical and physical subjects, the mere enumeration of which would far transcend our present limits.

Before leaving this subject, it is proper to say that the deflagrator of Hare in 1822 enabled Prof. Silliman to announce the fusion and volatilization of carbon, and the actual transfer of the volatilized portion of the positive electrode to the negative pole, by which the former is made cup-shaped and diminished in length, while the latter is sensibly elongated (*Am. Journ. Sci.*, [i.] v. 108). This fact was disputed by Vanuxem and others, but was amply confirmed much later by Despretz, who further detected on the walls of the inclosing glass egg, within which the arch for 600 Bunsen couples was brought to bear on the diamond, minute crystals of carbon obtained from the vapor of the volatilized diamond.

On the 15th of May, 1858, Dr. Hare died at the advanced age of seventy-eight years. In the following number of the *American Journal of Science*, his old friend and associate, himself then in his eightieth year, presented the following tribute to his early and life-long co-laborer, which we reproduce in this connection, even at the risk of some repetition of what has already been said, as a proper supplement to our notice of two of the best known contributors to chemical science in this country of the past generation.

" *The late Dr. Robert Hare.*—During the progress of the forty years of our editorial labors, sorrow has often been awakened as we have been called to record the departure from life of friends and fellow-laborers in the common cause.

" Robert Hare, the distinguished chemist and philosopher, who died in Philadelphia on the 15th of last May in the seventy-eighth year of his age, is entitled to a grateful commemoration in this Journal, to whose pages his contributions were for many years more numerous than those of any other correspondent. The enumeration of the titles merely of about one hundred and fifty articles furnished by him, occupies five columns of the general index of the first fifty volumes of the Journal. He appears in forty-one of those volumes, and in seven volumes of the Second Series.

"For more than half a century his name has been familiar to men of science as a chemical philosopher, and to the cultivators of the useful arts throughout the civilized world.

"Dr. Robert Hare was born in Philadelphia, January 17th, 1781. His father was an Englishman, a man of strong mind, and honored in his adopted country by the public confidence. His mother was from a distinguished Philadelphia family. In early life he managed the business of an extensive brewery, which his father had established, but his strong leaning toward physical science very early manifested itself, and soon led him to abandon the pursuits of a manufacturer and devote his talents and fortune to science. Before the age of twenty he gave evidence of this predilection for scientific pursuits by following the courses of lectures on chemistry and physical science in his native city, and by uniting himself with the Chemical Society of Philadelphia, then embracing the names of Priestley, Sybert, and Woodhouse.

"In 1801 he communicated to this Society a description of the oxyhydrogen blowpipe, which he then called a '*hydrostatic blowpipe.*' Prof. Silliman, having been much engaged with him in a series of experiments with this instrument in 1802–3, subsequently distinguished it as the 'compound blowpipe,' having, in fact, on his return from Philadelphia in 1803, constructed for the laboratory of Yale College the first pneumatic trough combining Dr. Hare's invention; an apparatus subsequently figured and described by Dr. Hare in his memoir 'on the fusion of strontia and volatilization of platinum.'* His memoir to the Chemical Society was separately published in 1801, and was republished in *Tilloch's Phil. Mag.*, London, 1802, and also in the *Annales de Chimie* (1st series), v. 45.

"This apparatus was the earliest and perhaps the most remarkable of his original contributions to science. It was certainly evidence of a highly philosophical mind, that Dr. Hare, in that comparatively early period in modern chemistry, and when the received notions of the true nature of combustion were so vague, not to say erroneous, should have had the acumen to conceive that a stream of oxygen and hydrogen burning together

* Trans. Am. Phil. Soc., vol. vi. p. 99, and plate 3 (June 17, 1803).

should produce so intense a heat. Lavoisier, certainly one of the most acute of chemical philosophers, and unsurpassed in his skill as an experimentalist, had beaten up the same path so far as to direct a jet of oxygen upon charcoal, and he thus produced a degree of heat by which he fused alumina and other bodies before deemed infusible. He had even brought the elements of water into the same vessel, and had there burned them from separate jets, in his famous apparatus for the recomposition of water. But it seems never to have occurred to him that here was a source of heat greater than any then known. In our view, Dr. Hare's merit as a scientific philosopher is more clearly established upon this discovery than upon any other of the numerous contributions he has made to science. His original experiments were repeated in 1802-3 in presence of Dr. Priestley, the discoverer of oxygen, then on a visit to Philadelphia, and of Silliman, Woodhouse, and others. They were subsequently greatly extended by Prof. Silliman, who, with the apparatus already alluded to, subjected a great number of refractory bodies to the action of the oxyhydrogen jet, and published an account of his results in the *Memoirs of the Conn. Acad.*, May 7th, 1812.

"The discovery of the oxyhydrogen blowpipe was crowned by the Amer. Acad. at Boston by the Rumford medal.

"The historian of science will, in view of the facts here quoted, find it needless to notice the disingenuous effort of Dr. Clarke of Cambridge, England, in his '*gas blowpipe*,' to overlook or appropriate the discovery of Dr. Hare, and the researches of Silliman and others, several years after (in 1819) this discovery had been fully before the scientific world—an effect which must ever remain as a sad stain upon the reputation of this otherwise distinguished man.*

"It is not our purpose here to rehearse the history of Dr. Hare's discovery in full, much less to describe all the modifications which the apparatus has received at the hands of its original discoverer and others. It is well

* The reader will peruse with interest, in this connection, Dr. Hare's elaborate defence of his own claims and those of his associate, Prof Silliman, against Dr Clarke's appropriation, in this Journal [1], vol. ii. pp. 281-302, 1820. Dr. Clarke, after a full and spirited protest had been communicated to him, stating fully Dr. Hare's claims and the wrong done him, failed to make any acknowledgment of his error, thus exonerating us from the force of the old maxim, "*Nil de mortuis nisi bonum.*" Dr. Hare heads his strictures on Dr. Clarke's book with the well-known lines of Virgil, "*Hos ego versiculos feci, tulit alter honores,*" etc.

known that in later years he constructed the apparatus on a gigantic scale, with large vessels of wrought iron capable of sustaining the pressure of the Fairmount water-works, and that with this powerful combination he was able to fuse at one operation nearly two pounds of platinum.* In these experiments the metal is held upon a refractory fire-brick, and both are heated as highly as possible in a wind furnace before submitting it to the gas-jet. The product of this fusion from the crude grains is found to be greatly purified, a result probably due to the volatilization at this intense heat of some of the associate metals.

"The employment of Dr. Hare's jet to illuminate lighthouses and signal reflectors under the names of Drummond light and Calcium light, is only another example of the mode of ignoring the name of the real discoverer, of which the history of science presents so many parallels.

"The fertility of Dr. Hare's inventive mind is illustrated by the numerous and ingenious forms of apparatus which he contrived for research or illustration. To many of these he was led by the necessity of preparing the illustrations for his lectures upon a scale of magnitude adequate to the instruction of the large classes of the Medical School of the University of Pennsylvania. He was called to fill the Chair of Chemistry in that institution in 1818, and continued in the discharge of its duties for nearly a third of a century, and until his resignation in 1847.

"He was fond of graphic illustrations; they abound in his memoirs and in his Compendium and other works, and aided by his lucid descriptions his inventions thus become quite intelligible. Where most instructors are satisfied with less perfect and more simple means and explanations, he seemed to be content with nothing short of perfection.

"During his long course of research and experimenting, he accumulated a vast store of instruments and materials. An inspection of his repositories and the treasures there accumulated filled the observer with astonishment, and in his lecture-room there was always a profusion of apparatus, often instruments of great dimensions, corresponding well with his large mind, with

* Roberts in New York has lately with Dr. Hare's apparatus succeeded in fusing perfectly 53 oz. of platinum at one operation, and Deville has by the same means more recently fused one hundred and fifty pounds of platinum at one operation, in obtaining the metal for the new standards of measure.

his great physical and intellectual power, and unquenchable ardor. He was himself an able and skillful mechanic, and often worked adroitly at the turning lathe and with the other resources of a well-furnished shop. In his operations he spared neither labor nor expense, and bestowed both munificently for the accomplishment of his objects.

"He devoted great labor and skill to the construction of new and improved forms of the voltaic pile, and it is easy to show, that, owing to his zeal and skill in this department of chemical physics, American chemists were enabled to employ with distinguished success the intense powers of extended series of voltaic couples long in advance of the general use of similar combinations in Europe.

"It was with one of Hare's deflagrators that Silliman in 1823 first demonstrated the volatilization and fusion of carbon, a result considered so extraordinary at the time that it was long received with incredulity. Since the general introduction of Bunsen's battery, these effects are no longer doubted; all Prof. Silliman's results having been confirmed and extended by Despretz, De La Rive, and others.

"The deflagrator was invented in 1820.* Four years earlier Dr. Hare had contrived another instrument which he called *the Calorimotor.* In this instrument great extent of surface was obtained from the combining of many large plates (18″ or 24″ square) of zinc and copper into two series, and plunging the whole at one movement into a tank of dilute acid. The magnetic and heating effects of this instrument were surprising, and to this day no other form of voltaic apparatus appears to occasion the movement of so great a *volume* of heat with so low a projectile or intensitive force. By it, large rods of iron or platinum, when clamped between its jaws, are first fully ignited and then fused with splendid phenomena, while at the same time its intensity is so low that hardly the least visible spark can be made to pass by it through poles of carbon.

"In the philosophy of chemistry, Dr. Hare has distinguished himself for the zeal and logical acumen with which he combated what he conceived to be the errors of the salt radical theory. He was ready at all times to engage in controversy upon any point of theory where he conceived there was an error latent. No one can review the numerous letters which he has addressed to the

* Sill. Journal [1], vol. iii. p. 105.

senior editor of this Journal, to Berzelius, to Liebig, and to Faraday, and published in this Journal, without perceiving that he was no ordinary antagonist.

"In his family and among his friends Dr. Hare was very kind, and his feelings were generous, amiable, and genial, although occasionally his manner was abrupt—from absence of mind occasioned by his habitual abstraction and absortion in thought; his mind was ever active, and conversation would sometimes seem to awaken him from an intellectual reverie. He had high colloquial powers, but to give them full effect, it was necessary that they should be roused by a great and interesting subject, and especially if it assumed an antagonistic form. He would then discourse with commanding ability, and his hearers were generally as willing to listen as he was to speak.

"He was a man of unbending rectitude, and a faithful friend both in prosperity and adversity.

"His frame was robust—powerful and ample in structure, and of strong muscular development, having been invigorated in earlier years by skilful training; and, had there been occasion, he would have made a formidable physical antagonist. His head was large and of noble model; no stranger could meet him without being impressed by a figure of such grandeur and a head and features so remarkable.

"Dr. Hare was an ardent patriot, who loved his country and cherished its institutions not for office or emolument, which he never sought or received, but from pure and lofty motives. He was of the school of Washington—an enthusiastic admirer of that great man—a federalist, while that primeval party had a name and retained vitality—and when it passed by an imperceptible transition into another form, he was found among the whigs. He occasionally wrote upon the great political and financial questions which agitate the public mind. These discussions, like all his writings, were always marked by vigorous thought, large views, and elevated patriotism.

"He was not, however, so exclusively a man of science as to ignore the charms of literature. His particular friends know that his philosophy was sometimes softened by listening to the Muses, and he occasionally indulged in poetical composition.

"Dr. Hare was one of the few life members of the Smithsonian Institution, to which he gave, soon after he resigned his professorship, all his chemical and physical apparatus, which has thus become the property of the nation."

Benjamin Silliman.—At the time when the chair of chemistry was first occupied by Prof. Silliman in Yale College, in 1802, chemistry as a science was almost unknown in the United States, and, as we have seen, very few contributions had then been made to it in this country. Prof. Silliman fully recognized his obligations to Dr. John Maclean, of Princeton, where he made a pilgrimage immediately after his appointment, and from whom he early obtained a list of books for the prosecution of his studies. Princeton was thus an authority in chemistry before Yale had taken her first lessons in this science. Priestley's arrival here in 1794, and his inspiring influence, both by his occasional presence in Philadelphia and by his communications to the American Philosophical Society, naturally made Philadelphia the point of chief attraction in the United States to the chemical student at the commencement of the nineteenth century. Here Professor Silliman found Dr. James Woodhouse filling the chemical chair in the University of Pennsylvania, on whose lectures he was a faithful attendant. But he was not long in discovering that he made more real progress in the study of chemistry by availing himself of the advantages of a small laboratory, which he and a young man by the name of Robert Hare united in fitting up with a little apparatus and limited means of research. There these zealous young students worked together, elaborating the compound blowpipe, previously contrived by Hare, and of which the history has already been given. His chemical work upon the Weston Meteorite has also been noticed. His "Elements of Chemistry in the order of the Lectures given in Yale College" was published in two volumes in 1830, and embraced the fruits of a long course of successful experience in demonstrative chemistry, and was, with the exception of Gorham's, the first systematic work on our science in this country, which was not a reproduction of some European treatise.

Prof. Silliman made important contributions to chemical science, as we have seen; but far more important than his researches, to the advancement of this department of knowledge, was his remarkable power as an expounder of its truths in his lectures. It is not for us to enlarge further upon this subjeet, nor is it needful, seeing that the work has already been done by the graceful pen of Dr. Fisher, his biographer. It is, however, but just to add, in passing, that between the years 1830 and 1850 Prof. Silliman appeared frequently as a public lecturer on science in other cities and in very distant parts of this country, and was the first college professor who ventured to step from his rostrum to teach the people. With what measure of success he accomplished this task, without loss to the dignity and high office of science, has already been recorded by other pens. That these lectures had an important influence as an active element in the great awakening of the popular mind toward science, elsewhere noticed in this essay, cannot be doubted, and it were easy to trace his influence in deciding the action of some of those who have since made important endowments for science.

His editorial labors, both in the successive editions of Dr. Henry's Chemistry, and far more in the *American Journal of Science*, have already been noticed. He filled the chairs of chemistry and mineralogy at Yale College for fifty years, during which geology, as a science, was developed and added to his duties. By securing early in his career the extensive mineralogical collection of Col. G. Gibbs to Yale College, he gave this department of science great prominence there, and rendered the development of the geological department comparatively easy.

Of his early contributions to chemistry we have already said something; it is hardly needful here to add the titles of his various papers, about sixty of which will be found in the catalogue of the Royal Society.

He was an industrious and zealous worker in the laboratory, and eminently successful as a demonstrator. In 1808 he, immediately upon the announcement of Davy's discovery of the metallic bases of the alkalies soda and potassa, repeated Davy's methods by the voltaic pile, and verified his results (see *Bruce's Journal*, pp. 88 and 134), and he reproduced in full the memoir by Gay-Lussac and Thénard on the furnace process for potassium, in his third American edition of Henry's Chemistry. His scientific life was at many points intimately associated with that of Dr. Hare, and we have already illustrated this fact by what has been said of the researches of the latter philosopher.

Prof. Silliman wrote on many subjects besides science. His "Journal of Travels in England, Holland, and Scotland and of two passages over the Atlantic in 1805 and

1806" (3 vols.), was very generally read, and early made his name widely known. A visit to Europe was then a remarkable event, and no educated American had, before him, recorded his experiences. "Europe Revisited" (2 vols.) was published in 1853, and an earlier volume, "Tour from Hartford to Quebec in the Autumn of 1819," is a pleasantly written narrative, full of interesting historical data with reference to the early occupation of the country by the French.

Adam Seybert is one of the few American chemists who enjoyed the advantage, rare at that time, of a training in the School of Mines at Paris, late in the last century. He has left but few papers, but his memoir, read before the American Philosophical Society, March 10, 1797, entitled "Experiments and Observations on Land and Sea Air," is of interest as the earliest example of such a research on our records. It relates the results of twenty-seven analyses of air made by the author at sea in a voyage across the Atlantic, and also the comparison of these results with other analyses made by him on land, near Philadelphia, by which comparison he reaches the conclusion that the air over the sea is purer than that over the land; that, while the latter varies with locality, the former is nearly constant: and he then modestly ventures the suggestion that "perhaps the impurities are absorbed by the agitation of the waves"—a conclusion to which modern investigation by the use of more exact methods has also arrived. Considering the imperfect condition of eudiometric methods in Seybert's time, his research and conclusions therefrom are decidedly creditable to his skill and sagacity. Dr. Seybert was the father of Mr. Henry Seybert, of whose contributions to chemical mineralogy we shall speak more at length. It was Adam Seybert, who a few years later performed the office of his great namesake in the Garden of Eden, by naming the few minerals then forming the collection of Yale College, when submitted to him in 1803 by Prof. Silliman.

Archibald Bruce, M.D., was both a chemist and mineralogist as well as a man of profound medical attainments. His name is associated with the *American Mineralogical Journal*, of which he was the projector and editor in 1810–14. It is pleasant to recall the fact also that his first chemical analysis "Of native magnesia from New Jersey" made known to science the beautiful mineral found in the magnesian rocks of Castle Point at Hoboken, New Jersey, which now bears the name of BRUCITE. He had also the sagacity to detect and correctly analyze the red zinc (zincite) of Sussex in New Jersey, associated with the Franklinite, two of the most distinctive and beautiful of American minerals. Some of the French authors still distinguish the zincite, erroneously, as Brucite. He also published a valuable paper "on the ores of titanium occurring within the United States." Dr. Bruce collected a valuable mineralogical cabinet. He died early (in 1818), in his 41st year. A fine engraved portrait of Dr. Bruce is preserved in the first volume of *Silliman's Journal*.

W. LANGSTAFF, M.D., New York.—Dr. Langstaff, when the assistant of Dr. Archibald Bruce, in 1811, made the first American analysis of chondrodite (then called *Brucite*). Indeed we may say this was the first mineral analysis of any difficulty (if we except the analysis of the Weston meteor by Prof. Silliman in 1807-8) made in this country. Berzelius had failed to detect the presence of fluorine as a factor in this species in his analysis of the variety from Finland. Dr. Langstaff's analysis of the Sparta mineral first detected the fluorine, and his analysis gives very nearly the correct constitution of the species (*Dana, Min.*, 1868. p. 364-65). This fact entitles Dr. Langstaff to honorable mention among American chemists, although I have failed to detect any other example of his work.

JOSEPH CLOUD, Assay Master in the U. S. Mint at Philadelphia, made, in 1807, an interesting research upon a native alloy of palladium and gold from Rio des Mortes, in Brazil. This metal had not before been found combined with gold, and all knowledge of it was confined to Dr. Wollaston's researches in 1802-1805 on its alloy with platinum. Mr. Cloud's paper on the Brazilian alloy of palladium was read before the American Philosophical Society, June 23, 1809, and is printed in the sixth volume of their Transactions, p. 497. This appears to be the earliest research of the kind made in this country. Mr. Cloud followed up the subject by an investigation into the platinum metals, and it is said (*Bruce's Journ.*, p. 43) that he obtained rhodium of remarkable purity, but his paper, if printed, has escaped my search.

WILLIAM JAMES MACNEVIN, M.D.—Dr. Macnevin was made Professor of Chemistry in the College of Physicians and Surgeons in New York in 1811. He was educated in Germany, receiving the degree of M.D. in Vienna in 1783, at the age of twenty years. There is a romantic interest connected with the political side of his career as one of the Irish patriots associated with Emmet, Fitzgerald, Tone, etc., with which we now have no concern. In 1826, he was one of the associates with Dr. Francis, Dr. John Griscom, and others in founding the Rutgers Medical College, and taught Materia Medica in addition to Chemistry. Dr. Macnevin published "An Exposition of the Atomic Theory," which was favorably received both in this country and in Europe. Besides editing an edition of Brande's Chemistry, he was also coeditor of the *New York Medical and Philosophical Journal*. His scientific papers, so far as recorded, are:—

Decomposition of Potash. *Am. Med. and Phil. Journ.*, ii. 204–208, 1811.

Chemical Examination of the Waters of Schooley's Mountain. *N. Y. Lit. and Phil. Trans.*, i. 540–557, 1815.

Analyse Eines Krystallisirter Dolomit aus Nord Amerika. *Schweigg, Journ.*, xxx. 89–94, 1820.

Exposition of the Atomic Theory of Chemistry and the Doctrine of Definite Proportions. *Thomson, Ann. Phil.*, xvi. 1820.

Chemische Unterschungen über eine neue art Baryt, den Schoharit. *Schweigg. Journ.*, xxxii. He died July 12, 1841, aged 78 years.

John Gorham, M.D.—Prof. Gorham was the Erving Professor of Chemistry at Harvard University from 1816 to his death in 1827. His one great and lasting contribution to our science was his systematic treatise, published in 1819, in two volumes, 8vo., embracing about eleven hundred pages, under the title of "The Elements of Chemical Science." This work bears ample testimony that the author was a man of ability and thoroughly familiar with his science. His "introduction" is an essay which every chemist to-day can read with pleasure and admire for its truly wide philosophic spirit as well as for its chaste and beautiful style. The whole treatise is, for the time, an admirable performance, and fully justifies the opinion then expressed of it by Prof. Silliman in his notice of the work (*Silliman's Journal*, 1822), that "this work is not surpassed by any one with which we are acquainted, as a perspicuous, chaste, and philosophical treatise." Dr. Gorham had been the fellow-student of Prof. Silliman under Dr. Hope in Edinburgh, in 1804–5.

Dr. Gorham's "Elements" was the first systematic treatise on the science of chemistry by an American author, and deservedly secures honorable mention to his name. His chemical papers appear to have been few. "An Analysis of Heavy Spar from Hatfield" (1815); "Contributions to Chemistry, No. 1;" "Indigogene" (*N. E. Journ. Med.*, vi. 1817); "Chemical Examination of Sugar, supposed Intentionally Poisoned" (*Thomson's Am. Phil.*, 1817, x. 197); "Chemical Analysis of Indian Corn" (*N. E. Journ. Med.*, ix. 1820; *Tilloch's Mag.*, lvii. 1821, 311); and "Examination of Calculi from the Sublingual Gland" (*N. E. Journ. Med.*, ix. 1820), are all I find mention of.

One of his pupils, whose own professional eminence gives weight to his words, in a private communication to the speaker, under date of July 27, 1874, says: "Dr. Gorham, who succeeded Dexter in the Chemical Chair (at Harvard), was an accomplished teacher, and exceedingly popular with all the students. The excellent treatise, to which you allude, was written for our benefit, and considered by us all as the sure guide to all the arcana of science, and the book of books, which no future discoveries could ever suffer to be laid upon the shelf as a thing of the past."

"Dr. Gorham died young, for the interests of science and the love of his professional brethren, who followed him as true mourners to an early grave."

Parker Cleaveland.—From 1803 until his death Prof. Cleaveland devoted his life with remarkable singleness of purpose and exclusive assiduity to the duties of his professorship at Bowdoin College, Maine. He at first did all the work there in mathematics, natural philosophy, chemistry, and mineralogy. He was relieved of mathematics by another colleague after some years. His name is inseparable from the early history of American science. Although a good chemist, and during his long life its successful teacher at Bowdoin, his fame rests chiefly and securely on his "Elementary Treatise on Mineralogy," which first appeared in 1816, and in a second revised edition in 1822. The *Edinburgh Review* for September, 1818, at a time when they were not much given to praising American books, said of Prof. Cleaveland's "Mineralogy," "that it would be found to be the most useful work on mineralogy in our language," and advises its republication in Great Britain.

There can be no doubt that the timely appearance of Cleaveland's "Mineralogy" did very much to stimulate scientific progress in the United States, and it was certainly, at the date of its issue, the most important contribution made to American scientific literature. A careful review of it by Prof. Silliman in 1818, will be found in the first volume of the *American Journal of Science*.

JAMES FREEMAN DANA.—The recognition of chemistry as an element of academic instruction at Dartmouth College in 1820, was signalized by the election of Dr. Dana as their first professor. He had been the assistant of Dr. Gorham at Harvard, where he graduated in 1813. He developed such ability in chemical studies, that in 1815, while yet in his novitiate under Dr. Gorham, he was selected by the university to visit London, and procure for the chemical department at Harvard a new ontfit of apparatus, which commission he executed to the complete satisfaction of the authorities. While in London he prosecuted his studies in practical chemistry in the laboratory of Accum, who also had been the instructor of Prof. Silliman in 1804–5, and who had at that time the only laboratory in London open to students. On his return to Cambridge he executed the needful repairs and alterations in the laboratory preparatory to receiving the new apparatus, and was almost immediately appointed assistant to the professor of chemistry.

In the autumn of 1817 he was appointed Lecturer on Chemistry at Dartmouth College, and in 1820 Professor of Chemistry and Mineralogy in the same institution. While yet a student at Cambridge, he received the award of the Boylston prize for a dissertation on the "Tests for Arsenic," and while on his voyage home from Europe he wrote a second dissertation on the "Composition of Oxymuriatic Acid," for which the Boylston premium was again assigned him in 1817. In all respects Dr. Dana was a man of superior qualities, and his brief career, cut short by an untimely death at thirty-three years, is marked by contributions to science of no ordinary merit. His most important original work was his "Epitome of Chemical Philosophy," Concord, New Hampshire, 1825, pp. 221. This treatise, in which he develops the philosophy of the science as it then existed, is an extended syllabus of the lectures delivered by Dr. Dana at Dartmouth College, and is altogether a creditable performance. He was an accomplished experimenter, skilful in devising apparatus and methods, and an eloquent, perspicuous lecturer.

He contributed original memoirs on a variety of subjects; for example:—

In 1819. On a New Form of Electrical Battery (which is a mode of Æpinus's condenser).

1819. "Chemical Examination of the Berries of Myrica Cerifera, or Wax Myrtle." He presents a proximate analysis of the berry.

1819. On the Effect of Vapor on Flame. This short paper has great significance, and the line of research it indicates has never yet been fully worked up.

1820. On the Existence of Cantharidin in the *Lytta Vittatæ*, or Potato Fly.

1822. "Chemical Examination of some Morbid Animal Products." In this paper Dr. Dana gives the results of his examination of a collection of urinary and other calculi in the Anatomical Museum of Harvard College. He detects the error of Brande in mistaking uric acid for muriatic acid in calculi, and shows his sagacity as an analyst by other evidence.

1823. Miscellaneous Notices: 1. Connection of Electricity, Heat, and Magnetism. 2. Preparation of Euchlorin Gas. 3. Concretion from the Tonsil.

1823. "Galvano-Magnetic Apparatus." This is a neat form of floating spiral, like Ritchie's, which was then unknown.

1824. "On the Theory of the Action of Nitrous Gas in Eudiometry." A creditable paper.

1824. "Ignition of Platinum," by Vapor of Ether on Warm Platinum Sponge. "New Locality of Cobalt." This was the "Danaite" or cobaltine of Fredonia, N. H., first noticed by Dr. Dana. Mr. Patten's Air-Pump. All the above in *Silliman's Journal*.

1827. Some Experiments on the Root of *Sanguinaria Canadensis* (*N. Y. Lyc. Nat. Hist.*, ii. 1828, 225). Dr. Dana discovered the alkaloid which he called *sanguinarine*, in the roots of this plant. Dr. A. A. Hayes, then assistant to Dr. Dana, had previously called the attention of his instructor to this plant. See *Silliman's Elements of Chemistry*, ii. 1831, pp. 503–505, for a statement of the case by Hayes. Dr. James Schiel, of St. Louis, has subsequently demonstrated the identity of sanguinarin with chelerythrine (*Sill. Journ.* [2], xx. 220, 1855. See *Gmelin's Hand-Book*, xvii. 156).

Samuel Luthur Dana, M.D., born 1795, died 1868. —Dr. Dana, of Lowell, was for fifty years the acknowledged authority in the United States as a technical chemist. After completing his medical studies in 1818, he soon devoted himself exclusively to manufacturing and technical chemistry, holding the position of chemist to the Merrimac print works in Lowell, Mass., from 1833 to the time of his death, thirty-five years. He is the inventor of what is known as the "American System" of bleaching, which he made known in 1838, in the Bulletin of the Société Industrielle de Mulhouse. By his researches upon the action of cow dung as a mordant, he discovered that this and similar manures acted by virtue of the phosphate of sodium they contain, and led to the use of dung substitutes, independently by Dana in the United States, and by Mercer in England. These researches upon cow dung also led him to investigate the nature of manures in general, of mould and muck, and finally to write his well-known book called "A Muck Manual for Farmers" and an essay on manures which received the prize of the Massachusetts Society for Promoting Agriculture. Dr. Dana, in point of time, originality, and ability, stood deservedly first among scientific writers on agriculture in the United States.

Dr. Dana published a translation of "Tanquerel on Lead Diseases" (translated chiefly by his daughters), his attention having been drawn to the importance of the subject by his researches upon the action of the waters of Lowell upon lead, undertaken by him at the request of the government of that city.

Dr. Dana was a man of a retiring, modest disposition, and he published but little, although the ample stores of his knowledge were always open to those who sought his advice.

John Griscom.—Dr. Griscom was one of the earliest teachers of chemistry in the United States, commencing as a private lecturer in 1806, in New York. Dr. Francis, who was subsequently his colleague in Rutgers Medical College, says, "for thirty years Dr. Griscom was the acknowledged head of all other teachers of chemistry among us" (in New York), "and he kept pace with the flood of light which Davy, Murray, Gay-Lussac, and Thénard and others shed on the progress of chemical philosophy at that day. His calm spirit, his deliberate and grave utterance, his exact diction, the simplicity of his manner, and his unostentatious life, were the characteristics which marked him."

Dr. Griscom contributed for many years abstracts of chemical papers from the foreign journals to the *American Journal of Science*, a service which he performed with habitual exactness. But I do not find record of any original researches by Dr. Griscom, whose activities were consumed chiefly in the duties of instruction, and in various philanthropic labors, to which he devoted himself with much zeal and success.

Prof. Silliman maintained a lifelong correspondence with Dr. Griscom, and in one of his letters written January 15th, 1850, says, in allusion to Dr. Griscom's contributions to the *American Journal of Science*, "but nothing in the miscellaneous department can ever rival those rich contributions which you made with so much punctuality and judicious selection."

THOMAS COOPER.—Dr. Cooper was among the early workers in chemistry in this country. He was a voluminous writer on a variety of subjects, political, ethical, economical, philosophical, and chemical. He filled the chemical chair at Dickinson College, in Carlisle, Pennsylvania, from 1811 to 1814, and after this at Columbia, South Carolina, from 1819 to 1834, where he became President of the University.

Dr. Cooper, in 1811, published in *Bruce's Journal*, pp. 134–139, an "Account of the Decomposition of Potash and Production of Potassium by Heat," accompanied by a plate, showing the apparatus he used. This was done in Priestley's laboratory, at Northumberland, and is the first account we have of the production of potassium in this country by the furnace process. In 1818 Dr. Cooper edited in Philadelphia an edition of Thomas Thomson's System of Chemistry, in 4 vols. 8vo.; and in the same year he published a work on Medical Jurisprudence. He had learned in France the secret of making chlorine from common salt, and attempted to turn bleacher and calico printer at Manchester, but was not successful. His radical politics led him to follow his friend Priestley to America, and he took up his residence at Northumberland as a lawyer, prior to assuming the duties of the chemical chair at Carlisle. He was a free-thinking materialist, and commonly accredited an unbeliever. He died May 11th, 1840, aged 81 years.

THOMAS G. CLEMSON, of Pennsylvania, was one of the small number of Americans educated at the School of Mines in Paris. He is the author of some mineral analyses, and proposed the name *seybertite* for the so-called bronzite, or clintonite of Amity, which he carefully analyzed, and both the name and analysis stand good to-day. Mr. Clemson was, I believe, the first to announce the discovery of the diamond in North Carolina, where he resided from an early period after his return from Europe. If he made later researches, I have failed to find the record of them.

Dr. John Redman Coxe, who in 1809 succeeded Dr. Woodhouse in the medical department of the University of Pennsylvania, has left us some records of his original researches. We may mention especially his paper in *Thomson's Annals of Philosophy*, in 1816, on a Plan for Electric Telegraphy, which long antedates any other American suggestion on this subject since the days of Franklin. Dr. Coxe also wrote on Phosphorus (*Thomson's Ann. Phil.*, 1813, i. 68); Observations on Crystallization (*Ibid.*, 1815, vi. 101–106); On Lead Pipes (*Ibid.*, 1816, viii. 237); Preparation of Phosphuret of Lime (*Journal Royal Instit.*, i. 1831, 172).

William Charles Wells, M.D., F.R.S., the author of the "Essay on Dew," crowned by the Royal Society of London, in 1814, with the Rumford medal, was an American, born in Charleston, South Carolina, in 1747. Few physical investigations can be found on the fair pages of science, undertaken in a purer spirit of research for truth's sake than those which this lonely, austere, and abstemious man carried out in his garden in Surrey, in 1812. His apparatus was of the simplest. With a few small thermometers, some plates of different kinds of metal, a few watch glasses, and small pledgets of swan's down and wool, on the greensward of his little garden in Surrey, during the livelong nights, with the silent stars his only companions, did this philosopher meekly and reverently enter the great temple of nature, an earnest seeker of her secrets—a humble worshipper at her shrine. There he evolved, by patient inductive research, those laws now seemingly so self-evident, which, from the days of Aristotle, had eluded the grasp of previous observers. "Few and simple as were the means with which Dr. Wells conducted his researches, his experiments were so various, so direct, and so conclusive—so sagaciously devised and so admirably executed—that the whole philosophy and economy of the subject which he studied were completely settled."* The simplicity of his recital of his experiences, in his life, is worthy of his earnest devotion to his work while suffering under the distressing disease which in a few years terminated his hard and checkered career.

There is a chastened intellectual joy which flows into

* From an eloquent tribute to the life and character of Dr. Wells, by Dr. Elisha Bartlett, 1849.

the soul, from the contemplation of any ideally perfect work of research like this, which has stood the test of time, and stands now, as it were, a life for a life. It seems like the sea-shell softly to murmur of its parentage, and, as Landor says of the shell—

> "Pleased, it remembers its august abodes,
> And murmurs as the ocean murmurs there."

[Professor Tyndall, in his late address, August 19, 1874, at Belfast, which comes to hand as this is passing the press, says: "In 1813 Dr. Wells, the founder of our present theory of dew, read before the Royal Society a paper in which, to use the words of Mr. Darwin, 'he distinctly recognizes the principle of natural selection; and this is the first recognition that has been indicated.' The thoroughness and skill with which Dr. Wells pursued his work, and the obvious independence of his character, rendered him long ago a favorite with me; and it gave me the liveliest pleasure to alight upon this additional testimony to his penetration."]

James Cutbush was the Professor of Chemistry at the U. S. Military Academy at West Point, and previously at St. John's College, Maryland. His paper "On the Formation of Cyanogen in some Chemical Processes not before noticed" (*Sill. Journ.*, 1822, vol. vi. pp. 149–155) describes the production of cyanogen from the action of nitric acid upon charcoal. He published an elaborate essay "On the Composition and Properties of the Chinese Fire and the so-called Brilliant Fires" in the seventh volume of the *Am. Journ. of Sci.*, pp. 118–140, with numerous pyrotechnic formulæ; and another article in the previous volume (vi. 302), "On the Composition and Properties of Greek Fire," which is full of curious learning. In the Memoirs of the Columbian Chemical Society of Philadelphia, of which society Dr. Cutbush was the president, is a short paper by him "On the Oxyacetate of Iron as a Test or Reagent for the discovery of Arsenic" (1812).

Julius T. Ducatel.—Dr. Ducatel, of Baltimore (born June 6th, 1796, died September 23d, 1849), was the Professor of Chemistry in the University of Maryland, and in 1830 was elected, on the death of Dr. De Butts, to the chemical chair in the medical department of the same university. Dr. Ducatel enjoyed the repute of being an accomplished and successful teacher and lecturer on his science. He had enjoyed in Paris the teachings of Brougniart, Brochant, and Gay-Lussac, with whom he ever maintained a correspondence. His only chemical contribution of which record is preserved, was his "Manual of Toxicology."

Lardner Vanuxem.—One of a small number of Americans who early enjoyed the advantages of a scientific training at the School of Mines in Paris, and the associate of Brougniart, Haüy, and other distinguished men, Vanuxem early contributed important chemical and physical memoirs upon American mineralogy, often in company with his friend Keating. These papers are mostly to be found in the *Proceedings of the Academy of Natural Sciences of Philadelphia.* His analyses of phosphate of iron from New Jersey; of tabular spar from Willsborough; of jeffersonite; of zircon, from Buncombe, North Carolina; of marmolite, and other serpentines, are not merely good analyses, but show their author to have had a thorough scientific training. The paper on the "Mineralogy of Sussex County, New Jersey," in connection with Keating (1822) is an admirably prepared memoir. Prof. Vanuxem was for a time in charge of the chemical instruction in the University of South Carolina, at Columbia, South Carolina, under Dr. Thomas Cooper's presidency. He later had charge of one of the divisions of the New York State geological survey, one volume of the final reports being devoted to the record of his labors. He was deservedly held in the highest esteem for his earnest simplicity and steady integrity of character. He died in 1848.

The University of Virginia has been fortunate in its chemical professors. Dr. J. P. Emmett was the first, from 1825, until his death in 1842. He was succeeded by Prof. Robert E. Rogers, who filled the chair until 1852, when it fell to Dr. J. Lawrence Smith, who was followed by Dr. S. Maupin, and he again by the present incumbent, Prof. J. W. Mallet.

John Patton Emmet, M.D.—Dr. Emmet was the Professor of Chemistry from 1824, until his death in 1842, at the University of Virginia. He contributed important memoirs upon both chemistry and physics. His papers "On Iodide of Potassium as a Test for Arsenic," "Upon the Solvent and Oxidating Powers of Ammoniacal Salts," "Bromine and Iodine in Kanawha Salts," "On Formic Acid," and "On the Solidification of Raw Gypsum," were all published in the *American Journal of Science*, where also he was a frequent contributor of papers on electro-magnetism and magneto-electricity, which showed originality and research. His method of evolving sparks and shocks from the common magnet was ingenious and original, and among the very earliest observations in magneto-electricity. I learn from Dr. J. Lawrence Smith that Dr. Emmet left valuable and extended notes of original experiments on light and other subjects, which have not yet been published.

John Torrey, of New York, for more than half a century deservedly esteemed for his exact attainment in science, and for every virtue, although one of the best read chemists and most successful chemical instructors in the United States, has left few records of his work to which reference can be made. He filled successively the Chemical Chairs at West Point; in the College of Physicians and Surgeons in New York; and at Nassau Hall, in Princeton; and for many years was at the head of the chemical department of the United States Assay Office in New York. His most important contributions to science were in the department of mineralogy and botany. His name is inseparably connected with the development of the North American flora. His fine botanical collections are now, by his gift, the property of Columbia College in New York, of which institution he was for many years a trustee.

Dr. Torrey in 1819 discovered that the remarkable fungus found underground in Virginia and elsewhere, and known as *tuckahoe*, or Indian-bread (*sclerotium gigantium*), was composed entirely of a new principle, not before described, and which he called *sclerotin*. Dr. Torrey's original paper on this subject was read before the New York Lyceum of Natural History in 1819, and was published in the *New York Medical Repository* for December, 1820. In 1827, after the publication of Braconnot's paper on *Pectic Acid* (in 1824, *Ann. de Ch. Phys.*, 28, 173; 30, 96). Dr. Torrey republished his earlier paper, with some additions in the *New York Medical and Physical Journal* (vi. No. 4), and showed the identity of the two substances. See *Silliman's Journal*, 2, xxvii. 439, for further remarks on pectic acid, and Dr. Torrey's original discovery of it.

Sketches of the scientific labors and services of Dr. Torrey will be found also in vol. v. *American Journal of Science*, 1873, pp. 324 and 411.

Dr. Torrey published in the *New York Lyceum of Natural History*:—

1824. On Yenite in the United States, p. 51, vol. i.

1824. Account of the Columbite of Haddam, i. pp. 89-93.

1836. Notes on American Minerals, vol. iii. p. 86.

1825. Vauquelinite in the United States.

1848. Vauquelinite in the United States, vol. iv. pp. 76-79.

In the *American Journal of Science and Arts:*—

1818. On Staurotide, vol. i. p. 435.

1820. On Siderographite, vol. ii. p. 176.

1822. On an ore of Zinc at Ancram, vol. v. 235.

1825. On West Point Minerals, vol. ix. p. 402.

1839. On the Condensation of Carbonic, Sulphurous, and Chlorochromic Acid Gases, vols. xxxv. 374 and xxxvi. 394.

Samuel Guthrie, M.D.—Dr. Guthrie, of Sackett's Harbor, New York, deserves honorable mention as one of the earliest laborers in practical chemistry in this country. He was an original discoverer of chloroform, quite independently of the contemporaneous researches of Soubeiran, Liebig, and Dumas—made at the same time, but completely unknown to Guthrie. I have elsewhere recited the main facts of this curious piece of chemical history, and may be permitted to quote it here.*

"So early as 1796, an association of four Dutch chemists, who had already discovered the rich hydrocarbon gas, long known as heavy carburetted hydrogen gas, or olefiant gas, and now called ethylene or hydrogen-dicarbide ($C_2H_4$), studied the effects produced from mingling this hydrocarbon with an equal volume of chlorine gas over water. They saw that the volume of the mixed gases rapidly diminished, with a notable elevation of temperature and the appearance of a dense oily-looking liquid, collecting on the sides of the bell-jar and the surface of the water, and quickly sinking to the bottom. Collecting this oily liquid and washing it clean of adhering chlorine, in alkaline water, and in pure water, it was found to be a new substance of a highly agreeable ethereal odor, and distinctly sweetish aromatic taste, neutral to tests, and nearly insoluble in water, to which, however, it imparted its taste and odor, but quite soluble in ether and alcohol. It was wholly unaffected by concentrated sulphuric acid even with the aid of heat. For many years its real constitution remained unknown, and it was shown only as one of the curiosities of the

* "A Century of Medicine and Chemistry:" A Lecture Introductory to the Course of Lectures to the Medical Class in Yale College, 1871.

chemist's laboratory, under the name of 'Oil of the Dutch Chemists;' the name olefiant gas having had its origin from the oil-producing property, which this gas developed in its action with chlorine. Analysis has long since shown that this chlorine compound of the Dutch chemists is a simple union of one molecule of ethylene with two of chlorine, and that it may properly be called the chloride of olefiant gas. I have been the more particular in noticing the discovery of this remarkable substance because it has acquired considerable notoriety from the fact that it was early and most naturally confounded with chloroform, to which, in sensible and physiological properties, it bears a remarkable resemblance. It was long known as 'Chloric Ether,' a name which conveys a false meaning, since there is nothing in the chemical constitution of the body which in the least resembles the ethers.

"In 1831 appeared the second volume of 'Silliman's Elements of Chemistry,' in the order of the lectures then given in Yale College, in which the Dutch liquid was spoken of in its physiological relations, with the remark that, 'Its medical powers have not been ascertained, but from its constitution and properties it is highly probable it would be an active diffusive stimulant.'

"This remark immediately attracted the attention of Dr. Samuel Guthrie, of Sackett's Harbor, New York, a man of an active and original mind, much devoted to practical chemistry, who at once conceived that he might obtain the so-called 'chloric ether' in greater abundance and at a cheaper cost by distilling together alcohol and chloride of lime (bleaching powder). His success was remarkable, and he obtained the alcoholic solution (of chloroform) in great abundance, describing his process in a short article in *Silliman's Journal of Science* for January, 1832; and subsequently, in July of the same year, he states with more detail the precautions he adopted to obtain the product pure, and especially, free from alcohol. It is remarkable that in his second paper he describes in full the method of testing the purity of the substance by agitation with concentrated sulphuric acid. There is no question that Dr. Guthrie was entirely original in his method of producing 'chloric ether,' as it was then called, and it is no abatement of his sagacity that he was not aware that, earlier in the same year in which he described his process, a French chemist, Mr. Soubeiran, had devised and described the same method in a memoir entitled, '*Re-*

*searches on some Combinations of Chlorine,'* which appeared in the *Ann. de Chemie et de Phys.* for Feb. 1831. Soubeiran calls the product 'a new ethereal liquid of a constitution unlike any before known to chemists,' and also gives us the name chloric ether (*ether chlorique*). The term 'chloric ether' had also been used by Dr. Thomson in 1820 to describe the oil of the Dutch Chemists. Soubeiran gave two analyses of this product, which, while they prove that the body is not the 'Dutch liquid,' failed to reveal its true constitution, which was first given by Dumas in 1834, in a memoir published by him in the same journal, and in this paper Dumas then gave to the new body the name by which it has ever after been known, *chloroform.*

"Such, in brief, is the history of one of the most remarkable bodies ever discovered. You will understand that while the 'chloric ether' of Guthrie was a misnomer, the substance which he produced was *chloroform,* and that the first use made of this agent in medical practice was at the suggestion of Prof. Silliman, to Dr. Eli Ives, formerly Professor of Theory and Practice in this college in 1832. Dr. Ives's note on his experience will be found in *Silliman's Journal,* vol. 21, for July, 1832. The case in which he employed it was one of asthma in an aged person, who was relieved of a severe paroxysm by its use 'more suddenly than she had been in any previous illness of the kind.' Thus the therapeutic history of chloroform had its commencement from the teachings and practice of the Yale Medical School."

The question of absolute priority of the discovery of chloroform may give it to the French chemists Souberaine, but a committee of the Medico-Chirurgical Society, of Edinburgh, have awarded to Dr. Guthrie the merit of having first published an account of its therapeutic effects as a diffusible stimulant in 1832. Chloroform is, therefore, fairly to be claimed as an American discovery. Guthrie also experimented with a boldness and intrepidity amounting almost to rashness in the preparation of fulminating compounds, of which he manufactured large quantities, of various and original constitution, for commercial purposes. His papers on this subject in vol. xxi. (1832) of the *American Journal of Science* disclose his power as an originator of new methods in chemistry. This is true, also, of his process for the rapid conversion of potato-starch into sugar, printed in the same volume.

George T. Bowen, whose early death, in 1828, at Nashville, where he had just assumed the duties of the chemical chair in the University of Nashville, deprived chemical science of a zealous votary. Such was his devotion to chemistry that, while an undergraduate at Yale College, he was permitted, contrary to all precedent in those days, to devote all the time he could spare from his other studies to laboratory work, under the instruction of Prof. Silliman. Here he made original observations (1822) "On the Electro-magnetic Effects of Hare's Calorimeter," and "On a Mode of Preserving in a Permanent Form the Coloring Matter of the Purple Cabbage as a Test for Acids and Alkalies." He has left us analyses and descriptions of several minerals, *e. g.*, of the scheelite of Lane's mine; of Sillimanite, which he proposed as a new species; of the silicate of copper from New Jersey; of a variety of serpentine which he called nephrite, from Smithfield, Rhode Island; and of pyroxene-sahlite from near New Haven. All this he did chiefly before 1822, and prior to commencing his medical studies in Philadelphia, where also he was a devoted follower of the meetings of the Academy of Natural Sciences, contributing to their memoirs and discussions. Dr. Bowen was born at Providence, Rhode Island, March 19th, 1803, graduated at Yale College in 1822, was elected Professor of Chemistry at Nashville in 1825, where he died October 25th, 1828, in the 26th year of his age.

DR. GERARD TROOST succeeded Dr. Bowen in the chemical chair of Nashville University in 1828, where he served as Professor of Chemistry, Geology, and Mineralogy until his death in 1850. Dr. Troost was a native of Bois le Duc, in Holland (born March 15th, 1776). He was educated at Amsterdam and Leyden, studying medicine and chemistry. Having great skill in crystallography, he was in 1807 sent to Paris by Louis Bonaparte, to pursue his favorite studies under the renowned French mineralogist Abbé Haüy. In 1810 he came to America and settled at Philadelphia, where he was one of the founders, and the first President of the Academy of Natural Sciences. He was a constant contributor to the early volumes of the Transactions of the Academy. His papers were chiefly mineralogical, and especially crystallographical. His paper on Pyroxene, in the *Annals of the Maclurean Lyceum*, is a valuable contribution.

In 1814 Dr. Troost established works for the production of alum at Cape Sable, Maryland, which was one of the earliest chemical industries in this country, and, if I mistake not, the first manufactory of alum.

To his well-directed zeal and industry science owes much for its progress west of the Alleghanies. He instituted the geological survey of Tennessee, and for eighteen years was the geologist of that State, carrying on his work of exploration under many discouragements, and almost unrequited, until his death on the 14th of August, 1850.

He added largely to our knowledge of meteoric bodies, having been fortunate in collecting a great number of both stony and iron masses, fallen or found in his immediate vicinity, and the chemical and physical history of which he accurately studied. His memoirs on these bodies will be found in the *Amer. Journ. of Sci.* With surprising industry and success, considering his remote and comparatively isolated situation, he amassed one of the most valuable collection of minerals and fossils ever formed in the United States, sparing neither labor nor expense to this end. Fortunately his collection escaped unharmed the ravages of war, thanks to the timely care and skill of one of Dr. Troost's sons, and of Dr. J. B. Lindsley, President of Nashville University, although his valuable scientific library was scattered and destroyed. The catalogue of Dr. Troost's mineral collections forms two stout manuscript volumes, written in the clear hand of the author, and describes 13,582 numbered and ticketed specimens, with their crystallographic and physical characters carefully distinguished. This collection, together with the fossils (which are also very valuable), has lately been secured to the Public Library of Louisville, Kentucky, chiefly by the exertions of Dr. J. Lawrence Smith, at a cost of $20,000. This collection is especially rich in crystallized specimens and varied forms, to the study of which Dr. Troost devoted special attention. The catalogue, we are informed, is to be printed in detail. A sketch of the life of Dr. Troost, by Dr. Philip Lindsley, will be found in vol. i. p. 539 of the works of the latter.

Denison Olmsted.—Although Prof. Olmsted's fame rests upon his astronomical and more especially upon his meteorological studies, and his discussion of the great meteoric shower of 1833, yet we remember with satisfaction that he was also a chemist. From 1817 to 1825 he filled the chair of chemistry in the University of North Carolina, where he signalized his term of duty by inaugurating and carrying forward, gratuitously, the first attempt ever made in the United States toward a geological survey of a State. His report, in two parts, appeared in 1824 and 1825, filling only about 140 octavo pages. He also read before the Connecticut Academy, in 1826, after his transfer to the physical chair at Yale College, a "Memoir on the State of Chemical Science," which may be read now with curious interest, as a record of the then existing state of philosophical opinion in our science. It may be found in the XIth and XIIth volumes of *Silliman's Journal.* It is noteworthy that no similar attempt has since been made by any American chemist, until Dr. Gibbs's Report on the Recent Progress of Organic Chemistry (*Proceed. Amer. Ass.*, ix. pp. 37-61, 1855).

Considering the rudimentary state of geology and its associate sciences in 1821, Prof. Olmsted's labors as the pioneer in this department of exploration must ever be considered as eminently honorable to his scientific grasp and ability.

Denison Olmsted, Jr.—This promising chemist, son of the former, died at the early age of twenty-two years, in 1846. He had been for two or three years before an assiduous student in the laboratory of Yale College, where the writer had the happiness to count him as one of the earliest of his pupils in the incipiency of the "Yale Scientific School." His analytical work during that period will be found on record. For a year before his death he held the post of chemist to the geological survey of Vermont, and he was honored shortly before his death by an appointment to a similar situation in Canada, to which our distinguished colleague Dr. Hunt, also taken from the Yale Analytical Laboratory, succeeded. His mineralogical cabinet, gathered by himself, now forms the nucleus of the collection in Beloit College.

W. W. Mather.—Prof. Mather, who died, acting President of the University of Ohio, at Columbus, is better known to this generation as the author of the Report on the First District, in the Geological Survey of New York (1843), than as a chemist. But, if we turn to the 27th volume of the *American Journal of Science* for 1835, pp. 241-267, we shall find an elaborate memoir entitled "Contributions to Chemical Science by W. W. Mather, Assist. Prof. of Chemistry at the U. S. Military Academy, West Point."

This memoir is upon—I. Chloride of Aluminium and its Analysis. II. Hydrated Chloride of Aluminium. III. Crystallized Tin from Solution. IV. Georgia Gold. V. Silver of Lane's Mine. VI. Iodide of Potassium and Platinum, or Iodo-platinate of Potassium. VII. Chloriodide of Platinum. VIII. Crystallized Perchloride of Platinum. IX. Amalgam of Platinum. X. Iodide of Mercury. XI. Solubility of Bitungstate of Ammonia. XII. Disulphuret of Bismuth.

An examination of this memoir will show that it is the work of a chemist of unusual ability. The author presents a great number of analyses by himself made with much care, and details all his processes. He gives a new determination for the atomic weight of aluminium, prompted to it by a discrepant statement in Berzelius (*Traité de Ch.*, ii. 373) by which the numbers representing the composition of alumina are transposed. The whole paper is a creditable one, and up to its date was the most elaborate original research in inorganic chemistry which had been made by any American chemist, so far as I have seen.

Prof. Mather also contributed papers "On the principles involved in the reduction of iron and silver ores, with a suplementary notice of some of the principal silver mines of Mexico and South America" (*Sill. Journ.*, 1, xxiv. 1833, pp. 213–237). In this elaborate memoir the author discusses the chemistry of the Mexican silver processes, before that time almost completely unknown in this country. His paper contains a great amount of useful information.

"On cupellation, an easy, an accurate, and new method" (*Sill. Journ.*, 1, xxxv. 321, 1839).

"On the crystalline form of iodine," with figures (*Sill. Journ.*, 2, xviii. p. 35, 1830).

George C. Schaeffer.—Prof. Schaeffer, who died in 1873, at Washington, was long justly esteemed as one of the best read chemists of his time. He published but little, but the student of American chemistry will find in his papers "On perchromic acid;" "On the manufacture of ice;" his "New test for nitrates and nitrites," and "On the origin of nitrites," evidence of his original power. He adopted what are now the accepted views in chemical philosophy long in advance of the great majority of chemists everywhere.

Nor can we forget his "Chemical abstracts," which for several years he supplied to the *American Journal of Science*, during the first decade of its second series, over the familiar initials of G. C. S.

Prof. Schaeffer for a time filled the chair of chemistry in the College at Danville, Ky. But the duties of instruction were less congenial to his tastes than the more quiet pursuits of original study, and he soon retired to the librarianship of the U. S. Patent Office, where he was in his element, and where he remained until his death, always honored and esteemed as a man of varied and exact learning.

All his memoirs here cited are to be found in the *American Journal of Science and Arts.*

LEWIS C. BECK.—Dr. Beck filled the chair of chemistry in Rutgers College, New Jersey, and at the Albany Medical College. His industrious habits and great devotion to science enabled him amid the constant drag of routine duty to make important contributions to science, in botany, medicine, and chemistry. His most important work was his "Mineralogy of New York" (1842) forming one of the quarto volumes of the Reports on the Geological Survey of the State. In this work occur many chemical analyses of minerals, mineral waters, and the like, made by the author, as well as of hydraulic limestones and other economic products. He was also an early contributor to general chemistry, and published, in 1827, "General views on the formation of phosphuretted hydrogen;" in 1828, "On the nature of bleaching and disinfecting compounds;" "On the functions of nitrogen in respiration;" "On the commercial potashes of New York;" "On wines and other fermented liquors;" and "On adulterations of various substances used in medicine and the arts," etc. At the request of Prof. Henry, Dr. Beck commenced in 1848 a laborious series of "Researches on the breadstuffs of the United States," afterwards published as a report by the United States Patent Office, at Washington.

He was a man of retiring habits, great modesty, and his personal character was such as to gain him numerous and attached friends. He died in April, 1853, in his fifty-fifth year. Dr. Beck was the author of "A Manual of Chemistry" (1831), which passed through four editions.

J. W. BAILEY.—The untimely death of Prof. Bailey deprived American science of one of her most devoted and successful workers in the fulness of his powers. Prof. Bailey was a chemist who, in the discharge of the duties of the chemical chair in the United States Military Academy at West Point, New York, gave good evidence of his ability, both as a teacher and investigator; although his devotion to microscopical researches, with such eminent success, has almost led us to overlook his earlier contributions to our science.

Thus, for example, his tests for nitric acid, the double cyanide and iodide of mercury, and for sulphur by Playfair's nitro-prusside when used indirectly to detect sulphur in bodies like albumen, horn, hair, feathers, mustard-seed, etc. His paper "On the Common Blowpipe," and his note on the curious effects of a current of air on the flame of lamps, are evidences of his tact and neatness in chemical manipulation. His papers on the non-existence of polarizing silica in the organic kingdoms, and especially his beautiful researches in 1843 "On the crystals which occur spontaneously found in the tissues of plants" (*Sill. Journ.*, 1, xlviii. pp. 17–32, with a plate, 1845) are fine examples of micro-chemistry, and are characterized by a neatness which is found in all the work of this eminent and lamented investigator, and fully illustrated by his own pencil, which he held with great skill. A sketch of Prof. Bailey's life and scientific labors, by Dr. A. A. Gould, will be found in the *American Journ. of Science*, 2, xxv. p. 133, 1858. He died February 27, 1857, at the age of forty-six years

Alexander Dallas Bache.—Few probably of the younger chemists of this day look upon the late renowned chief of the United States Coast Survey as a chemist. But his encyclopædic knowledge embraced almost the entire circle of the sciences. He was chosen, only three years after his graduation at West Point, and when only twenty-two years of age, to the chair of Natural Philosophy and Chemistry in the University of Pennsylvania, at Philadelphia, which he held for seven years. During this time he published several chemical and chemico-physical articles, as that "On the Specific Heat of the Atoms of Bodies," in which he maintained that the best data then known (1828) failed to support the doctrine that the specific heat of atoms is the same for all bodies; and "On the Inflammation of Phosphorus in a Vacuum or Highly Rarefied Medium," 1830, a research he never fully completed. In 1832 he published a translation in *Silliman's Journal*, of the "Essay on Chemical Nomenclature Prefixed to the Treatise on Chemistry; by J. J. Berzelius," in which, as is well known to all students of the literature of our science, the distinguished chemist of Stockholm proposed the terminology which is now, after more than fifty years, come fully into vogue. In his paper entitled "Remarks on a Method proposed by Dr. Thomson for Determining the Proportions of Potassa and Soda in a Mixture of the Two Alkalies, with the Application of a Similar Investigation to a Different Method of Analysis," he generalizes the special case given, and shows that the principle to which these results refer themselves may be used with great effect in avoiding a difficult step in chemical analysis, by the substitution of a less direct but more simple one, aided by easy calculations, and well deserving the attention of analytical chemists (*Franklin Institute Journal*, 1836, xvii. pp. 305–309).

In molecular physics Prof. Bache's "Inquiry in Relation to the Alleged Influence of Color on the Radiation of Non-luminous Heat" (*Silliman's Journal*, 1836, I, xxx. pp. 16–28), has become classic. It is almost needless to say that he proved by it the fallacy of the notion, till then commonly received, that color did influence the radiation of non-luminous heat. It is plain, that, had he not been called to a wider field of usefulness in the administration of great public trusts for science at Girard College, and later and chiefly of the Coast Survey, he could easily have obtained great prominence in chemical research.

Wm. J. Taylor.—This chemist has left us a number of mineral analyses. He was a critical mineralogist and competent analyst. His most elaborate research was an extended memoir on Rock Guano, published in 1857 (*Proceedings of Academy of Natural Sciences*, and *Silliman's Journal*, xxiv. No. 71, pp. 177–188), with numerous exhaustive analyses, and copious references to the literature of the whole subject. He has also published an "Examination of the Meteoric Iron from Xiquipilco, Mexico," with minute analyses (*Silliman's Journal*, 1856, xxii. p. 374, and *Proceedings of the Academy of Natural Sciences*, Philadelphia, viii. No. 3): and has described lecontite, a new mineral species, a double sulphate of ammonia and soda with potash, containing two equivalents of water, and yet homomorphous with the group of anhydrous sulphates. Mr. Taylor, besides publishing other mineralogical notes, has translated Janoyer on the "Influence of Sulphur on Iron (*Silliman's Journal*, 2, xxiv. 330). We have to lament Mr. Taylor's early death.

J. E. Teschemacher of Boston is well remembered as an acute and exact scientist, expert especially in analytical chemistry and in the determination of mineral species, using the blowpipe with remarkable skill and facility. A full list of his scientific papers will be found in the *American Journal of Science*, vol. xvii. p. 294, 1854, more than thirty in number, mineralogical, chemical, and chiefly botanical. Mr. Teschemacher was all his life engrossed in commercial affairs, and made science his recreation, doing more good work than some who have command of all their time for science.

James Davenport Whelpley.—Dr. Whelpley contributed a remarkable paper to the philosophy of chemistry in 1845, entitled "Idea of an Atom, suggested by the Phenomena of Weight and Temperature" (*Silliman's Journal*, 1, xlviii. 352–368). This paper embodies views entirely original with the author, but in which he was partly anticipated by Faraday's paper in 1844, on the "Nature of Matter" (*Phil. Mag.*, February, 1844, p. 136). But Whelpley's paper anticipated the subsequent notions of Faraday as set forth in his "Thoughts on Ray Vibrations" (*Phil. Mag.*, May, 1846). A review of these opinions showing the priority of Whelpley's statements will be found in *Silliman's Journal*, 1846, 2, ii. 401. Dr. Whelpley is also the author of two remarkable "Letters on Philosophical Induction," and on "Philosophical Analogy," which discuss principles fundamental in scientific methods.

John Pitkin Norton, Professor of Scientific Agriculture in Yale College, was appointed to the place he filled so well in 1847. Cut off at the early age of thirty years he has yet left us the record of a well directed life, crowned with honorable distinction as an original investigator in chemistry. After spending two years in attending the lectures of Prof. Silliman, and in study and research in the analytical laboratory of B. Silliman, Jr., he went to Scotland, where, as the student of Prof. James F. W. Johnston, he won the prize of the Highland Society, of fifty guineas, for his comprehensive and able research upon the Oat; an investigation which led the way to the later researches of the same class in this country and in Europe. In Utrecht, under Mūlder, he prosecuted his studies in agricultural and physiological chemistry, of which his memoir on the protein bodies of peas and almonds is in evidence. In 1847 he joined Prof. Silliman, Jr., as a colleague in the duties of the Analytical Laboratory of Yale College, which drew to its walls an increasing number of pupils, and soon developed into the "Yale Scientific School," now the "Sheffield Scientific School." Prof. Norton was an industrious author and published during his term of duty his "Elements of Scientific Agriculture," and edited with valuable notes and corrections, Stephen's "Book of the Farm," in two volumes. He wrote a memoir on the potato disease, and was a constant contributor to the *Albany Cultivator*, in a series of letters written both from Europe and after his return. These letters were always remarkable for sound judgment, thorough accuracy and fulness, and the lively style in which they were written.

Among the class of practical agriculturists and students who came up to attend Prof. Norton's first course of lectures on Scientific Agriculture, in January, 1848, were several young men, then unknown to fame, upon two of whom his mantle fell, and is now borne in the persons of Prof. William H. Brewer, and Prof. Samuel W. Johnson, of the Sheffield School, worthy successors in his own chosen field of study and authorship.

In the winter of 1851–52, Prof. Norton entered with zeal into the plan of establishing at Albany a university in which agriculture and its connected sciences should receive the direct patronage of the State. In carrying out this effort he was compelled to travel twice in each week during the winter from New Haven to Albany and back, giving three lectures in each place. This exertion proved too much for his powerful frame, and developed the latent seeds of pulmonary disease, which cut him down just as he had fairly entered on the wide field of his usefulness, perfectly fitted for the work, and enjoying the entire confidence alike of the agricultural community and of men of science. He was a man of noble generosity and the highest moral and scientific excellence.

Evan Pugh, Ph.D., F.C.S.*—Few American teachers of chemical science have attained a nobler fame than Dr. Evan Pugh, late President of the Agricultural College of Pennsylvania. A blacksmith's apprentice at the age of nineteen, he bought out the residue of his time and supported himself by manual labor while he received a year's instruction at the seminary of Whitestown, N. Y. He had fallen heir to a small estate, including a small academy, or private school, at Oxford, Chester County, Pennsylvania, his native place; and, removing thence, he conducted the school successfully for about two years. At this time Dr. Pugh manifested great interest in the educational reform which had lately

* This notice of Dr. Pugh has been prepared by Mr. W. S. Waring.

commenced in Pennsylvania, and the manner in which he discussed the various subjects which engrossed the attention of the educators of that time, showed that he possessed in an eminent degree those logical and analytical qualities of mind which are characteristic of truly scientific men. He was an ardent advocate of phonetic spelling, and had himself attained great proficiency in the use of phonetic short-hand, a method of writing which he continued to employ, on account of its labor-saving qualities, for making notes, etc., throughout his life.

In 1853 he decided to sell his estate and academy, which had become under his management a flourishing institution, in order to obtain means by which he might secure for himself a European course of scientific instruction. His friends protested vigorously against this step, but he was not to be deterred; he went the same year to Europe and spent four years in the universities of Leipsic, Göttingen, and Heidelberg, and in Paris, a most diligent and successful student of natural and mathematical science. At Göttingen he honorably sustained the examinations for the degree of Doctor of Philosophy.

Although he seemed, while in Europe, to allow his course of studies to shape themselves by a sort of prescience, as it were, definitely towards his future career, he yet found time to study, as he had the capacity to master, the highest mathematics, besides making a number of chemical investigations of no slight importance, and which form the subjects of his principal published contributions to science, viz.:—

"Hämatinsalpetersäure identisch mit Pikraminsäure," *Journ. für Prakt. Chemie*, lxv. 362.

"Miscellaneous Chemical Analyses," Inaugural Dissertation, Göttingen, 1856.

"On a New Method of Estimating Nitric Acid," *Quart. Journ. Chem. Soc.*, xii. 35, and

"On the Sources of the Nitrogen of Vegetation, with special reference to the question whether plants assimilate Free or Uncombined Nitrogen," *Philosophical Transactions*, part ii., 1861, 146 pp., 4to., with plates.

This last-mentioned investigation was made in connection with Messrs. Lawes and Gilbert; but Dr. Pugh's share in the work was by no means the least. It appears that while in Paris Dr. Pugh addressed to Mr. J. B. Lawes, the distinguished English agriculturist, so well known by the numerous and valuable researches carried on at his estate of Rothamstead, a proposition to undertake a new investigation of the question, then so vigorously mooted in France between Boussingault and Ville, as to the assimilability of free nitrogen by vegetation. Mr. Lawes received this proposition favorably, and signified his willingness to have the research carried on in his laboratory and to defray all the costs, provided Dr. Pugh could satisfy him of his ability to estimate nitrogen with a certain degree of precision. Dr. Pugh repaired to Rothamstead, and his skilful application of volumetric methods satisfied Mr. Lawes.

The question which Dr. Pugh undertook to decide was one that had been raised more than half a century before by Priestley and Ingenhouse on the one hand, who thought they had observed that plants absorbed the free nitrogen of the atmosphere, and Sennebier and Woodhouse on the other hand, who negatived this opinion. In 1837 the subject was taken up again by Boussingault, who had the sagacity to apprehend the importance of closely investigating the sources of the nitrogen periodically yielded by a given area of land, over and above that which was artificially supplied to it. After a series of experiments extending over a period of 17 years, Boussingault concluded that plants did not assimilate free nitrogen. But it happened in the mean time that M. Georges Ville, of Paris, had, from a series of investigations made by him from 1849 to 1852, which seemed to show an enormous assimilation of nitrogen by the plants with which he experimented that could not be accounted for otherwise by him, announced that the free nitrogen of the atmosphere was assimilated by vegetation. Such strikingly different results at once excited great interest among chemists and vegetable physiologists, and a commission was appointed from the French Academy of Sciences to superintend the conducting, under M. Ville, of a new set of experiments at the Muséum d'Histoire Naturelle, in 1854–5. The report of this commission only tended to confirm the conclusions already drawn by M. Ville. Other experiments were made by MM. Cloez, Gratiolet, DeLuca, Harting, and Petzholdt, whose conclusions were nearly as conflicting as those of MM. Boussingault and Ville themselves.

The researches, however, which were instituted by Dr. Pugh, and to which he devoted two years of nearly constant labor, were characterized with such comprehensiveness in their details, skill and ingenuity in the construction of apparatus and cautions against error, and withal such a rare degree of penetration to discover the many collateral questions involved, and acuteness in their solution, that the conclusions which they established have never since been questioned.

Besides establishing the conclusions of M. Boussingault, these investigations supplied a great amount of evidence in relation to rotation of crops, etc. etc., of vast importance to agricultural science, and opened a rich field of inquiry in vegetable physiology which promised the most important results, had Dr. Pugh remained at Rothamstead to prosecute these researches.

But, while yet there, he received the offer of the presidential chair of the Agricultural College of Pennsylvania from its trustees, who had heard of the rare ability he had already evinced; and although Mr. Lawes, who not only admired his abilities, but was greatly attached to him in friendship, was anxious to retain Dr. Pugh in his laboratory at a handsome remuneration, and notwithstanding the latter was passionately fond of cultivating the fields of scientific research, he returned home in the autumn of 1859 to assume the position which had been offered him.

Willingly renouncing the brilliant career which he was doubtless aware lay before him in case he should continue his researches, he recognized the duty he owed his country, and assumed the nobler and more enduring work. It was a controlling idea with him, that the teacher lives a second generation in the mental developments of the taught, and that to be a benefactor to his race the student must be the medium through which he should operate upon the great world around him.

When Dr. Pugh assumed the presidency of the Pennsylvania Agricultural College, the expediency of combining manual labor with thorough study in an institution of learning was an open question, all previous attempts of the kind both in Europe and America having resulted in signal failures. He had, however, perfect faith in a system which he believed was calculated, above all others, to develop mental and physical strength as well as practical knowledge. Referring once to the well-known fact that it is not sufficient to have spent a certain number of years within the walls of a college or university in order to secure a respectable education, he said, "An English friend, himself a university graduate, once remarked to me that he could point to artisans in the workshops of England with better trained minds, as evinced by greater power of following up any connected train of thought, than could be found with many persons who had spent years at the time-honored universities of Oxford or Cambridge."

With the eyes of the friends of agricultural education in every civilized country resting upon the experiment, he had the courage to undertake to demonstrate its practicability. He had previously visited and carefully studied the chief agricultural academies and schools of Europe, and his idea of what an American agricultural college should be was as definite as it was comprehensive and just. He found the college a struggling institution, its buildings not half finished, and its exchequer awaiting the action of a hesitating legislature for funds to carry on the enterprise. With characteristic energy he organized a new plan of instruction, planned and superintended the erection of the college buildings, secured endowments, and, besides taking the general guidance of the institution, he gave instruction and superintended the practical investigations of the students in chemistry, scientific agriculture, mineralogy, and geology.

He had just succeeded in establishing a thoroughly scientific institution upon a broad and enduring basis, and in convincing a sceptical public of the ultimate success of such a noble enterprise, when death cut short his work. He died in Bellefonte, Pa., on the 29th of April, 1864, after less than a week's illness, at the age of thirty-six.

C. M. Wetherill, M.D.—Prof. Wetherill's researches, like his lamented and sudden death, are fresh in our memories. His early papers in 1848, in the *Annalen der Chem. und Pharm.*, were "On the Neutral Sulphates of Ethyloxyd, their Decomposition Products with Water" ("Ueber Neutrales Schwefelsaures Æthyloxyd und dessen Zersetzung Strodercte mit Wasser"), and "Analysis of the Subsulphate of Cinchona." The first of these papers is reproduced in the *Proc. Am. Phil. Soc.*, 1848. His last papers are "Experiments with the Ammonium Amalgam" (*Sill. Journ.*, 2, xl. pp. 160–165, 1865), and "On the Existence of the (so-called) Ammonium Amalgams" (*Sill. Journ.*, 3, i. pp. 369, 371, 1871), both of which are most creditable contributions. The first demonstrates that the ammonium amalgam, so called, is a metallic froth; the second that the compound ammonias, *e. g.*, methyl-ammonium-oxalate, may form the so-called amalgam. Dr. Wetherill published a number of other papers, chiefly analyses, *e. g.*, "Concretion from the Stomach of a Horse;" "Molybdate of Lead;" "Food of the Queen Bee;" "Mexican Honey Ant," etc.; "A New Apparatus for the Determination of Carbonic Acid" (May, 1873, *Journ. Frank. Inst.*, xxx. 333). "Examination of Fusel Oil from Indian Corn" (May, 1873, *Journ. Frank. Inst.*, xxx. 385). This is a valuable contribution, with a fractional distillation of the crude oil, an ultimate analysis of the silver salt of one of the fatty acids from the distillate ($C_{16}H_{15}O_4Ag$), and an examination of the alcohol of fusel oil. "Examination of Gas of the Philadelphia Gas Works" (1854, *Journ. Frank. Inst.*, xxviii. 35). "An apparatus for Organic Analysis by Illuminating Gas, and on the use of this Gas in Experimental Analysis" (1854, *Journ. Frank. Inst.*, xxviii. 107–115; 184–191; 274–279). "Description of an Apparatus for Broiling by Gas" (1854, *Journ. Frank. Inst.*, 121). His paper on "Adipocire and its Formation" (*Trans. Am. Philo. Soc.*, xi. 1855) contains the results of both chemical and microscopical examinations of adipocire, with an account of experiments on the decomposition of muscular fibre by water with a view to the formation of adipocire. In 1859 he published "Analysis of the White Sulphur Water of the Artesian well of Lafayette, Indiana" (*Sill. Journ.*, 2, xxvii. pp. 241–249); a carefully conducted investigation of permanent value. "On the Crystallization of Sulphur, and upon the Reaction between Sulphid of Hydrogen, Ammonia, and Alcohol" (*Sill. Journ.*, 2, xl. pp. 338–344); a research undertaken to determine the conditions requisite to produce octohedral and prismatic sulphur. "On the Crystalline Nature of Glass" (*Sill. Journ.*, 2, xli. pp. 16–27). This curious research has demonstrated the fallacy of the common opinion that glass is quite amorphous, and demands further investigation.

"Experiments on Itacolumite (Articulite), with the Explanation of its Flexibility and its Relation to the Formation of the Diamond" (*Sill. Jour.*, 2, xliv. pp. 61–71). This is a most ingenious and suggestive paper, and is an excellent illustration of the skill and ingenuity which the author brought to bear on a seemingly unpromising subject, whether we accept his conclusions or not.

The only volume published by Dr. Wetherill was his technical treatise, called "The Manufacture of Vinegar; its Theory and Practice, with Special Reference to the

Quick Process," 1860, pp. 300, which is a very useful book.

There are other names of early laborers in the common field which are not forgotten, but time fails us that we should enumerate all in a summary which does not claim to be complete. The names of Renwick, Chilton, Dewey, T. Dwight Eaton, Elisha Mitchell; Thos. D. Mitchell, Steel, E. Hitchcock, Webster, Hall, Godon, S. G. Morton, Keating, W. R. Johnson, and others, are among the unrecorded ones in our Address.

No definite line of division can be drawn between the two moieties of our century of chemistry. The notice we have taken of those whose names have already been mentioned has, almost unavoidably, been somewhat biographical. For those who are yet in active work this course is, for obvious reasons, undesirable, and our notice of the contributions of living men must generally be much less personal. Before resuming our enumeration of contemporaneous work, it will be proper to touch briefly on some general considerations which naturally suggest themselves in this connection.

It is easy to see, by a review of the ground gone over, that, in the early history of chemistry in the United States, there were a few workers whose labors have made a sensible impression on the history of the science. Such were Rumford, Priestley, Hare, Silliman, Gorham, J. F. Dana, Wells, Bache, Seybert, Bruce, Torrey, Mather, Troost, Bowen, and others. As a department of academic training chemistry was generally provided for in most of the colleges, but it was usually coupled with natural philosophy and natural history, and was never made the subject of personal laboratory training other than by didactic and demonstrative lectures. Practical and analytical laboratories of instruction were unknown. With a few honorable exceptions, the incumbents of professorial chairs made no contributions to the advancement of science, or the stock of human knowledge. Text-books and manuals were supplied, prior to the appearance of those of Gorham and J. F. Dana, by the republication of European manuals, such as those of Henry, Murray, Brande, Chaptal, and the like. The subjects which very naturally occupied the attention of chemists here, as elsewhere, in the early part of this century were largely physical, growing naturally out of the excitement following the discovery of the pile of Volta, and its use by Davy in evolving potassium, sodium, and the other like metals from their combinations.

The "New Chemical Philosophy" of the French school had gradually won its way to complete supremacy over the phlogistic theory, although, as we have seen, Dr. Priestley to the last did battle valiantly for the doctrines of Stahl. But, although Davy's determination of the real nature of chlorine was the *coup de grace* to the old ideas, we still find the literature of chemistry full of desperate struggles to resist the dualistic philosophy which for more than half a century since has, until within the past twenty years, held almost undisputed dominion.

A few American chemists very early sought the advantages offered to students by the School of Mines in Paris—for example, the two Seyberts, Keating, Vanuxem, Clemson, etc., or, like Silliman and Gorham, found guidance in London and Edinburgh. But the advantages thus obtained were neither easy of access, nor otherwise well suited to the wants of students. Private laboratories of eminent chemists were at that time nearly closed to the access of students, few of whom enjoyed such advantages as the brothers Róse found in the laboratory of Berzelius. No chemical schools or laboratories were then organized for chemical training of students in the arts of analysis, and the methods of research were unknown, in fact, until Liebig, in 1826, first threw open wide the doors of access to the laboratory at Geissen, and welcomed cordially all students without distinction of nationality to his scientific hospitality. It was there that Hoffmann, Will, and Fresenius were his assistants, and we find the names of Johnston, Lyon Playfair, and Gregory among his English-speaking students before the tide of American followers had set in. This marks an era in the scientific history of the world that made itself felt far and wide, and nowhere more than in the United States, although nearly twenty years later, when it contributed its quota to the events next to be considered.

Great Scientific Awakening about 1845.—The year 1845 marks the beginning of a new era in the scientific life of America, which is still in active progress, and chemistry has had its full share in this advance. Many circumstances conspired to bring about this increased activity, some of which we will briefly enumerate:—

Louis Agassiz arrived in the United States in the autumn of 1846, and commenced his wonderful course of scientific labor which has made itself felt in all departments of research, and has infused a zeal for scientific studies and research in the public mind before unknown. Coming only as a guest, and for a special mission, he found here a home which with joy opened to receive and adopt him as an American citizen, and has made his name a household word in every hamlet of this broad land.

The Smithsonian Institution, founded by an Englishman, was organized at Washington in 1846, and commenced its labors under the guidance of Prof. Joseph Henry in 1847. Opening wider and yet more freely the various paths of scientific research with every passing year, and placing the science-workers of America in intimate fellowship with their co-workers in all parts of the civilized globe, its influence for good is steadily increasing.

The United States Coast Survey had in 1845 just passed under the comprehensive direction of Prof. Alexander Dallas Bache, and was at the commencement of this new epoch in American science already making its power felt in all departments of research: co-ordinating, systematizing, and directing not only its own special methods, but extending its hospitality and encouragement alike to physicists, chemists, naturalists, and explorers—what a power it has ever been in this country for the advancement of science, and what a school for special training, is the cheerful acknowledgment of all who have any knowledge of scientific progress in the United States during the past thirty years.

Astronomical Observatories.—In 1845 Professor Ormsby Macknight Mitchel effected the establishing of the Astronomical Observatory at Cincinnati, since so renowned in astronomical history. Observatories had existed before in the United States at Yale (1830), Williams (1836), Western Reserve (1838), etc., but they were more or less imperfectly organized, and we believe that the efforts of General Mitchel at Cincinnati may be fairly looked upon as the starting point of that great activity in astronomy in this country, which has since developed itself, and has so unexpectedly, by aid of the spectroscope, connected astronomy and chemistry so intimately as to render them in some sense co-ordinated sciences.

The American Association for the Advancement of Science commenced its enlarged existence in 1848, being evolved out of the Association of American

Geologists and Naturalists, which body at its last meeting in Boston, in 1847, resolved to enlarge its sphere of action, to include physics, chemistry, astronomy, and the allied physical sciences. This latter organization has itself been an outgrowth from an earlier organization, the American Association of Geologists, founded originally by the joint action of those who, in 1840, were charged with the conduct of the geological surveys of the States then prosecuting such explorations. The *Proceedings* of the American Association for the Advancement of Science at once opened a new channel of communication for the workers in science, while the migrations of the association tended doubtless to quicken the public interest in scientific pursuits.

The American Philosophical Society had a little earlier, in 1843, held its centennial celebration in Philadelphia, an event which stimulated to renewed activity the oldest of American scientific societies, and drew together a large number of co-workers from distant places to participate in this scientific festival. It was fit that the oldest scientific organization in this country, with a noble record of work in the first quarter of our chemical century, should join with fresh vigor in the great awakening which has distinguished the latter quarter of the same century.

The American Journal of Science closed its first half century of volumes in 1845, and commenced its second series in the year 1846 under an enlarged editorial management, and with more frequent issues, thus offering to investigators more frequent contact with their fellow-workers.

The year 1847 witnessed also the inauguration of the system of schools for science training in some of the older colleges, which has since led the way to the establishing of like schools far and wide.

At Yale College in 1847 was instituted the "Depart ment of Philosophy and the Arts," and work was commenced under it in the "Yale Analytical Laboratory" under the instruction of Professors Norton and Silliman, Jr. This effort was almost without any endowments in money, and was carried on for some years exclusively at the personal charge of the two professors, who not only paid their own salary, but furnished the laboratories, library, apparatus, and collections, and even paid a rent to the academical department for the use of the old presidential house, which they had also paid for fitting up for the use of the school. From the very commencement of this work by Professor Silliman, Jr., some four or five years before, in a small way, evidence was not wanting in the gathering of pupils of the existing necessity for such instruction.

At Harvard in the same year Mr. ABBOTT LAWRENCE had just made an endowment of fifty thousand dollars, at that time of unparalleled munificence, which became at once the starting point of the "Lawrence Scientific School" under the direction of Professor E. N. Horsford, who had then but recently returned from the instructions of Liebig. How suggestive, and fruitful in noble emulation, this good example of Lawrence has been in the scientific endowments of seats of learning, we may see on every hand. It is only necessary to mention the names of Sheffield, of Peabody, of Williston, of Hopkins, of Chandler, of Judd, of Packer, of Pardee, of Edwin A. Stevens; the endowments of Agassiz's Museum of Comparative Zoology of the Harvard Observatory, of the Winchester Observatory at Yale, and, lastly, of the more than regal munificence to science by the gifts of James Lick upon the Pacific coast, and of others which might properly be mentioned—to see at once the cause and effect of our increased activity in all departments of scientific research.

But this is not all.

The conquest of Mexico by the United States in 1845, the acquisition of California, and the subsequent discovery of its gold and of the gold of Australia, are events which have most obviously added their powerful stimulus to the general activity of the entire country, and, we may add, of the world, awakening the public mind to the importance of physical studies, and aiding to give them a rank in the general estimate they had never before attained, whether as means of intellectual and general culture, or as ends for the attainment of wealth and power. Without the almost convulsive shock thus imparted to the old-time system of education, by the union and focalization of all these and other like causes, the inertia with which the arguments for a more comprehensive training in our institutions of learning were so long successfully resisted, would still continue, and the "humanities" of mediæval scholasticism would have never relaxed their almost exclusive dominion in a polite education. That we are here to-day as chemists, and to celebrate this new Atlantis "for the glory of the Creator and the relief of man's estate," is in testimony that a great advance has been made upon the old traditions—a victory achieved, and with a yet more fruitful future before us and those who are to follow.

Thus on every hand, under the inspiration of these combined influences, and others of a like nature not so conspicuous, was the educated mind of America directed with new intent toward all departments of scientific study, and a revival of learning followed, which happily is still in full progress. The work in the various geological and other explorations already undertaken, or, like the Wilkes expedition, just completed, had, in 1845, furnished a small band of picked men trained for original research. Chemical students, drawn to Europe by the attraction of the writings of Liebig and the laboratory training of Wöhler and others were returning to infuse new activity and accuracy into chemical studies, establishing laboratories for research in various departments of original investigation.

There had, indeed, been a partial kindling of a like nature twenty-five or thirty years before, when the early munificence of William Maclure aroused in Philadelphia and New Haven, and to some extent in other cities, a remarkable zeal for the study of geology, mineralogy, and general natural history, followed by the publication of his geological map of the United States, by the establishing of the "Academy of Natural Sciences" in Philadelphia, the "Lyceum of Natural History" in New York, and the "American Geological Society" in New Haven. But the failure of Mr. Owens's educational scheme at New Harmony, where Mr. Maclure had made a heavy investment, and had carried an important part of his collection of books and natural history specimens, accompanied by Say, Leseur, and others, ending in his removal to Mexico, where his delicate health compelled him to reside, led the way to a considerable suspension of this new activity in science. Nearly all the publishing societies in America became dormant, or languished with intervals of spasmodic activity. Some of them died entirely. *Bruce's Journal* died, and a period of general stagnation in scientific activity prevailed for some years. This gradually yielded to better influences. Chemistry was making slow but steady progress. Evidence of original work began to appear in this and the cognate sciences, as will be seen by what has already been recorded, and thus the way was opened for the entrance of those combined influences which developed themselves, as we have just specified, about the years 1845–47, under circumstances so auspicious.

[In the following enumeration of chemical contributions by authors now living, an effort has been made, as far as practicable, to preserve a chronological order; but this could not be very strictly observed. It was at first intended to classify the contributions to chemistry in this country subjectively; but this was found to be inconsistent with the effort to do each worker the fairest amount of justice possible. Nor has it been thought essential to preserve a strict order in the mode of enumerating papers. The author has desired to make this list as complete as possible, but he is sensible of its imperfections, while he is at the same time unconscious of any intentional omissions, and hopes for a friendly indulgence where omissions exist. To those who have kindly responded to his request for assistance in preparing the lists which follow, he returns his thanks, and he takes this occasion to remind others if they find their lists incomplete, that they have had an opportunity to make them otherwise.]

JOSEPH HENRY, Washington, D. C.—Professor Henry, now the Nestor of American science, has devoted his great powers, during a long and active life, chiefly to other branches of science and administrative duty, and with what eminent success need not be recounted here. But we find him early in his scientific studies at work in the laboratory of Dr. T. R. Beck, in Albany, and afterwards, in the absence of Dr. John Torrey, delivering the chemical lectures at Nassau Hall, in Princeton. While in Albany with Dr. Beck, he devised and published an improved form of Wollaston's sliding scale of chemical equivalents, in which hydrogen was adopted as the radix, a contrivance which is hardly known, even by name, to the present generation of chemists.

Prof. Henry, in the discharge of his duties as the Secretary of the Smithsonian Institution, has had it in his power greatly to advance chemical science, both by encouraging original researches in the laboratory of the institution and elsewhere, and also in his Annual Reports and in the Smithsonian Contributions and Miscellaneous Collections, by publishing chemical memoirs by American chemists, and promulgating a knowledge of those undertaken, either by encouragement of the Smithsonian, or elsewhere.

By his own original researches in electro-magnetism, commenced in Albany in 1826, and continued at Princeton after his removal to Nassau Hall, Prof. Henry has contributed more than any other American to the advancement of that important department of physics, which has been so fruitful in the hands of inventors in new and important practical applications closely affiliated to chemistry.

Prof. Henry's original contributions to science have been chiefly physical, but they fall largely into the department of chemical physics.

The following is a brief enumeration of his scientific investigations and discoveries:—

1. A sketch of the topography of the State of New York, embodying the results of the survey before mentioned.

2. In connection with Dr. Beck and the Hon. Simeon De Witt, the organization of the meteorological system of the State of New York.

3. The development, for the first time, of magnetic power, sufficient to sustain tons in weight, in soft iron, by a comparatively feeble galvanic current.

4. The first application of electro-magnetism as a power, to produce continued motion in a machine.

5. An exposition of the method by which electro-magnetism might be employed in transmitting power to a distance, and the demonstration of the practicability of an electro-magnetic telegraph, which, without these discoveries, was impossible.

6. The discovery of the induction of an electrical current in a long wire upon itself, or the means of increasing the intensity of a current by the use of a spiral conductor.

7. The method of inducing a current of quantity from one of intensity, and *vice versa.*

8. The discovery of currents of induction of different orders, and of the neutralization of the induction by the interposition of plates of metal.

9. The discovery that the discharge of a Leyden jar consists of a series of oscillations backwards and forwards until equilibrium is restored.

10. The induction of a current of electricity from lightning at a great distance, and proof that the discharge from a thunder cloud also consists of a series of oscillations.

11. The oscillating condition of a lightning-rod while transmitting a discharge of electricity from the clouds, causing it, though in perfect connection with the earth, to emit sparks of sufficient intensity to ignite combustible substances.

12. Investigations on molecular attraction, as exhibited in liquids, and in yielding and rigid solids, and an

exposition of the theory of soap bubbles. [These originated from his being called upon to investigate the causes of the bursting of the great gun on the United States Steamer Princeton.]

13. Original experiments on and exposition of the principles of acoustics, as applied to churches and other public buildings.

14. Experiments on various instruments to be used as fog signals.

15. A series of experiments on various illuminating materials for light-house use, and the introduction of lard oil for lighting the coasts of the United States. This and the preceding in his office of Chairman of the Committee on Experiments of the Light-House Board.

16. Experiments on heat, in which the radiation from clouds and animals in distant fields was indicated by the thermo-electrical apparatus applied to a reflecting telescope.

17. Observations on the comparative temperature of the sun-spots, and also of different portions of the sun's disk. In these experiments he was assisted by Professor Alexander.

18. Proof that the radiant heat from a feebly luminous flame is also feeble, and that the increase of radiant light, by the introduction of a solid substance into the flame of the compound blowpipe, is accompanied with an equivalent radiation of heat, and also that the increase of light and radiant heat in a flame of hydrogen, by the introduction of a solid substance, is attended with a diminution in the heating power of the flame itself.

19. The reflection of heat from concave mirrors of ice, and its application to the source of the heat derived from the moon.

20. Observations, in connection with Professor Alexander, on the red flames on the border of the sun, as observed in the annular eclipse of 1838.

21. Experiments on the phosphorogenic ray of the sun, from which it is shown that this emanation is polarizable and refrangible, according to the same laws which govern light.

22. On the penetration of the more fusible metals into those less readily melted, while in a solid state.

Besides these experimental additions to physical science, Professor Henry is the author of twenty-five [1846–71] reports, giving an exposition of the annual operations of the Smithsonian Institution. He has also published a series of essays on meteorology in the Patent Office Reports, which, besides an exposition of established principles, contain many new suggestions; and, among others, the origin of the development of electricity, as exhibited in the thunder-storm; and an essay on the principal source of the power which does the work of developing the plant in the bud, and the animal in the egg.

He has also published a theory of elementary education, in his address as President of the American Association for the Advancement of Education, the principle of which is, that in instruction the order of nature should be followed; that we should begin with the concrete and end with the abstract, the one gradually shading into the other; also the importance of early impressions, and the tendency in old age to relapse into the vices of early youth. Youth is the father of old age rather than of manhood.

He was successful as a teacher, and never failed to impart to his students a portion of his own enthusiasm. His object was not merely to impart a knowledge of facts, but mainly to give clear expositions of principles; to teach the use of generalizations, the method of arriving at laws by the process of induction, and the inference from these of facts by logical deduction.

Henry Seybert, of Philadelphia, like his father, Adam Seybert, was educated in the School of Mines in Paris, and was an early contributor to our knowledge of the chemical constitution of American minerals. In 1822 he analyzed the sulphuret of molybdenum from Chester, Pa.; chromate of iron from Maryland and Pennsylvania; the tabular spar, pyroxene, and colophonite of Willsborough, N. Y., and the maclureite (chondrodite) of New Jersey (in which he independently discovered fluorine as Dr. Langstaff had done before). He also analyzed the manganesian garnet found with the chrysoberyl at Haddam, Conn., and the chrysoberyl of the same locality. In 1830 he analyzed the Tennessee meteorite of Bowen, since which date I have been unable to find any further contributions from Mr. Seybert, whose attention was unfortunately diverted from science, to which his early life was so advantageously devoted, to other and less fruitful lines of investigation.

Charles Upham Shepard, M.D., New Haven.—From the year 1824 to this time Prof. Shepard's name has been intimately associated with the progress of

American mineralogy and the study of aerolites. His chemical work has been largely given to the examination of meteoric masses, to which he has devoted special attention, amassing probably the finest collection of these remarkable bodies which exists in America. Nearly all his papers on mineralogy and meteorites have appeared in the *American Journal of Science* and in the Proceedings of the American Association for the Advancement of Science, and for a full list of titles reference may be had to these works. The catalogue of the Royal Society contains, prior to 1863, titles of seventy-eight papers by Prof. Shepard. In 1832 he published his "Treatise on Mineralogy," based on the natural system of Mohs, and subsequent editions have appeared in 1844, 1852, and 1857.

No observation or original research of Dr. Shepard has been fruitful of so much good in its consequences as his discovery, about 25 years ago, of the deposit of phosphate of lime in the Eocene marl of South Carolina, and the distinct recognition of the fact of its great value for agriculture. This discovery led, in 1859–60, to finding, in the immediate vicinity of Charleston, the richest phosphates directly above and upon the Eocene, and to its introduction into commerce on a vast scale, and the manufacture of superphosphate fertilizers, not alone for this country, but for foreign export, and the growth in consequence of an important industry in the chemical arts at Charleston.

Augustus A. Hayes, Brookline, near Boston, Mass.—Dr. Hayes has been an industrious worker in chemistry from an early date until the failure of his health some ten years since. His papers are scattered over a wide range, and the following is only a partial list:—

1831. Production of Hydrocyanic Acid under unusual circumstances. *Journ. Royal Inst.*, i. 169.

1848. Native Copper from Lake Superior. *Am. Acad. Proc.*, ii. 195.

1848. On the Urinary Deposit called Red Sand. *Ibid.*, 196.

1848. On Stereopene, or Camphor from Crude Oil of Valerian. *Ibid.*, iii. 99–100.

1850. On the Assumed Existence of Ammonia in the General Atmosphere. *Proc. Am. Ass.*, iv. 207–213.

1852. On a New Species of Wax. *Am. Acad. Proc.*, ii. 190.

1852. On Native Iron from Siberia. *Ibid.*, iii. 149.

1852. On Aluminium. *Ibid.*

1852. Bessemer Process; New Points of Chemical Interest. *Ibid.*, iii. 322.

1852. Fossilized Egg from the Guano Island. *Proc. Boston Nat. Hist. Soc.*, v. 165.

1852. On Cochituate Water. *Ibid.*, 169.

1852. Analysis of a Saline Mineral from South America. *Ibid.*, v. 192–390.

1852. On the State in which Phosphate of Lime Exists in Sea-Water. *Ibid.*, vi. 48.

1852. Analysis of a Specimen of Gum from Africa. *Ibid.*, vi. 129.

1852. On a kind of Sugar developed in Sorghum. *Ibid.*, 200–203, 207–209.

1852. On some Modified Results attending the Decomposition of Bituminous Coals by Heat. *Ibid.*, vii. 50–51; also, in *Am. Journ. Sci.*

1857. On the Composition of the so-called Guano of the Atlantic Islands. *Edinb. N. Phil. Journ.*, ii. 107.

1857. Corrosion of Yellow Metal. *Am. Acad. Proc.*, iv. 28.

1857. Chemical Examination of a Substance found in the Medullary Cavity of Trees in the Sandwich Islands. *Proc. Boston Soc. Nat. Hist.*, vii. 209.

1861. On the Occurrence of Soluble Compounds of Copper, Lead, and Zinc in Alcohol. *Lond. Chem. News*, iv. 117.

1870. On the Cause of the Color of the Water of Lake Leman, Geneva. *Am. Journ. Sci.* [2], xlx. 186.

1872. On the Red Oxide of Zinc of New Jersey. *Ibid.* [3], iv. 191.

Lewis Feuchtwanger, M.D., New York.—Dr. Feuchtwanger has been known to American chemists by his commercial establishment for the manufacture and sale of rare chemicals for over forty years. He has also added something to our literature.

1831. Remarks on Arsenic, with Drawings of the Color of its Precipitates formed by Reagents applied to them. *Sill. Journ.*, xix. 339, with a colored plate.

1837. Expeditious Mode of Manufacturing Vinegar. *Ib.*, xxxi. 272.

1867. A Popular Treatise on Gems, 12mo. pp. 505, and a new edition in 1872.

1872. Remarks on Glass Making. *Proc. Am. Ass.*, xxii. 88.

Robert Peter, M. D., Professor of Chemistry in the University of Transylvania, Lexington, Ky.—Dr. Peter, who is one of the oldest chemists in the United States, has been connected with the geological surveys of Kentucky and Indiana, as well as with various institutions of learning. His published papers are in part as follows:—

1834. Thoughts on the Application of Chemistry to Medicine. *Transyl. Med. Journ.*, vol. vii.

1834. An Account of the Vegetable Alkalies, including their Therapeutic Action when applied internally or by the Endermic Method. *Ibid.*

1835. Notice of the Crab Orchard Mineral Springs (Lincoln County, Ky.), with a Chemical Analysis of Four of the Waters. *Ibid.*, vol. viii.

1846. Chemical Analysis of Urinary Calculi in the Museum of the Medical Department of Transylvania University, with Remarks on the Relative Frequency of Calculi in Lexington, Ky., and the Probable Causes. *Western Lancet*, vol. v.

This paper was subsequently reproduced with thirty-four additional pages, and several new analyses in the *Transylvania Med. Journ.*, N. S.

1849. Remarks on the Agriculture of the Blue Limestone of Kentucky, with its Analysis. *Albany Cultivator*, Albany, N. Y., vol. v.

1849. On Ozone. On Magnesia as an Antidote to Arsenic. } In the *Trans. Med. Journ.*, vol. i., N. S.

1850. The Quantitative Analysis of the Water of the Lower Blue Lick Spring, in Nicholas Co., Ky., with remarks on some other Salt Springs of the Blue Limestone Formation. *Quar. Med. Journ.*, Lexington.

1852. A series of lectures (contributed to same Journal) on the Chemical Relations of Organic Bodies, and on the Chemistry of the Urine.

1856. Chemical Analysis of Soils, Minerals, Rocks, Ores, Coals, Waters, etc. etc., with remarks covering 124 pages of vol. i. of the Reports on the Kentucky Geological Survey. 8vo.

1857. To vol. ii. of same Report, 184 pages containing the account of 206 chemical analyses contributed to the work by Dr. Peter.

1857. To vol. iii. of same report, Dr. Peter contributed 247 pages, and 220 chemical analyses with remarks.

1861. To vol. iv. of same report, he contributed 291 pages, with 529 chemical analyses, etc.

1860. In the Second Report of a Geological Reconnoissance of the Southern and Middle Counties of Arkansas, made during the years 1859–60, by Dr. David Dale Owen, Geologist (Phila., 8vo. pp. 433), etc., Dr. Peter, as the chemist to the survey, contributed an account of 271 chemical analyses by himself of the soils, subsoils, under-clays, nitre-earths, etc., of Arkansas, with remarks covering 125 pages.

1860. In Report of a Geological Reconnoissance of Indiana by Dr. D. D. Owen, made during 1859–60, Dr. Peter contributed the chemical analyses of thirty-three soils, subsoils, etc. Indianapolis, 1862, pp. 368, 8vo.

1873. Dr. Peter adds to his former chemical work on the Geological Survey of Kentucky (Prof. N. S. Shaler Chief Geologist), a new chapter in the report now about to be published.

John William Draper, Prof. of Chemistry New York University, New York.—Few men of science now living in America have been so long and so favorably known in the various departments of scientific investigation, which he has followed, as Dr. Draper. His reputation is cosmopolitan, and many of his publications have been reproduced in several European languages. The following is believed to be a full list of Dr. Draper's scientific papers, arranged in chronological order. Many of them are not, properly speaking, chemical, but belong rather to the department of molecular physics.

1834. "On Capillary Attraction," showing that it is an electrical phenomenon, and containing an explanation of endosmosis, *Journ. Frank. Inst.*, Sept., 147.

1834. "Analysis of Native Chloride of Carbon," *Journ. Frank. Inst.*, Nov., 295.

1834. "On a Galvanic Battery of Four Elements," *Journ. Frank. Inst.*, Nov., 289. It contains the voltaic decomposition of fused salts, and reducing effect of liberated hydrogen.

1835. "Experiments to determine whether Light has any Magnetic Action," *Journ. Frank. Inst.*, Feb.

1836. "Experiments on the Tidal Motions of Conductors Free to Move," being an investigation of the figure of equilibrium, and the motions of masses of mercury under the influence of a voltaic current, *Frank. Inst. Journ.*, January.

1836. "Analysis of some Ancient Coins," *Silliman's Amer. Journ.*, vol. xxix., 157.

1836. "Experiments on Endosmosis," *Frank. Inst. Journ.*, March.

1836. "Endosmosis through Water Strata and Soap Bubbles," *Frank. Inst. Journ.*, July.

1836. "On Interstitial Movements," *Amer. Journ. Med. Sci.*, May.

1836. "Observations on Microscopic Chemistry," *Journ. Frank. Inst.*, Dec.

1837. "Experiments on Solar Light," *Frank. Inst. Journ.*, June, July, Aug., Oct. These contain, among many other things, experiments on the absorption of the chemical rays, decomposition of carbonic acid by light, diffraction of the chemical rays, deposition of camphor crystals, and effects of light on vegetation.

1838. "On the Physical Theory of Capillary Attraction," *Amer. Journ. Med. Sci.*, Feb.

1838. "On the Great Mechanical Force Generated by the Condensing Action of Tissues," showing that gases will diffuse into each other against the pressure of many atmospheres and the voltaic decomposition of water under heavy pressures, *Amer. Journ. Med. Sci.*, May.

1838. "On the Physical Theory of Endosmosis," *Amer. Journ. Med. Sci.*, Aug.

1838. "On the Constitution of the Atmosphere," *Lond. Phil. Mag.*, Oct.

1839. "On the Measurement of the Tension of Electrical Currents," *Phil. Mag.*, Oct., Nov.

1840. "Some Experiments on the Sun's Light, made in the South of Virginia," *Phil. Mag.*, Feb.

1840. "On the Electromotive Power of Heat," containing a description of improved thermo-electrical couples, *Phil. Mag.*, June.

1840. "On the Taking of Portraits from the Life by the Daguerreotype," *Phil. Mag.*, Sept. This memoir contains the first description published on photographic portraiture.

1841. "On some Analogies between the Chemical Rays and Radiant Heat," *Phil. Mag.*, Sept.

1842. "On a New Imponderable Principle," *Phil. Mag.*, Dec.

1843. "On Certain Spectral Appearances connected with Photography, and on Latent Light,' *Silliman's Journal*, vol. xliv.

1843. "On the Law of the Conducting Power of Wires for Electrical Currents," an investigation connected with Morse's invention of the telegraph, *Silliman's Journal*, vol. xlv.

1843. "Photographic Copies of the Fixed Lines of the Spectrum." This memoir contains the description of many new lines, both in the ultra red and ultra violet spaces. *Phil. Mag.*, May.

1843. "On the Decomposition of Carbonic Acid by Plants in the Prismatic Spectrum." Up to this time it was supposed that the deoxidation of carbonic acid is accomplished by the violet rays; this memoir showed that it is by the yellow rays. *Silliman's Journal*, vol. xlvi., *Phil. Mag.*, Sept.

1843. "On a Change Impressed by Light in the Properties of an Elementary Substance," *Phil. Mag.*, Nov.

1843. "Description of the Chlorine and Hydrogen Photometer (Tithonometer)," an instrument subsequently used extensively by Bunsen and Roscoe in their photo-chemical researches. *Silliman's Journal*, vol. xlvi., *Phil. Mag.*, Dec.

1844. "On Tithonized Chlorine," *Phil. Mag.*, July.

1844. "On a Fourth Imponderable," *Phil. Mag.*, Aug.

1845. "On Capillary Attraction," *Phil. Mag.*, March.

1845. "On the Interference or Diffraction Spectrum," *Phil. Mag.*, June.

1845. "On the Allotropism of Chlorine as Connected with the Theory of Substitutions," *Silliman's Journal* vol. xlix.

1845. "On the Light of Ignited Lime and the Electric Spark," *Phil. Mag.*, Dec.

1846. "On the Circulation of the Blood as depending on Chemical Action," *Silliman's Journal*, 2d series, vol. ii.

1847. "On the Negative or Protecting Rays of the Spectrum," *Phil. Mag.*, Feb.

1847. "On the Production of Light by Heat." This memoir contained many facts published subsequently (1860) without due acknowledgment by M. Kirchoff in his celebrated memoir as mathematical deductions. *Silliman's Journal*, 2d series, vol. iv., *Phil. Mag.*, May.

1848. "On the Production of Light by Chemical Action," *Silliman's Journal*, 2d series, vol. v., *Phil. Mag.*, Feb.

1849. "On the Allotropism of Living Beings," *Phil. Mag.*, April.

1851. "On Phosphorescence," *Phil. Mag.*, Feb.

1851. "On the Chemical Action of Light," *Phil. Mag.*, May.

1853. "On a New Method for the Quantitative Estimation of Urea," *Phil. Mag.*, Oct.

1857. "On the Diffraction Spectrum," *Phil. Mag.*, March.

1857. "On Photometry," *Phil. Mag.*, Sept.

1857. "On the Modification of Chlorine," *Phil. Mag.*, Nov.

1858. "On the Nature of Flame and Condition of the Sun's Surface," *Silliman's Journal*, 2d series, vol. xxvi., *Phil. Mag.*, Feb.

1872. "On the Distribution of Heat in the Spectrum," *Silliman's Journal*, 3d series, vol. civ., 161.

1873. "On the Distribution of Chemical Force in Spectrum," *Silliman's Journal*, 3d series, vol. cv., 25, 91.

Besides these he published in 1844 a volume entitled "A Treatise on the Forces which Produce the Organization of Plants." In this were collected many of his memoirs on photo-chemical and other subjects, and among them:—

"On the Influence of Physical Agents on Organization and Life."

"On the Action of the Sunbeams in Producing Organized Bodies."

"On the Mechanical Cause of the Flow of Sap in Plants—it is due to the Carbonization of Water on the Leaves by the Light of the Sun."

"On the Physical Constitution of the Sunbeam, and on the Prismatic Spectrum."

"On the Diffraction Spectrum" (with a colored plate).

"Experiments proving that it is in the Yellow Region of the Spectrum that Reduction of Carbonic Acid by the Leaves of Plants takes place."

"On the Theory of Ideal or Imaginary Coloration."

Many of the above memoirs have been translated into French, German, Italian, and republished in various European journals.

In 1856 Dr. Draper published a Treatise on Human Physiology, containing, in like manner, the solution of many chemico-physiological and physical questions respecting digestion, absorption, the flow of the chyle and lymph in their special vessels, the mechanical action of the heart, the dependence of circulation on respiration, the nature of nervous action, the functions of the different portions of the ear, the tympanum, cochlea, semicircular canals; the nature of vision, and explanation of the functions of different portions of the eye; the influence of physical agents on the organic series. This work has been translated into Russian, and is largely used in the schools of that country.

It may be added that Dr. Draper took the first photographic portrait of the human face, and thereby laid the foundation of what has since become an important branch of industry; the first photograph of the moon; the first photograph of the diffraction spectrum. Simultaneously with Becquerel, he photographed the Fraunhofer fixed lines of the spectrum, and the ultra violet ones, and was the first to discover the great bands in the ultra red region.

In the midst of so much scientific activity, Dr. Draper has found time for relaxation in purely literary pursuits. He has published historical works on the Intellectual Development of Europe, and on the American Civil War, which have been translated into almost every European language; but these are sujects outside of the present memoir.

ROGERS.—There have been five persons of this name in the United States who have been more or less intimately connected with the history of the science by their contributions and labors. They are all of one family, the father and four sons, whose names are familiar the world over. The father—

DR. P. K. ROGERS was the Professor of Natural Philosophy and Chemistry at the College of William and Mary in Virginia, from 1819 to 1829. If Dr. Rogers had made no other contribution to the progress of chemistry in the United States than to have trained four sons to the pursuits of science, he has left record which is probably without a parallel. But we know that he was an able and faithful teacher of the science, and his labors live in the lives of his pupils.

WM. B. ROGERS, so well known in many departments of scientific research in this country, succeeded his father in the same chair at William and Mary, where he remained until his transfer to the University of Virginia at Charlottesville, in 1836. His scientific labors have been largely geological and physical, but he has also conducted many chemical researches, both alone and in connection with his brothers Robert E. and Henry D. Rogers. We note the following researches by himself alone:—

"On the Existence of Bi-malate of Lime in the Berries of the Sumac (*Rhus glabrum* and *R. Copallinum*) and the Mode of Procuring it from them in the Crystalline Form." (*Am. Journ. Sci.*, xxvii., 1835, pp. 294–299.)

"Apparatus for Analyzing Marl and other Carbonates," and "Self-filling Syphon for Chemical Analysis." (*Am. Jour. Sci.*, xxvii. 299–303.)

"Analysis of (recent) Shells." (1834, *Am. Jour. Sci.*, xxvi. 361.)

"On the connection of Thermal Springs, in Virginia, with Anticlinal Axes and Faults." (1843, *Reports Am. Asso. Geol. and Nat.*, pp. 323–347.) In this important memoir Prof. Rogers gives in a tabular form the results of his Analysis of twenty-eight of the Virginia thermals, and points out particularly the preponderance of free nitrogen among the gaseous contents, much exceeding the $CO_2$ and $H_2S$ in volume. This paper contains but a small part of the chemical work of the years when, as geologist of Virginia, Prof. Rogers was engaged in an examination of the thermal waters of that vast State. Unfortunately for science the arrest of that work has kept the full results of Prof. Rogers' labors from seeing the light.

"On Ozone Observations" (1858, *Edinb. N. Phil. Jour.*, vii. 35–42). The experiments detailed in the treatise confirm the observations of M. Cloez (*Ann. de Chem.*, 1857, l. pp. 80–96), showing that the effects supposed to be due to ozonized oxygen evolved from growing plants are really due to sunlight and moisture.

"An account of Apparatus and Processes for the Chemical and Photometrical Testing of Illuminating Gas." (*Brit. Asso. Report*, 1864, ii. p. 39.)

Many minor papers by Prof. R. will be found in the *Journ. of the Franklin Inst.*, *Proceed. Am. Phil. Soc.*, of the *Am. Acad.*, and *Am. Ass.*

W. B. Rogers and Robert E. Rogers.—These chemists have together published a number of important chemical contributions, relating chiefly to new or improved methods in chemical analysis and research. Such is their

"New Process for Obtaining Pure Chlorine." (*Sill. Jour.*, 2, i. 428, 1840.)

"On a New Process for obtaining Formic Acid, and on the Preparation of Aldehyd and Acetic Acid by the Use of Bichromate of Potassa." (*Sill. Jour.*, 2, ii. pp. 18–24.)

"On the Absorption of Carbonic Acid by Liquids." Part I. (*Sill. Journ.*, 2, vi. pp. 96–109.) Part II. is in *Proc. Am. Ass.*, 1850, pp. 298–311.

"Oxydation of the Diamond in the Liquid Way." (*Proc. Am. Asso.*, vi. 110.)

"On the Decomposition of Rocks by Meteoric Waters." (*Proc. Am. Ass.*, 1848, p. 60; *Sill. Journ.*, 2, v. 401.)

"On the Volatility of Potassa and Soda and their Carbonates." (*Proc. Am. Ass.*, 1848, pp. 36–38.)

"On the Use of Hydrogen Gas and Carbonic Acid Gas, to Displace Sulphuretted Hydrogen in the Analysis of Mineral Water," etc. (*Sill. Jour.*, 2, xviii. 213–216, 1854.)

"On a New Method of Determining Carbon in Graphite." (*Sill. Journ*, 2, v. 352.) This process turns out to be one of the best methods known of determining carbon in the analysis of cast-iron, and is now in constant use in many laboratories for this purpose.

"On the Oxydation of the Diamond in the Liquid Way." (*Sill. Journ.*, 2, vi. 110.) Chromic acid is the agent used.

"On New Instruments and Processes for the Analysis of the Carbonates." (*Sill. Journ.*; 1, xlvi. 346–359.)

Robert E. Rogers and M. H. Boyé.—"On the Analysis of Limestone, especially of the Magnesian kind, and a method of completely separating limes from Magnesia, where both are present in large quantity." (*Frank. Inst. Journ.*, 1840, xxv. pp. 158–162.)

Robert E. Rogers and James B. Rogers.—"On the Alleged Insolubility of Copper in Hydrochloric Acid, and on Fuch's Method of Analyzing Iron Ores." (*Sill. Journ.*, 2, vi. pp. 395 (abstract), and *Am. Asso. Proc.*, Philadelphia, 1848.

Henry D. Rogers wrote chiefly on geology, to which science his contributions are among the most important made in the United States. The joint memoir by himself and Wm. B. Rogers on the structure of the Appalachian, presented at the Boston Meeting of the American Association of Geologists and Naturalists in 1843 (*Trans.*, pp. 474–532), is too well known to require comment from us.

In connection with his brother, W. B. Rogers, Prof. H. D. Rogers in 1835 communicated an important chemico-physical paper entitled "Experimental Inquiry into some of the Laws of the Elementary Voltaic Battery." (*Sill. Journ.*, 1, xxvii. pp. 39–61.)

Some years before his death (in May, 1868) Prof. H. D. Rogers removed to Scotland, where, in 1857, he assumed the duties of the chair of geology and natural history. His enduring monument as a man of science is found in the "Report on the Geology of Pennsylvania." (3 vols. 4to. and atlas.)

It will never be forgotten that the Massachusetts Institute of Technology owes its conception and successful inauguration among the science-teaching institutions of America almost solely to the personal efforts of Prof. Wm. B. Rogers, who presided over its councils until compelled a few years since by failing health to resign its arduous duties.

JOHN JOHNSTON, Professor of Chemistry at Wesleyan University, Middletown, Connecticut, has published the following articles in the *American Journal of Science*:—

1836. [1] Vol. xxx. p. 387. Description of a large Crystal of Columbite.

1839. [1] Vol. xxxviii. 297. Description of Apparatus for preparing liquid and solid $CO_2$.

1838. [1] Vol. xxxiv. 86. Description of a peculiar Air-pump.

1841. [1] xl. 41. Description of Precious Beryl.

1864. [11] xxxvii. 115. Electric Properties of Pyroxilin Paper.

Prof. Johnston has also published:—

1840. Text-book of Chemistry; on the Basis of Dr. Turner's Elements of Chemistry. This has been revised three or four times in as many new editions.

Elements of Chemistry; an abridgment of the foregoing.

JAMES C. BOOTH, Ph.D., Philadelphia.—Dr. Booth has contributed the following papers which we have found, and probably others of which I have no notice.

1836. On the Deutarseniuret of Nickel, from Riechelsdorf in Hessia. *Sill. Journ.* [1], xxix. 241.

1841. Analysis of Various Ores of Lead, Silver, Copper, Zinc, Iron, etc., from King's Mine, Davidson County, North Carolina. *Ibid.* [1], xli. 348.

1842. On Beet Root Sugar. *Journ. Frank. Inst.*, and Sturgeon, *Ann. Elect.*, v. 388.

1842. Chrome Iron Analysis. *Ibid.*

1848. Constitution of Glycerine and Oily Acids. *Journ. Frank. Inst.*, xx. 365.

1852. On Remingtonite, a New Cobalt Mineral. *Sill. Journ.* [2], xiv. 38.

In joint authorship with MARTIN H. BOYÉ.

1842. Analysis of Well Water in Philadelphia. *Journ. Frank. Inst.* [3], iii. 249.

1842. On the Extraction and Decolorization of Gelatine. *Ibid.*, May, 1842.

1842. On the Preparation of Aluminous Mordants. *Ibid.*

1843. Conversion of Benzoic Acid into Hippuric Acid. *Am. Phil. Soc. Proc.*, iii. 129.

1844. Analysis of Three Kinds of Feldspar. *Ibid.*, ii. 53.

In joint authorship with T. H. Garrett:—

1862. Experiments on Illumination with Mineral Oils. *Journ. Frank. Inst.*, xxv. 193.

In joint authorship with C. Morfitt.

1853. On the Analysis of Cast Iron. *Ibid.* [3], xxv. 193, 247, 317.

1862. Recent Improvements in the Chemical Arts. *Smithsonian Miscellaneous Collections.*

In joint editorship with Martin H. Boyé.

1844. The Encyclopedia of Chemistry. Phila., 8vo.

Report on the Geology of Delaware with Chemical Notes. 8vo.

Charles T. Jackson, Boston.—Dr. Jackson was one of the earliest chemists in the United States to open a laboratory (1838) for instruction and research in analytical chemistry in Boston, where several of the active men of our time obtained their first lessons in the art of chemical analysis. Most of Dr. Jackson's contributions to chemistry have been made in connection with the work of the Geological Surveys of which he had charge, as those of Rhode Island, Maine, New Hampshire, Lake Superior, etc. His memoir, in connection with Francis Alger, on the Geology and Mineralogy of Nova Scotia was an important contribution to science, and gave us our first exact knowledge of that interesting region. He has been recognized and decorated by many European governments as the discoverer of the anæsthetic powers of ether. His alcohol blast-lamp for alkaline fusions of silicates was a powerful heating apparatus which, before the introduction of street gas into laboratory use, was a familiar instrument in most analytical laboratories in America. In the Royal Society Catalogue there are sixty-nine titles under Dr. Jackson's name of papers prior to 1863. These are scattered in the pages of many journals and transactions, and relate mostly to mineral analyses. He first demonstrated, by his analysis of the meteoric iron of Alabama, the presence of chlorine as a factor in this class of bodies. He was long an active member, and for many years the President, of the Boston Society of Natural History, in whose Proceedings many of his contributions appeared. He has for some time been an inmate of an insane asylum, his case being regarded as hopeless.

James Blake, of San Francisco, is one of the few chemists in this country who has undertaken researches on the difficult department of physiological chemistry by experiments on the living subject. As early as 1839 he published "Observations on the Physiological Effects of Various Agents Introduced into the Circulation as Indicated by the Hæmadynamometer," and "Experimental Researches on the Mode of Operation of Poisons." Dr. Blake is the pioneer in this line of research.

Dr. Blake has also published "On Electrical Currents Produced during the Process of Fermentation and Vegetation." (*Phil. Mag.*, London, xii. pp. 539–541.)

His important memoir* "On the Effects of Various Saline Substances Injected into the Circulatory System" proves that there exists a close relation between the chemical properties of the substances experimented upon and their physiological effects; his experiments, going to prove that when introduced into the blood substances which are isomorphous exert similar actions on the living tissues; and that salts with the same base have analogous actions.

He tested the action of salts of magnesia, which were found, when introduced in any quantity into the blood, to arrest the action of the heart, with complete prostration of muscular power. The salts of zinc, isomorphous with those of magnesia, have a similar action, but produce the same effects in smaller quantities. The salts of copper, of lime, of strontia, of baryta, and of lead are considered in the order in which they are more closely related by their physiological actions. The peculiar action which the salts of the three last named substances exercise upon the muscular tissues, occasioning contractions in them during many minutes after death produced by their introduction into the blood. These muscular movements were in some cases observed forty-five minutes after the cessation of the heart's action. His experiments on the salts of silver and soda reveal a remarkable similarity in action upon the pulmonary tissue, on the heart, and on the systemic capillaries; for while in the case of all the other salts already mentioned, death seems to be produced by the destruction of the irritability of the heart, the fatal result with the salts of silver and soda is the consequence of their

* Published in the French Archives Générales de Medicine for Nov. 1839. See also Brit. Asso. Rept., 1846, pp. 240–244, and Roy. Soc. Proceedings, iv., 1839, p. 155; Am. Journ. Med. Sci., 1849.

action on the tissues of the lungs. The physiological actions of the salts of ammonia and of potassa were found by Dr. Blake not to correspond with any of the preceding. Although agreeing perfectly with one another in their action upon the heart and the systemic capillaries, they differ extremely in their effects on the nervous tissues, ammonia being particularly distinguished from all inorganic compounds in this respect, and being very analogous to poisons derived from organic products, which it also resembles in its chemical properties. This last observation respecting ammonia, a nitrogenous compound, has received ample confirmation in the researches of later chemical physiologists, and especially in those of Dr. Richardson on the nitrites of the alcohol radicals and of Drs. Crum Brown and Fraser on the salts of the ammonium bases, derived from strychnia, brucia, and other alkaloids.

Dr. Blake has more recently extended his observations on this interesting subject to embrace the molecular weight as well as the isomorphism of the metallic salts and compounds of some of the metalloids. His paper will be found in the *Am. Jour. Sci.* for March, 1874, and his deductions are:—

1. In the changes induced in living matter by inorganic compounds, the character of the change depends more on the physical properties of the reagent than on its more purely chemical properties.

2. That the character of the changes is determined by the isomorphous relations of the electro-positive element of the reagent.

3. That among the compounds of the more purely metallic elements, the quantity of substances in the same isomorphous group required to produce analogous changes in living matter, is less as the atomic weight of the electro-positive element increases.

4. That the action of inorganic compounds on living matter appears not to be connected with the changes they produce in the proximate elements of the solids and fluids, when no longer forming part of a living body, at least in so far as our present means of research enable us to judge.

5. That in living matter we possess a reagent capable of aiding us in our investigations on the molecular properties of substances.

Wolcott Gibbs, Rumford Professor at Harvard College, has published:—

1840. "A Description of a New Form of Magneto-

Electric Machine, and an Account of a Carbon Battery of considerable energy, communicated for this journal by Oliver Wolcott Gibbs, member of the junior class in Columbia College." *Am. Journ. Sci.* [1], xxxix. 132. This was the first mention of the use of carbon as the negative element in a voltaic couple.

1845. Dissertation on a Natural System of Chemical Classification. Brochure, New York, and *Am. Journ. Sci.* [1], xlix. 384.

1847. Chemischer-Mineralogischer Untersuchungen. *Pogg. Ann.*, lxxi. pp. 559–67.

1849. Analysis of Dust of a Sirocco which fell at Malta May 16th, 1846. *Sill. Journ.* [2], xi., 374, 1851. Also, *Abhandlungen der Akad.*, Berlin, 1847, and *Pogg. Ann.*, *loc. cit.*

1851. January 1st Dr. Gibbs announced his intention to prepare for the columns of the *American Journal of Science* "Abstracts of the more important physical and chemical papers contained in foreign scientific journals, accompanied by references and by such critical observations as the occasion may demand." *Am. Jour.* [2], xi. 105. This purpose was steadily carried out by Dr. Gibbs for over twenty years; his well-known initials, W. G., appearing in almost every subsequent issue of the *American Journal of Science*, until 1873: an important service to science, the value of which was greatly enhanced by his notes and criticisms, which, of themselves, form a valuable contribution to chemistry. These abstracts and notes cover over 500 closely printed pages. It is far beyond our limits to cite all these "Notes" in detail. They are all referred to in the decade Indices of the *Journal.*

1852. Contributions to Analytical Chemistry. *Am. Journ. Sci.* [2], xiv. 204; also, *Pogg. Ann.*, lxxviii. 162.

1854. Note on a New Electro-Chronometric Method. *Proc. Am. Assn. Adv. Sci.*, viii. 103.

1854. On the Volumetric Determination of Nitric, Arsenic, Antimonic, and Stannic Acids, and on the Separation of Manganese, Cobalt, and Nickel. *Ibid.*, viii. 247.

1854. On two New General Methods of Chemical Analysis. *Ibid.*, 248. These two papers were read but not printed in the volume of Proceedings, the titles only appearing there.

1855. Report on the Recent Progress of Organic Chemistry. *Ibid.*, ix. 37–61.

1858. On the Theory of the Polyacid Bases. *Ibid.*, xii. 190–197. In this paper the author relegates the discovery of the theory of water-types to Dr. Sterry Hunt; having, in his Report on the Progress of Organic Chemistry, read at Providence, ascribed it to Gerhardt and Williamson.

1858. Preliminary Notice of New Bases, containing Metals Associated with Ammonia. *Ibid.*, xii. 197–200.

1858. On the Rational Constitution of Certain Organic Compounds. *Am. Journ. Sci.* [2], xxv. 18–38.

1857. In joint authorship with F. A. GENTH. "Researches on the Ammonia-cobalt Bases" (for full references see GENTH).

1858. Also with Genth. Preliminary notice of a New Base, containing Osmium and the Elements of Ammonia. *Am. Journ. Sci.* [2], xxv. 248.

1860. Researches on the Platinum Metals (preliminary note.) *Am. Journ. Sci.* [2], xxix. 427.

1861. Remarks on the Atomic Weights of the Elements. *Am. Journ. Sci.* [2], xxxi. 248–256.

1861. Researches on the Platinum Metals. § 1 and § 2. *Am. Journ. Sci.* [2], xxxi. 63–70.

1862. The same continued, § 3. *Ibid.*, xxxiv. 341–356.

1864. The same continued, § 3. *Ibid.*, xxxvii. 57–61.

[This memoir was destined to appear in the Smithsonian Contributions, and was permitted by that Institution to appear in advance in the *Am. Journ. Sci.* Reference to it will be found in Smithsonian Reports for 1859, p. 35, and 1860, p. 39. The conclusion of the research has not yet been published.]

1864. "Contributions to Chemistry, from the Laboratory of the Lawrence Scientific School," viz.:—

1. "On the Relations of Hyposulphite of Soda to certain Metallic Oxides."
2. "On the Determination of Nitrogen by Weight."
3. "On the Separation of Cerium from Didymium and Lanthanum."
4. "On the Separation and Estimation of Cerium."
5. "On the Quantitative Separation of Cerium from Yttrium, Aluminium, Glucinum, Manganese, Iron, and Uranium."
6. "On the Employment of Fluoride of Potassium in Analysis." *Am. Journ. Sci.* [2], xxxvii. 344–358.

1865. "Contributions to Chemistry from the Laboratory of the Lawrence Scientific School, No. 2," viz. :—

1. "On the Separation of Chromium from Aluminium and Iron, etc. etc."

2. "On the Employment of Sodium for the Separation of Iron and Aluminium from other Bases."

3. "On the Separation of Manganese from Cobalt, Nickel, and Zinc."

4. "On the Separation of Cobalt from Nickel."

5. "On the Separation of Uranium from Cobalt and Nickel."

6. "On the Electrolytic Precipitation of Copper and Nickel as a Method of Analysis." *Am. Journ. Sci.* [2], xxxix. 58–65.

1867. On the Construction of a Normal Map of the Solar Spectrum. An abstract of a memoir read before the National Academy of Sciences, Aug. 7, 1866. *Am. Journ. Sci.* [2], xliii. 1–10.

1867. Contributions to Chemistry from the Lawrence Scientific School, No. 3, viz.:—

1. "On a New General Method of Volumetric Analysis."

2. "On the Precipitation of Copper by Hypophosphorous Acid."

3. "On the Precipitation of Copper and Nickel by Alkaline Carbonates."

4. "On the Employment of Sand and Glass Filters in Quantitative Analysis."

5. "On the Estimation of Manganese as Pyrophosphate." *Am. Journ. Sci.* [2], xliv. 207–217.

1867. "On certain points in the Theory of Atomicities." *Ibid.*, pp. 409–416.

1868. "On the Measurement of Wave-lengths by the Method of Comparison." Abstract of a paper read before the National Academy of Sciences, Aug. 16, 1867. *Ibid.*, xlv. 298–301.

1868. "On the Molecular Structure of Uric Acid and its Derivatives." *Ibid.*, xlvi. 289–298.

1869. "On the Wave-lengths of the Spectral Lines of the Elements." *Ibid.*, xlvii. 194–218.

1869. Contributions to Chemistry from the Laboratory of the Lawrence Scientific School, viz.:—

"On the Action of Alkaline Nitrites upon Uric Acid and its Derivatives." *Ibid.*, xlviii. 215–226.

1870. "Contributions to Chemistry, from the Laboratory of the Lawrence Scientific School," viz.:—

1. On a Simple Method of avoiding Observations of Temperature and Pressure in Gas Analysis.

2. On the Application of Sprengel's Mercurial Pump in Analysis. *Ibid.*, xlix. 370–371.

1870. "Miscellaneous Optical Notices." *Ibid.*, l. 45-54.

1873. Analytical Notices, viz.:—

1. On the Quantitative Estimation of Chromium and the Separation of Chromium from Uranium.

2. On the Estimation of Magnesium as Pyrophosphate. *Ibid.* [3], v. 110-117.

1873. "Researches of the Hexatomic Compounds of Cobalt" (being Part II. of the Researches on the Ammonia Cobalt Bases, by Gibbs and Genth). *Ibid.*, vi. 116-126.

1874. The same continued. *Ibid.* [3], viii. 189, 200, and 284-296.

James Lawrence Smith, Louisville, Ky.—Dr. Smith's name appears as a contributor to chemistry as early as 1841, when he wrote "On the Means of Detecting Arsenic in the Human Body," while he was yet a student in medicine in Paris. From that date to the present chemical readers are familiar with his contributions and researches, which have been both varied and important. For some years Dr. Smith was the chemical correspondent of the *American Journal of Science* in Europe. He has quite recently published a volume of his more important papers under the title of "Mineralogy and Chemistry, Original Researches," Louisville, Ky., 1873, 8vo., pp. 401. This volume contains the titles of forty-seven memoirs and papers. It opens with a memoir on Emery communicated to the Academy of Sciences of the French Institute in 1850. Before Dr. Smith's residence in Asia Minor very little was accurately known of the geology, mineralogy, and chemical history of emery. By this memoir, in two parts, we are put in possession of an exact and full history of its geology, mineralogy, and chemical constitution, as well as of that of its associated minerals, with descriptions of new species, and many chemical analyses. In this research Dr. Smith devised a new method for determining the effective hardness of emery, and adopted, after many trials, the mode of attack by sodic-bisulphate as the only satisfactory means of breaking up the constitution of emery in an ultimate analysis. In the report of the commission of the Academy, Messrs. Cordier, Élie de Beaumont, and Dufrénoy, to whom Dr. Smith's memoir was referred, it is spoken of in terms of high encomium, and its insertion in the *Mémoire des Savants étrangers* was recommended.

In 1866 Dr. Smith extended his researches upon

emery and its associate minerals to the interesting mine of that substance at Chester, Mass., first made known by Dr. C. T. Jackson, and this paper properly follows that on the emery of Asia Minor.

The minerals of Chili collected by the Astronomical Expedition to that country under Gillis were submitted to Dr. Smith for examination, and the results appeared in the first volume of Gillis's Report. They are now made accessible in Dr. Smith's volume of Memoirs.

The chemical examination of the "Thermal Waters of Asia Minor" has made known for the first time the constitution of some of the oldest thermals of a district renowned from the earliest historic period as the resort of invalids.

The most extended memoir in Dr. Smith's volume is that on the "Re-examination of American Minerals," which covers 76 pages of the work. The first part of this research was made jointly with Mr. Geo. J. Brush in 1853, at the University of Virginia, where Dr. Smith was then in charge of the chemical chair, and the paper appeared originally in the XVth and XVIth volumes of the *American Journal of Science*, in three parts. It included examinations, with analyses, of thirty-seven mineral species, or reputed species, the joint work of Smith and Brush, forming at the time the most important contribution to mineral chemistry yet made by any American chemists. The subsequent portion of this memoir is occupied with an examination, both physical and chemical, of the minerals of the Wheatley mine, and with the analyses of certain other species, the exclusive work of Dr. Smith. In these analyses the method used for the determination of the alkaline elements is that known as Smith's method, a detailed statement of which is given in a separate paper, pp. 200–221 of this volume, on the "Determination of Alkalies in Minerals," with a supplemental paper on the same subject "by ignition with carbonate of lime and sal-ammoniac" on pp. 293–401. These methods have passed into the literature of analytical chemistry. The American edition of Fresenius, by Johnson, says of the last named process, "Prof. Smith's method is by far the most convenient and accurate for separating alkalies from a silicate, and is universally applicable, except, perhaps, in presence of boracic acid." p. 303, vol. ii.

Dr. Smith's memoirs and researches upon meteorites have added much to our former knowledge of this interesting class of bodies, and are too well known to require more detailed mention here. Over one hundred pages of his volume of "Original Researches" are devoted to these memoirs.

Dr. Smith has added many ingenious appliances to our art in the way of apparatus, none of which is, perhaps, more noteworthy than his inverted microscope for chemical work.

Of his contributions to technical chemistry it is not our purpose to speak here, but his report on the "Progress and Condition of Several Departments of Industrial Chemistry," forming one of the series of documents published by the United States Government on the Paris Exposition of 1867, is familiar to all.

With Dr. Smith's volume of memoirs at hand, it is hardly needful to give here a detailed list of titles of his papers.

TRAILL GREEN, Lafayette College, Easton, Pa.—Prof. Green's papers are as follows:—

On the Atmosphere in Relation to Vegetation.

On Carbon and its Compounds. *The Educator.*

On Humine or Geine, the Food of Plants. *Agriculturist.*

On the Manufacture of Sugar from the Potato.

On Spontaneous Combustion.

MARTIN H. BOYÉ, Ph.D., Philadelphia.—Dr. Boyé's chemical papers have mostly been in joint authorship with others. I find the following titles:—

1846. Acetate of Lime formed in Coal Pits. *Proc. Chem. Phil. Soc.*, iv. 239.

1846. Oxide of Cobalt, with Brown Hematite, of Chester Ridge, Pa. *Ibid.*

1844. Analysis of the Bittern of a Saline on the Kiskiminetas River, near Freeport, Pa. *Sill. Journ.* [2], vii. 74, and *Proc. Am. Asso. Adv. Sci.*, 1848.

1850. Analysis of Schuylkill Water. *Sill. Journ.* [2], lx. 123.

In joint authorship with CLARK HARE.

1842. On the Perchlorate of the Oxide of Ethyl, or Perchloric Ether. *Ibid.* [1], xlii. 63.

1842. On the Perchlorate of the Oxide of Ethyl, or Perchloric Ether. *Ibid.* With R. E. ROGERS.

1842. On Magnesian Limestones. *Journ. Frank. Inst*

1842. On Magnesian Limestones. *Ibid.* With H. D. ROGERS.

1841. New Compound of Deuto-chloride of Platinum, Nitric Oxide, and Chlorohydric Acid. *Am. Phil. Trans.*, viii. 59–65.

1846. New Compound of Deuto-chloride of Platinum, Nitric Oxide, and Chlorohydric Acid. *Ibid.* With C. M. WETHERILL.

1846. Analysis of a Concretion from a Horse's Stomach. *Proc. Am. Phil. Soc.*, ix. 330. With J. C. BOOTH (see under BOOTH).

BENJAMIN SILLIMAN.—Professor of Chemistry, Yale College, New Haven, Conn. His chemical and physical papers are—

1841. Electrography, or the Electrotype. *Am. Journ. Sci.* [1], xl. 157–164.

1841. Analysis of the Soil of the Nile. *Ibid.*, 190.

1842. A Daguerreotype Experiment by Galvanic Light (with Dr. W. H. GOODE). *Ibid.*, xliii. 185.

This experiment was made in 1840, and is the earliest record of the fact, then an unexpected result, that the voltaic arc has photographic efficacy.

1842. On the Use of Carbon in Grove's Battery. *Ibid.*, xliii. 393.

1843. Description of a Carbon Voltaic Battery. *Ibid.*, xliv. 180–186.

1844. Review of Dana's Mineralogy. *Ibid.*, xlvi. 362–388.

1844. Analysis of Meteoric Iron from Burlington, Otsego Co., N.Y. *Ibid.*, xlvi. 401.

1845. Analysis of Blue Mud of New Haven Harbor. *Ibid.*, xlviii. 337.

1845. Notice of a Mass of Meteoric Iron found at Cambria, near Lockport, in the State of New York. *Ibid.*, xlviii. 388–392.

1845. Analysis of the Water of the Dead Sea. *Ibid.*, 10.

1846. On the Chemical Composition of Calcareous Corals. *Ibid.* [2], i. 189–199.

This investigation was undertaken upon the zoophites, collected by Prof. Dana on the Wilkes Exploring Expedition, and appeared in the work on Zoophites by that author. By it the occurrence of phosphoric acid and fluorine as constant factors of these organisms was first demonstrated.

1846. Chemical Examination of Several Natural Waters. (Report of the (Boston) Water Commissioners.) *Ibid.* [2], ii. 218–224.

1846. On the Meteoric Iron of Texas and Lockport (with T. S. Hunt). *Ibid.* [2], ii. 370–376.

1847. Hydrate of Nickel, a New Mineral. (Emerald Nickel.) *Ibid.* [2], iii. 407.

1847. "First Principles of Chemistry." A chemical manual revised in 1850 and 1853, and in which the fundamental ideas of the so-called "New Chemistry" were first distinctly brought out in a text-book in the organic portion prepared by Dr. Hunt. Over fifty thousand copies of this manual were distributed.

1847. Description (and analysis) of a Meteoric Stone which fell in Concord, New Hampshire, in October, 1846. *Ibid.* [2], iv. 353.

1848. On Chloroform. *Ibid.* [2], v. 240.

1849. On Gibbsite and Allophane, from Richmond, Mass. *Ibid.* [2], vii. 411-417.

1849. Description and Analysis of Several American Minerals. The subjects treated of in this article are as follows:—

I. Description and Analyses of Several Mineral Species belonging to the family of Micas.

II. Description and Analyses of Unionite, a new mineral species.

III. Description and Analyses of a Species resembling Worthite.

IV. Identity of Sillimanite, Bucholzite, and Fibrolite with Kyanite.

V. Analysis of a Granular Albite, associated with Corundum of Pennsylvania, and a new Analysis of the Indianite of Bournon.

VI. On Boltonite and Thomson's Bisilicate of Magnesia.

VII. On Nuttalite of Brooke.

*Ibid.* [2], viii. 377–394.

1850. On the New Mineral Lancasterite. *Ibid.*, ix. 216.

1850. Optical Examination of Several American Species. *Ibid.* [2], 372–383.

In this memorial the specific characters of Muscovite, Phlogopite, and Biotite, were first distinctly demonstrated as resting on optical phenomena.

1850. Analysis of Emerylite. *Ibid.*, p. 117.

1851. On Mammoth Cave. *Ibid.* [2], xi. 332–340.

1852. Daguerreotypes by Galvanic Light. *Ibid.*, 417.

1852. An Excursion on Etna. *Ibid.* [2], xii. 178.

1857. Notice of a Photometer, and of some Experiments therewith upon the Comparative Power of several artificial means of Illumination (with Chas. H. Porter). *Ibid.* [2], xxiii. 315.

1858. First Principles of Natural Philosophy, and—

1860. New edition of the same.

1859. Meteor of Aug. 11, 1859. *Ibid.* [2], xxviii. 300.

1860. On the Combustion of Wet Fuel in the Furnace of Moses Thompson. *Ibid.* [2], xxx. 243–253.

1860. Note on the Loss of Light by Glass Shades. *Ibid.*, 423.

1865. Examination of Petroleum from California. *Ibid.*, xxxix. 341.

1866. On Gaylussite from Nevada Territory. *Ibid.* [2], xlii. 220.

1867. On Naphtha and Illuminating Oil from heavy California Tar (Maltha). *Ibid.* [2], xliii. 242.

1869. On the Effect of Atmospheric Air when mixed with Gas in Reducing its Illuminating Power. (Joint paper with H. Wurtz.) *Ibid.* [2], xlviii. 41.

1869. Note on Wollongonite, a remarkable Hydrocarbon from N. South Wales. *Ibid.*, 85.

1870. On the Relation between the Intensity of Light produced from the Combustion of Illuminating Gas and the volume of Gas consumed. *Ibid.* [2], xlix. 17–24.

1870. On Flame Temperatures in their Relations to Composition and Luminosity (jointly with Henry Wurtz). *Ibid.*, 339–347.

1870. Note on Mr. Stimpson's Paper on Farmer's Theorem. *Ibid.* [2], 377.

1870. On the Determination of the Photometric Power of a Rich Gas by Dilution with a Poor Gas of known value. *Ibid.*, 379.

1873. On the Meteoric Iron found near Shingle Springs, Eldorado County, California. *Ibid.* [3], 18.

1873. Mineralogical Notes on Utah, California, and Nevada, with a description (and analyses) of Priceite, a new Borate of Lime. *Ibid.*, 126–133.

1874. Mineralogical Notes. Tellurium ores from Colorado. *Ibid.* [3], 25.

In the *Amer. Chemist*, July, 1871, vii. p. 18, 23:—

1871. "Report on the Rock Oil, or Petroleum, from Venango County, Pa."

This is a reproduction of a printed but unpublished report of 1855 (April), which is believed to be the earliest investigation into the chemical and physical properties of American petroleum, then collected only in surface pools, of a dark color and viscous quality, long before any Artesian borings had made known the vast extent and importance of this remarkable product.

F. A. P. Barnard, D.D., LL.D., President of Columbia College, New York. Nearly all Dr. Barnard's contributions to science, which are numerous and important, are physical. We note the following papers as falling within the scope of this essay.

1841. Improvement in the Daguerreotype process of Photography. *Am. Journ. Sci.* [1], lxi. 352.

1859. Means of preventing the Alteration of Metallic Surfaces as employed to close and break a voltaic circuit. *Proc. Am. Assn. Adv. Sci.*, vol. xiii. 1819, 208–216.

Fredk. A. Genth, Professor of Chemistry and Mineralogy in the University of Pennsylvania, has no superior in this country as an analytical chemist. His early chemical papers are to be found in the European journals, before his coming to America, in Berzelius's Jahresbericht; Liebig's Annalen; in Leonhard and Bronn's Jahrbuch; in Erdmann's Journal, and also in the German-American Keller-Tiedemann's Monatsbericht, etc. In Keller-Tiedemann's Monatsbericht appeared the first description of the ammonia cobalt bases, which he had discovered in Germany, in 1846. His first paper which I have seen is, "Chemische Unterschung des Masopins eines neuen Hartzartigen Körpers," in Wöhler and Liebig's Annalen, 1843, 116–124.

Dr. Genth has published most of his papers since coming to the United States in the *Am. Journ. of Sci.*

1853. "On the Allotropic Modification of Oxide of Cobalt" [2], xv. 120. "This corresponds to the allotropic modification of oxide of nickel," first noticed by Dr. Genth in 1845. *Ann. der Chem. und Pharm.*, liii. p. 139.

1853. "On a probable New Element with Iridosmine and Platinum, from California." [2], xv. 246.

1853. "On Rhodophyllite," xv. 438, and *Proc. Acad. Nat. Sci.* Phila. 1852, 121.

1853. "Contributions to Mineralogy: 1. Tetradymite; 2. Gray Copper; 3. Apophyllite; 4. Allanite" [2], xvi. 81–86, and continued; "5. Owenite; 6. Kämmerite, Emerald, Nickel." *Ibid.*, 167.

1854. "Contributions to Mineralogy: 1. Pyrophyllite; 2. Chrysotile; 3. Scolecite; 4. Owenite, identical with Thuringite" [2], xviii. 410, and continued; "5. Tetradymite; 6. Bismuthine; 7. Aciculite; 8. Barnhardite, a new mineral; 9. Gray Copper (Fahlerz); 10. Geokronite; (?) 11. Garnet; 12. Allanite; 13. Tungstates of N. Carolina; 14. Scorodite; 15. Wavellite." [2], xix. 15. In all these "contributions" are numerous and exhaustive analyses of minerals.

1854. "On a New Meteorite from New Mexico." xvii. 239.

1855. "Analysis of a Meteorite from Tuczon, Province of Sonora, Mexico." [2], xx. 110. Also in *Pro. Acad. Nat. Sci.*, vii. 317.

1855. "Herrerite identical with Smithsonite." *Ibid.*, 118.

1857. "Contributions to Mineralogy: 1. Bismuthine from Riddwehyttan in Sweden; 2. Harrisite (Shepard), a Pseudomorph of Copper Glance after Galena; 3. Cantonite, a Pseudomorph of Covelline, after Galena; 4. Linnæite; 5. Enargite; (?) 6. Coracite (LeConte) is Pitch blende; 7. Epistilbite; 8. Shepard's Plumbo-Resinite is Cyanosite; 9. Cherokine (Shepard) is Pyromorphite; 10. Vivianite; 11. Wavellite; 12. Dufrenite; 13. Hitchcockite (Shepard); 14. Lanthanite; 15. Bismuthite." [2], xxiii. 415–427.

1857. In joint authorship with WOLCOTT GIBBS. "Researches on the Ammonia-cobalt Bases. Part I." [2], xxiii. 234–265. *Ibid.*, 319–341; concluded in xxiv. 86–107. This memoir, more elaborate and fuller of new results than any chemical research before accomplished in this country, and which occupied the leisure of the authors for several years, formed part of the ninth volume of the "Smithsonian Contributions to Knowledge," from which it was reprinted as above.

1859. "Contributions to Mineralogy: Whitneyite, a New Species." [2], xxvii. 400.

1859. "Contributions to Mineralogy; 1. Native Iron; 2. Native Bismuth; 3. Whitneyite; 4. Barnhardite; 5. Gersdorffite; 6. Molybdate of Iron; 7. Albite; 8. Ripidolite; 9. Pholerite; 10. Scheelite; 11. Rhombic Tungstate of Lime; 12. Wolfram; 13. A few observations on the occurrence of gold." [2], xxviii. 246–255.

1862. "Contributions to Mineralogy: 1. Gold, pseudomorph after Aikinite; 2. Antimonial Arsenic and Arsenolite; 3. Arsenids of Copper; 4. Copper Glance, pseudomorphous after galena; 5. Millerite; 6. Proustite; (?) 7. Automolite; 8. Pyrope; 9. Lime Epidote; 10. Leopardite, a true porphyry; 11. Staurotide (?); 12. Chrysolite and Minerals resulting from its alteration; 13. Serpentine; 14. Kerolite; 15. Rammelsberg's Mineral Chemie." [2], xxxiii. 190–206.

1868. "Contributions to Mineralogy, No. VII.—1. Whitneyite; 2. American Tellurium Minerals. In this paper is described *Melonite*, a new mineral, $Ni_2Te_3$(?);

*Calaverite*, a new mineral, Au $Te_4$; *Montanite*, a new mineral $BiO_3TeO_32HO$; and *Cosalite*, a new mineral $2PbS + BiS_3$. This paper, like all the former numbers of this series, has numerous analyses.

1870. "North Carolina's Mineral Resources, etc." *Franklin Inst. Journ.*, 1871 and 1872.

1874. "Contributions from the Laboratory of the University of Pennsylvania."

I. "Corundum, its alterations and associated minerals," *Proc. Am. Phil. Soc.*, September 19, 1874, p. 56, with many analyses.

There are a few other notices in the *Pro. of the Acad. Nat. Sci.*, and, on the occurrence of tin in America, in the U. S. Railroad and Mining Register, which we have not enumerated.

Henry How, D.C.L., Professor of Chemistry and Natural History University of King's College, Windsor, N. S., has published the following papers on chemistry and chemical mineralogy :—

1. Analysis of Ancient Peruvian Alloy. Read before Chemical Society of London, and published in their *Journal*, 1846.

2. Analysis of the Ashes of the Orange Tree, viz., of Root, Stem, Leaves, Fruit, and Seed, in conjunction with T. H. Rowney. Read before Chem. Soc. Lond., and published in their *Journal*, 1847.

3. Analyses of Coals of Great Britain, etc. Published in Blue Books for Houses of Parliament, containing reports by Sir H. De La Beche and Dr. Lyon Playfair on Coals suited to the Steam Navy, 1848–49.

4. On certain Salts and Products of Decomposition of Comenic Acid. Read before Roy. Soc. Edin., and published in *Transactions*, 1851.

5. On the Decomposition of Citrate of Lime in contact with Putrefying Curd. Read before Chem. Soc. Lond., and published in their *Journal*, 1851.

6. On Meconic Acid and some of its Derivatives. Read before Roy. Soc. Edin., and published in *Transactions*, 1852.

7. On some New Basic Compounds, obtained from Vegetable Alkaloids. Read before Chemical Soc. Lond., and published in their *Journal*, 1853.

8. On Platinum accompanying Silver in Solution in Nitric Acid. Read before Chemical Soc. Lond., and published in their *Journal*, 1853.

9. Report on Torbane Hill Mineral, so-called Coal,

for the Instruction of Counsel in the case of Gillespie *v.* Russell. Edin., 1853.

10. On the Action of Halogen Compounds of Ethyl, and Amyl, on some Vegetable Alkaloids. Read before Roy. Soc. Edin., and published in *Transactions*, 1854.

11. On the Hyposulphites of the Organic Alkaloids. *Edin. New Phil. Journ.*, 1855.

12. Additional Experiments on the Ethers and Amides of Meconic and Comenic Acids. *Edin. New Phil. Journ.*, 1855.

13. On the Occurrence of the Mineral Natro-boro-Calcite in Gypsum of Nova Scotia. *Am. Journ. Sci.*, and *Edin. New. Phil. Journ.*, 1857.

14. Chemical Analyses of Faröelite and some other Zeolitic Minerals occurring in Nova Scotia. *Am. Journ. Sci.*, 1858.

15. Analysis and Description of Three New Minerals from Trap of Bay of Fundy. *Edin. New Phil. Journ.*, 1859.

16. On an Oil-Coal from Pictou Co., N. S., and the Comparative Composition of Minerals often included in the term "Coals." *Am. Journ. Sci.*, and *Edin. New Phil. Journ.*, 1860.

17. On the mineral Gysolite occurring in Trap of Bay of Fundy. Read before Roy. Soc. Edin.; published in *Am. Journ. Sci.*, and *Edin. New Phil. Journ.*, 1861.

18. On Natro-boro-Calcite and another Mineral, containing Boracic Acid in Gypsum of Nova Scotia. Read before Roy. Soc. Edin.; published in *Am. Journ. Sci.*, and *Edin. New Phil. Journ.*, 1861.

19. On Pickeringite occurring in Slate in Nova Scotia, and on the Class of Salts to which it belongs. Read before Chem. Soc. Lond. and published in *Qu. Journ.*, 1863.

20. On some Mineral Waters of N. S. Read before Nat. Hist. Soc. Montreal; pub. in *Canadian Naturalist*, 1863.

21. On the Waters of the Mineral Springs of Wilmot, N. S. Read before N. S. Inst. Natural Science; pub. in *Transactions*, 1864.

22. On Mordenite; a New Mineral from Trap of N. S. Read before Chem. Soc. Lond.; pub. in *Qu. Journ.*, 1864.

23. Notes on the Economic Mineralogy of Nova Scotia, Part I., Iron Ores. Read before N. S. Inst. Nat. Sci.; published in *Transactions*, 1864.

24. Note on Purification of Oxalic Acid. *Chemical News*, 1864.

25. On a Dense Brine from Salt Springs, N. S. Read before Chemical Soc. London; published in *Journal*, 1865.

26. On some Brine Springs of Nova Scotia. Read before N. S. Institute Nat. Sci.; pub. in *Transactions*, 1865.

27. Notes on Economic Mineralogy N. S., Part II. Ores of Manganese. Read before N. S. Inst.; pub. in *Transactions*, 1865.

28. Notes on Econ. Min. N. S., Part III. Limestone and Marbles. Read before N. S. Inst.; published in *Transactions*, 1866.

29. On the Comparative Composition of some Recent Shells, a Silurian Fossil Shell, and Shell Limestone of Carboniferous Age. *Am. Journal of Science*, 1866.

30. Contributions to the Mineralogy of N. S., Part I., Pyrolusite, etc. *Lond., Edin., and Dub. Phil. Mag.*, 1866.

31. Contributions to the Mineralogy of N. S., Part II., Wichtyne, etc. *Lond., Edin., and Dub. Phil. Mag.*, 1867.

32. Contributions to the Mineralogy of N. S., Part III., Silico-boro-calcite, etc. *Lond., Edin., and Dub. Phil. Mag.*, 1868.

33. Notes on Econ. Min. N. S., Part IV., Gypsum and Anhydrite. Read before N. S. Inst. Nat. Sci.; pub. in *Transactions*, 1868.

34. On an Oxalate of Manganese. *Chemical News*, 1869.

35. On the New Precipitation of Manganese by Sulphide of Ammonium in Presence of some Organic Ammoniacal Salts. *Chem. News*, 1869.

36. Mineralogy N. S. Report to Provincial Government, pp. 217; Halifax, 1869.

37. Contributions to Mineralogy N. S., Part IV., Lignite, etc. *Lond., Edin., and Dub. Phil. Mag.*, 1869.

38. Notes on Econ. Min. N. S., Part V., Coals and Allied Minerals. Read before N. S. Inst. Nat. Sci.; pub. in *Transactions*, 1869.

39. Contributions to Mineralogy N. S., Part V., New Forms of Borates, etc. *Lond., Edin., and Dub. Phil. Mag.*, 1870.

40. Contributions to Mineralogy N. S., Part VI., Winkworthite, etc. *Lond., Edin., and Dub. Phil. Mag.*, 1871.

41. On an Acid Feed Water from Stellarton, N. S. Read before Chem. Soc. Lond.; published in their *Journal*, 1870.

42. On a Water from Coal Measures at Westville, N.S. Read before Chem. Soc. Lond.; pub. in their *Journal*, 1871.

43. On Two Coals from Cape Breton, their Cokes and Ashes, with some Comparative analyses. Read before Chemical Society London; published in *Qu. Journal*, 1874.

Thomas Sterry Hunt, Professor of Geology at the Massachusetts Institute of Technology, Boston.—The name of no American chemist occurs more frequently, or in a more important relation to the progress and development of our science, during the past quarter of a century than that of Dr. Hunt. His contributions to our science have been equally valuable in theoretical chemistry, in chemical philosophy, and in geological and mineralogical chemistry. No author has covered a wider range than he. Not less than one hundred and thirty entries are found under his name in the second and third series of the *American Journal of Science;* and adding those published in Canada, England, and France, and some memoirs in the proceedings of various American societies, the total roll of his papers amounts to about one hundred and sixty titles. A dry enumeration of these would be of little interest; we will rapidly allude to a few of them in the classified order named below.

I. *Theoretical Chemistry.*—The views of Laurent and Gerhardt found their first advocacy in this country at the hands of Dr. Hunt in his able review of the *Précis* of the latter in 1847 (*Amer. Journ. Sci.* [2], iv. 93–171), and his own papers in the years next following have contributed in no small degree to extend the bounds of theoretical chemistry and its philosophy. We mention in particular his paper "On the Anomalies in the Atomic Volume of Sulphur and Nitrogen," in 1848 (*Amer. Journ. Sci.* [2], vi. pp. 170–178). This paper contains also remarks on Chemical Classification and a notice of Laurent's Theory of Binary Molecules. In his paper, 2. "On some Principles to be considered in Chemical Classification," read at the Philadelphia meeting of the American Association, etc., in 1848, Dr. Hunt freely criticizes the systems of Liebig and of the French school, the rather to show their merits than their defects, and to exhibit their real harmony with each other and with nature. In this paper he advances his own views, showing what we all now recognize as the true constitution of gaseous nitrogen—NN—and that the various saline forms are reducible to two, the types of which are seen in water, $H_2O$, and the protoxyds, $M_2O$, and in the hydrogen, $H_2$, or the metals $M_2$, the first including all the oxygenized acids, and the second, the hydracids. 3. "On the Chemical Constitution of Gelatine and its Transformations."

4. "Remarks on the Constitution of Leucine and the Ureas" (*American Journal of Science* [2], ix. 63–67).

5. "On the Compound Ammonias and the Bodies of the Cacodyle Series," published in 1852 (*Amer. Journ. Sci.* [2], xiii. 206–211).

6. "On the Action of Sulphuretted Hydrogen upon Nitric Acetene," published in 1847, *Amer. Journ. Sci.* [2], iv. 350.

7. "On the Decomposition of Aniline by Nitrous Acid."

The last investigation points out a new mode of decomposition of organic bases, and in the case cited phenol was regenerated.

8. "On the Theoretical Relations of Water and Hydrogen." In this paper, published in March, 1854, Dr. Hunt reviews the opinions of the European chemists on the water-type, and reclaims (Dec. 30, 1853) for himself the priority of authorship in this important conception which the English edition of Gmelin's Handbook (vol. vii. pp. 17 and 201) ascribes to Williamson.

9. "On the Theory of Types in Chemistry," is the title of a memoir of Dr. Hunt's, dated January 5, 1861 (*Amer. Journ. Sci.* [2], xxxi. pp. 256–263), in which he ably reviews the history of the subject, and shows that in the series of papers whose titles are above quoted, 1 to 9, were first developed the views of the *water-type* and of *multiple or condensed types* which were subsequently adopted by Williamson, Gerhardt, and Ad. Wurtz. Dr. W. Gibbs, in an essay presented by him at the Baltimore meeting of the American Association for Ad. Science, May, 1858, remarks that in a previous paper of his (his "Report on the Progress of Organic Chemistry") he had attributed the theory of water-types to Williamson and Gerhardt, and adds, "in this I find I have not done justice to Mr. T. Sterry Hunt, to whom is exclusively due the credit of having first applied the theory to the so-called oxygen-acids and to the anhydrids, and in whose earlier papers may be found the germs of most of the ideas on classification usually attributed to Gerhardt and his school."

10. "Theory of Nitrification and Nature of Gaseous Nitrogen" (*Amer. Journ. Sci.*, 1848), further developed with experiments on the oxidation of nitrogen by permanganic acid, and the origin of nitrous acid, forming a key to the true origin of nitrites and nitrates in nature. This view was adopted without change or addition by Schönbein in 1862, and without acknowledgment. See Hunt's Reclamation in the *Amer. Journ. Sci.* [2], xxxv. pp. 271–273, 1863.

Other views of fundamental importance have been put forth by Dr. Hunt on Theoretic Chemistry, but we must pass them and make brief mention of some of his more important contributions to—

II. *Chemical Philosophy.*—1. "Considerations on the Theory of Chemical Changes, and on Equivalent Volumes." This paper appeared in 1852 (*Amer. Journ. Sci.* [2], xv. 226), and is a more condensed statement of the same views developed by the author in an "Introduction to Organic Chemistry," which appeared in Silliman's Chemistry in the same year.

2. "Thoughts on Solution and the Chemical Process" (*Amer. Journ. Sci.* [2], xix. 100). In this paper the ground is taken that all solution is chemical union.

3. "On the Objects and Method of Mineralogy" (*Amer. Journ. Sci.*, [2], xliii. 203.)

4. "On the Constitution and Equivalent Volume of some Mineral Species." This is an elaborate memoir (*Amer. Journ. Sci.*, Sept. 1853), in which the author develops his views respecting the homology of chemical formulas, and the similarity of volume in isomorphous species, looking to an enlargement and simplification of the plan of chemical science, and leading to a correct mineralogical system.

5. "Illustrations of Chemical Homology." In this paper, read at Washington, in 1854, before the American Association for Advancement of Science (viii. 237), the author gives a greater extension to his former paper just named (4) and discussed many points with regard to the homologies of organic and mineral species. Here will be found developed his views on the constitution of the feldspars, which were some years later adopted without acknowledgment by Tschermak.

Besides these contributions already cited, Dr. Hunt has been a constant worker in the analyses of minerals, and has made many important—

III. *Studies in Geological and Mineralogical Chemistry.*—We can only mention in passing:—

1. Analyses of Warwickite, Columbite, Samarskite, Rutherfordite, in early volumes of the *Amer. Journ. Science.*

2. On Euphotide, Saussurite, and related Diorites, an elaborate study with many analyses, published in 1859 in the *Amer. Journ. Science.*

3. On the Labrador Feldspars, printed in the *London Phil. Magazine* for 1855.

4. Contributions to the Chemistry of the Ophiolites, vols. xxv. and xxvi., *Amer. Journ. Sci.*, 1858. An elaborate research with numerous analyses forming part of the Geological Reports of Canada.

5. "Contributions to Lithology. I. Theoretical Notions. II. Classification and Nomenclature. III. On some Eruptive Rocks" (*Amer. Journ. Sci.* [2], xxxvii. 248, and xxxviii. 91 and 248, 1864). This elaborate memoir gives the composition of the various eruptive rocks of the district of Montreal, with the author's theoretical deductions therefrom.

6. "Contributions to the History of Natural Waters" (*Amer. Journ. Sci.*, 1865). In this memoir is given the theory of the origin of mineral-waters, with studies of their composition, illustrated by the waters of the St. Lawrence basin, and the chemical relations of each element. This research is in part in the Geological Survey of Canada for 1867.

7. "On Some Reactions of the Salts of Lime and Magnesia and on the Formation of Gypsum and Magnesian Rocks" (*Amer. Journ. Sci.*, 1859). This very elaborate memoir exhibits a great amount of chemical work, and treats—I. of the action of solutions of bicarbonate of soda on salts of lime and magnesia. II. On the reaction between solutions of bicarbonate of lime and the sulphates of soda and magnesia. III. On the formation of double carbonate of lime and magnesia. IV. Facts in the history of gypsums, dolomites, magnesites, and limestones. V. On the mode of formation of the preceding rocks. This was followed by a supplementary paper, entitled "Farther Contributions to the Chemistry of Lime and Magnesia Salts" (*Amer. Journ. Sci.*, 1866).

In this connection it is but just to mention that in addition to the work here recorded, Dr. Hunt has in the volumes of the Geological Survey of Canada given analyses of a vast number of rocks, soils, ores, etc., contributions toward the chemistry of ore-deposits in Canada, etc.

But time fails us even to name the work of Dr. Hunt in many other important researches of a like nature. "Researches on the Artificial Production of Earthy Silicates, and some points in Chemical Geology and the Chemistry of the Metamorphic Rocks," published in the *Quarterly Geological Journal*, London, from 1859 to 1863. His "Chemical Theory of the Globe;" "The Chemistry of Chaos;" "Chemical Origin of Rocks, Sea, Atmosphere, Ore Deposits, Mineral Species, Volcanoes," developed in various papers in the *Amer. Journ. Sci.*, the *Smithsonian Report* for 1869, and the author's address at Indianapolis before the American Association for the Advancement of Science, on the "Origin of Crystalline Rocks," and his "Contributions to the Chemistry of Copper" (*Amer. Journ. Sci.*, 1870).

A volume containing some of the more important of Dr. Hunt's original papers here enumerated, and others, is now in press, and will soon appear, simultaneously, in Boston and in London.

John L. LeConte, M.D., Philadelphia.—This eminent naturalist made his inaugural dissertation on a chemical investigation, which has been published as follows:—

On a New Species of Urinary Concretions, by John L. LeConte, M.D. *New Journal of Medicine and the Collateral Sciences*, 1846, vol. vii. p. 172.

E. N. Horsford, Cambridge, Mass.—Prof. Horsford's chemical papers are as follows:—

1846. Uber den Werth Verschiedener Vegetabilischer Nahrungsmittel, hergeleit aus ihrem Stickstoffgehalt *Liebig's Annal.*, lxiii. 166, translated in *Sill. Journ.*, ii. 264.

1846. Analyse der Ashe des Kleies Trifolium praetense. lviii. 391, *Liebig Annal.*

1846. Uber den Ammoniakgehalt der Gletscher. *Liebig Annal.*, lix. 113.

1846. Uber Glycocoll (Leimzucker) und einige seiner Zersetzungs producte. *Liebig Annal.* lxi. Translated in *Sill. Journ.*, iii. 369, iv. 58, 326.

1846. List of Sweet Bodies. *Proc. Am. Acad.*, i. 303. Chemical Essays Relative to Agriculture. *Sill. Journ.*, ii. 144.

1847. Warrentrapp and Will's Method for the Determination of Nitrogen improved. *Sill. Journ.* [2], iv. 267.

1848. Strecker's Researches on Ox-gall. *Ibid.* [2], v. 17.

1848. Resistance presented to Fluids by Electric conduction. *Ibid.* [2], v. 36.

1848. New Blast Lamp. v. 36, *Ibid.* [2].

1848. Liebig's New Mode of separating Nickel and Cobalt. *Ibid.* [2], v. 411.

1848. On Motions of Fluids in Animal Bodies. *Ibid.* [2], v. 415.

1848. Contamination of Water, etc. *Am. Acad. Proc.*, ii. 62–99.

1848. Explosion of Burning Fluids. *Proc. Am. Ass.*, ii. 178, 179.

1849. On the Moisture, Ammonia, and Organic Matters of the Atmosphere. *Ibid.*, ii. 124, *Liebig Annal.*, lxxiv. 243, 1850.

1849. Note on Soda in the Ashes of Anthracite Coal. *Proc. Am. Ass.*, 233.

1849. On Color of Fused Sulphur. *Proc. Am. Ass.*, 234.

1851. Occurrence of Placid Waters in the Midst of large Areas where Waves are constantly breaking. vi. 41, *Proc. Am. Ass.*

1850. On the Relation of Barium, Strontium, etc. *Sill. Journ.* [2], ix. 176.

1851. Plasticity of Sulphur. *Proc. Am. Ass.*, vi. 63.

1851. Relation of Chemical Constitution to Light. *Proc. Am. Ass.*, 74.

1856. Ammonia in the Atmosphere. *Ibid.*, x. 145.

1863. Salts of Zinc, Aluminium, Sodium, Potassium. *Mem. Am. Acad.*, viii. 354–360.

1851. Analyses of Teas. *Sill. Journ.* [2], xi. 249.

1851. Relation of Chemical Constitution to taste. *Ibid.* [2], xii. 195.

1852. Permeability of Metals to Mercury. *Ibid.* [2], xiii. 305.

1853. Solidification of the Coral Reefs of Florida, and the Source of Carbonate of Lime in the Growths of Corals. *Proc. Am. Ass.*, vii. 122.

1868. Source of Free Hydrochloric Acid in Gastric Juice. *Ibid.*, xvii. 178.

1868. Phosphoric Acid a Constituent of Butter. *Ibid.*, xvii. 114.

1869. Phosphoric Acid, Iron, and Potassium, Constituents of Chlorophyl. *Ibid.*, 147.

John W. Mallett, Professor of Chemistry in the University of Virginia, at Charlottesville, Va., has for many years been an industrious worker, publishing original researches on chemical subjects, which form important contributions to our science. The destruction of the buildings of the University of Alabama, by the Federal Cavalry during the late civil war, has deprived Prof. Mallett (who was formely Prof. of Chemistry at Tuscaloosa) of all means of responding to the call for his papers, but the following list is as complete as it could be conveniently made by us from the materials at hand.

1850. On the Minerals of the Auriferous Districts of Wicklow. *Phil. Mag.* [3], xxxvii. 392.

1845. Chemical Examination of Killinite. *Dub. Geol. Soc.* iv. *Chemist*, I. 47–49, 1849–50.

1851. Occurrence of Gadolinite in Ireland. *Phil. Mag.* [4], i. 350.

1851. Beobachtungen über das Telluräthyl. *Liebig Ann.* [4], xxix. 223.

1852. On a New Fossil Resin. *Phil. Mag.* [4], iv. 261.

1853. Analysis of Euclase. *Phil. Mag.* [4], v. 127.

1853. On a Siliceous Deposit from the Hot Volcanic Springs of Taupo. *Phil. Mag.* [4], v. 285.

1854. Analysis of Tin Pyrites. *Sill. Journ.* [2], xvii. 23.

1854. Analysis of Idocrase from Ducktown, Polk Co., Tenn. *Ibid.* [2], xx. 85.

1854. On Phosphates of Iron and Manganese from Norwich, Mass. *Ibid.* [2], xviii. 33.

1855. On Crystallization of Platinum from Fusion. *Ibid.* [2], xv. 340.

1856. Redetermination of Lithium. *Am. Assn.*, x. 144.

1856. On a Zeolitic Mineral from the Isle of Skye. *Phil. Mag.* [4], xii. 406–552.

1857. Atomic Weight of Aluminium. *Brit. Assn. Report*, p. 53.

1857. On the Atomic Weight of Lithium. *Phil. Mag.* [4], xiii.

1857. Results of some Analyses made for the Geol. Survey of Alabama. *Sill. Journ.* [2], xxiii. 181.

1857. Notice of a supposed new case of Fluorescence. *Ibid.* [2], xxiii. 434.

1857. On the Separation of Lithia and Magnesia. *Ibid.* [2], xxiii. 427.

1857. On the Rose-colored Mica of Goshen, Mass. *Ibid.* [2], xxiii. 180.

1857. Separation of Magnesia and Lithia. *Ibid.* [2], xxiv. 137.

1858. Schrotterite from Cherokee Co., Alabama. *Ibid.* [2], xxvi. 79.

1859. On Brewsterite. *Ibid.* [2], xxviii. 48.

1860. Metallic Copper and Dinoxyd of Copper. *Ibid.* [2], xxx. 253.

1859. Nitrate of Zirconium. *Am. Assn.*, xiii. 217.

1859. Atomic weight of Lithium. *Am. Assn.*, xiii. 221.

1860. Osmious Acid and the position of Osmium in the list of elements. *Phil. Mag.* [4], xix. 293.

1861. Chemical and Physical Conditions of the Culture of Cotton. *Proc. Royal Soc.*, xi. 340.

J. D. Whitney, Cambridge, Mass.—Mr. Whitney's chemical work has been in mineral chemistry. He has published as follows:—

1849. Examination of American Minerals. *Sill. Journ.* [2], vii. 433, 434. *Proc. Boston Nat. Hist. Soc.* 1849, p. 48.

1849. On some Silicates containing Carbonic Acid, Chlorine, and Sulphuric Acid. *Sill. Journal*, vii. 435. *Pogg. Ann. der Ph. und Ch.*, lxx. 431.

1849. On Chloritoid and Masonite; and Black Oxide of Copper, Lake Superior. *Sill. Journ.* [2], viii. 273. *Proc. Boston Nat. Hist. Soc.* 1849, p. 100.

1854. Analysis of Algerite and Apatite. *Sill. Journ.*, xvii. 206.

1860. On Pectolite. *Ibid.* [2], xxix. 205.

1860. Analysis of Pyroschists. *Ibid.*, lxvi. 160.

William Phipps Blake has written chiefly on geological and kindred topics; but we find in 1850 an article by him on the "Occurrence of Crystallized Oxyd of Chromium ($\ddot{\text{Cr}}$) in Furnaces for the Manufacture of Chromate of Potash," giving the crystallographic and other physical characters of the substance. *Am. Jour. Sci.*, 2, x. No. 30, Nov. 1850.

Mr. Blake was the first to recognize the *tellurids* among the mineral products of California. His Report on the Precious Metals, forming one of the governmental volumes on the Paris Universal Exposition of 1867, is replete with valuable information. Mr. Blake first drew attention to the platinum metals associated with the gold washings of California, and published an analysis of the mass made for him in Dr. Genth's laboratory in 1854. "Report of a Geological Reconnaissance of California," 4to. pp. 300.

1850. "On Dimorphism of Copper," *Am. Ass. Proceedings*, iv. p. 151.

1850. "New Instrument for Measuring the Angles contained between the Optic Axes of Crystals and for Goniometrical Purposes," *Ibid.*, pp. 378–221.

JOHN M. ORDWAY, Chemical Laboratory of the Massachusetts Institute of Technology, Boston.—All of Prof. Ordway's papers, with a single exception, have been published in the *Am. Journ. of Sci.*, 2d series. They are as follows:—

*Memoirs.*

1850. Nitrates of Iron, Alumina, and Chromium. *Am. Journ. Sci.*, ix. 30.

1865. Nitrates of Iron. *Id.*, xl. 316.

1859. Some Facts respecting the Nitrates. *Id.*, xxvii. 14.

1857. Some Soluble Basic Salts of Tin. *Id.*, xxiii. 220.

1858. Examination of the Soluble Basic Sesquisalts. *Id.*, xxvi. 197.

1858. A new Mode of making Commercial Caustic Soda. *Id.* xxvi. 364.

1861–1865. On Waterglass, a series of five articles. *Id.*, xxxii. 153, 337; xxxiii. 27; xxxv. 185; xl. 173.

*Reviews.*

1856. Wetherill's Manufacture of Vinegar. *Am. Journ. Sci.*, xxxi. 450.

1867. Schützenberger's Traité des Matières Colorantes. *Id.*, xliii. 421.

1867. Mulder's Die Chemie der auströckende Oele. *Id.*, xliv. 438.

1868. Assmass' Die Trockne Destillation des Holzes. *Id.*, xlv. 274.

*Obituary Sketches.*

1868. Dr. S. L. Dana. *Id.*, xlv. 424. Author of the same in *Proc. Am. Acad. Arts and Sci.*, viii. 26.

WM. H. BREWER, New Haven, Connecticut.—Prof. Brewer's contributions to chemistry are:—

1850. Determinations of Nitrogen in two Varieties of Indian Corn. *Proc. Am. Assoc. Adv. Sci.*, iv. 386.

Prof. Brewer has also contributed Analysis of Minerals to Dana's Mineralogy, etc.

GEORGE J. BRUSH, Sheffield Scientific School, New Haven.—All the chemical researches of Prof. Brush fall under the head of chemical mineralogy, to which he has made important contributions. Besides the subjoined list, he has contributed analyses of minerals to the third, fourth, and fifth editions of Dana's *Mineralogy*, and to the various supplements. Of the latter he edited the eighth, ninth, and tenth, published in the *American Journal of Science*, and also the appendix to the fifth edition, recently published by Wiley. So large a part of the work of American chemists has been devoted to mineralogy, which, in the larger sense, is only a department of chemistry, that we have no right to consider such researches as not falling within the scope of our essay.

Papers on chemical mineralogy published by Prof. Brush are found in the *American Journal of Science*, viz.:—

Second series:—

Vol. x. pp. 370. Analyses of American Spodumine.
" xv. pp. 207. }
" vvi. pp. 41. } Re-examination of American Minerals. By J. Lawrence Smith and George J. Brush. Parts I.–III.
" xvi. pp. 365. }

This joint work of Profs. Smith and Brush includes the examination of the following minerals:—

Part I. Emerylite, euphyllite, Litchfield mica, unionite, kerolite, bowenite, williamsite, lancasterite, hydromagnesite, magnesite.

Part II. Chesterlite, loxoclase, Danbury feldspars, Haddam albite, Greenwood mica, biotite, margarodite, Chesterlite talc, rhodophyllite, cummingtonite, hydrous anthophyllite, monrolite, ozarkite, dysyntribite, gibbsite, emerald nickel.

Part III. Danburite, carrollite, thalite, hudsonite, jenkinsite, lazulite, kyanite, elæolite, spodumene, petalite.

Vol. xviii. pp. 407. On the Chemical Composition of Clintonite (Seybertite).
" " pp. 415. On a New Test for Zirconia.
" xx. pp. 273. On Prosopite.
" xxiv. pp. 128. On the Chemical Composition of Antigorite.
" xxiv. pp. 116. On Dechenite and Eusynchite.
" xxiv. pp. 124. Note on Parathorite.
" xxv. pp. 198. Chemical Composition of Chalcodite.
" xxvi. pp. 64. Mineralogical Notices: Analyses of Gieseckite (?) from Diana, Compact Pyrophyllite, Unionite, Danbury Feldspar.
" xxvii. pp. 395. Chemical Examination of Boltonite.

Vol. xxxii. pp. 94. On Crystalline Hydrate of Magnesia.
" xxxiv. pp. 243. On Amblygonite from Maine.
" " pp. 402. On Triphyline from Norwich, Mass.
" xxxvi. pp. 122, 257. On Childrenite from Hebron, Maine.
" " pp. 152. On the Tucson Meteoric Iron.
" xxxvii. pp. 66. On Tephroite.
" xxxix. pp. 132. On Artificial Diopside.
" xli. pp. 246. On Cookeite and Jefferisite.
" xliv. pp. 219. On Native Hydrates of Iron.
" xlvi. pp. 140, 240. On Sussexite.
" xlviii. pp. 17. On Hortonolite.
" " pp. 17. On Durangite.
" " pp. 179. On a Meteoric Stone from Frankfort, Alabama.
" " pp. 360. On Magnetite in the Pennsville Mica.

Third series:—
Vol. I. pp. 28. On Galenite from New Jersey.
" II. pp. 30. On Ralstonite.
" V. pp. 421. On Compact Anglesite.

HENRY WURTZ, Hoboken, New Jersey.—Prof. Wurtz, who was at one time professor of chemistry in the Columbian Medical College at Washington, D. C., is now chemical editor of the Gas Light Journal in New York. His chemical contributions date from 1850, as follows. [Prof. Wurtz has furnished us the following notes on his papers.]—

1850. On a Supposed New Mineral Species. *Am. Journ. Sci.* [2], x. p. 80, July.

1850. On the Green Sand of New Jersey as a Source of Potash. Read to the American Association at New Haven, August, 1850. *Ibid*,, p. 326, November. [Analyses given of two raw green sand marls containing 6·38 per cent., and 4·94 per cent. of KO. The fact first announced that dilute sulphuric acid yields *alum* directly, readily crystallizing out from solution of the green sand granules. Previous ignition peroxidized the iron chiefly, and the alum then obtained was mostly free from iron. The fact was first announced that when the grains, even without pulverization, were fused at a low temperature with chloride of calcium, in sufficient proportion to form a pasty mass, complete double decomposition was effected, and the mass yielded to water, "all the potash which was contained in the green sand employed in the form of chloride of potassium." Upon this was founded "a method of decomposing minerals in the process of analysis," presented to the Association at the same meeting. Sulphate of potash was obtained by fusing together alum and chloride of potassium.]

1850. On a New Method of Decomposing Silicates in the Process of Analysis. Read to the American Association at New Haven, August, 1850. *Ibid.* [2], x. p. 323, November. [Feldspar and hornblende were found, when fused with chloride of calcium, to be completely fluxed, and decomposable by muriatic acid. It was suggested to use, at times, chloride of barium, instead of chloride of calcium, because of its freedom from deliquescence. A mixture, in equivalent proportions, of the chlorides of barium and strontium was found very advantageous, from its far greater fusibility. An analysis was given, made by this method, of the pink scapolite of Bolton, Massachusetts.]

1851. On Bromine as a Toxicological Agent. By Henry Wurtz, Assistant in the Yale Analytical Laboratory. *Ibid.* [2], xi. 405, May. [Bromine with water and heat was used to replace chlorine to destroy the organic matter of stomachs, etc., to isolate mineral poisons.]

1852. On the Preparation of Pure Hydrate and Carbonate of Potash. *New York Journ. Pharm.* February, 1852, i. 33. [Elimination of silica from solutions of potassic carbonate by evaporating with the addition of carbonate of ammonia in lumps. Superiority of flint-glass bottles for solutions of potassic hydrate, on account of their greater resistance to corrosion. Preparation of pure hydrate from pure potassic sulphate, by reduction to sulphide, and boiling with oxide of copper, manganese, or iron. Residual undecomposed sulphate removed by solution of baric hydrate.]

1852. Preparation of Chemically Pure Hydrate and Carbonate of Soda. *Ibid.*, i. 36, February, 1852. [Commercial bicarbonate of soda is freed from sulphate, phosphate, and chloride by washing with water by decantation, then dried on the sand-bath, and exposed to a heat below redness, to expel $CO_2$. On solution in water, the silica is chiefly left in flakes. Remaining traces of silica then removed by evaporation with addition of lumps of ammonic carbonate, and resolution. To obtain dry pure carbonate, the last solution is then re-evaporated in vessels of Pt, Ag, or clean Fe, avoiding glass and porcelain. To obtain pure sodic hydrates, the carbonate must be decomposed by lime, which is free from silica.]

1852. Preparation of Pure Barium Compounds (with other subjects). *Ibid.*, June, 1852, i. 161. [The important point is here the first announcement of the power of baric carbonate, either precipitated, or pulverized witherite, to precipitate gypsum totally from its solutions; with the first suggestion to utilize this property for purifying waters for steam purposes, sea-water included. Brine of salt works also mentioned as a proper subject.]

1852. Preparation of Pure Magnesia. *Ibid.* i. 199. [Commercial *magnesia alba* dissolved in nitric acid, and by digestion with an excess of the carbonate, all silica, ferric oxide, alumina, and $PO_5$ separated. To eliminate lime, some magnesic sulphate and alcohol added, the latter in quantity insufficient to cause immediate precipitation. In the course of time the lime crystallizes out as gypsum. The liquid is then evaporated and heated, with stirring and addition of powdered carbonate of ammonia, to expel the nitric acid. On ignition, and washing with distilled water after cooling —to remove sulphates and alkaline salts—chemically pure magnesia remains. Oxalate of lime was found to be appreciably soluble in magnesic solutions, and hence lime could not be eliminated as oxalate from such solutions.]

1852. On the Preparations of Iron used in Medicine. *Ibid.*, i. 229. [Preventing oxidation of ferrous compounds by introducing into the bottle fragments of quicklime wrapped in paper. Alcohol will not preserve ferrous salts, as generally supposed, as it absorbs oxygen from the air, and conveys it thereto. To obtain ferrous sulphate free from ferric salt, baric carbonate employed. Another new mode, by agitation with pulverized protosulphide of iron. To obtain pure ferric oxide, dissolve separately in hot water five of recrystallized copperas, six of crystallized sodic carbonate, and one of nitrate of soda, filter, mix, evaporate to dryness, and heat the mass to faint redness. Water then leaves undissolved a heavy impalpable, but perfectly soluble, ferric oxide. Coal gas is proposed to be used, instead of hydrogen, in making *pulvis ferri.*]

1853. Purification of Sal Ammoniac. *Ibid.*, ii. 1, January, 1853. [The yellowish portions of loaves of sal ammoniac were known to be ferriferous. The transparent colorless parts were found to be equally so, and the iron found to be present as FeCl. The yellow color is not due to iron. Neither sublimation nor crystallization eliminated the iron, though so asserted in the books. Brewer's process of purification here first published—with Cl and $NH_3$.]

1856. On the Composition of the Water of the Delaware River. By Henry Wurtz, New Jersey State Chemist. *Am. Journ. Sci.* [2], xxii. 124, November, 1856. [Includes also an analysis of the water of springs proceeding from the crystalline gneiss rocks at Trenton, New Jersey.]

1858. Action of Nitric Acid on the Metallic Chlorides. *Am. Journ. Sci.* [2], xxv. 39, May, 1858. [This extended research, which is continued in the same journal, vol. xxvi. page 81, covered the behavior of hot nitric acid upon the chlorides of K, Na, Li, $NH_4$, Mg, Ca, Sr, Ba, Al, Gl, Fe, Mn, Co, Ni, Zn, Cd, Cu, Cr, U, Hg, Pb, Ag, Au, Pt, Sn, As, Sb, Bi, Ce, La, Di, Th, Zr, Mo, and V. Many new and important facts were developed, too numerous to detail here.]

1858. Detection of Nitric Acid in Solution, with Observations on the Action of Ferric Salts upon Indigo and Metallic Gold, and on the Neutralization of the Colors of Metallic Solutions. *Ibid.*, xxvi. 49, April. Read to the American Association in Baltimore, in April, 1858. [Containing the first observations of the power of ferric solutions to dissolve metallic gold and platinum.]

1858. A Method of Separation of Magnesia from the Alkalies. Read to the American Association in Baltimore, April, 1858. *Ibid.*, xxvi. 83. [The bases, as chlorides, are converted into nitrates by evaporation with nitric acid, ignition, and washing with water.]

1858. Action of Nitric Acid in the Cold upon some Metallic Solutions, with new modes of obtaining pure Compounds of Barium, Strontium, and Cadmium. *Ibid.*, 188. Read to the American Association, at Baltimore, April, 1858. [BaCl and CdCl, in strong solution, gave instantly, and SrCl more slowly, crystalline precipitates of pure nitrates. HgCl was also instantly precipitated, but went down as such, and not as nitrate. KCl and NaCl gradually form nitrates in the cold.]

1858. Suggestions regarding Economical Applications of Glycerine. Read to the American Association at Baltimore, April, 1858. *Ibid.*, xxxi. 195. [Mixing with mustard and other condiments, confectionery, chocolate, chewing tobacco, filling gas meters, making copying ink, etc.]

1858. Preparation of Pure Sulphates, etc. By Henry

Wurtz, Professor of Chemistry in the National Medical College, Washington, D. C. *Ibid.*, xxvi. 367. [Elimination of iron from cupric sulphate by conversion to ferric oxide by ebullition with a little plumbic deutoxide, or even with minium, and then adding baric carbonate. The same method is applied to a great number of other sulphates, including Epsom salt. Referring to former paper, in which the precipitation of gypsum by baric carbonate is brought out, it is further suggested that plumbic carbonate be used for this, the lead being recovered again.]

1858. Improvements in the Preparation of Hard Minerals for Analysis. Read to the American Association at Baltimore in 1858. *Ibid.* 190. [Proposed to crush always in a hard iron mortar, and then to remove the abraded iron with iodine-water, also with a neutral solution of ferric chloride. When earthy carbonates are present, remove them first by boiling with ammonic chloride or nitrate, then iodine. Pyrrhotine was found to be separable from pyrites, by dissolving in iodine-water, the pyrites being insoluble therein. Elutriation of minerals in the iron mortar *with alcohol* recommended.]

1858. Chemical Examinations connected with a Bullet which had been imbedded for more than forty years in a Human Lung. *Ibid.*, 192. [The bullet was found corroded and partly encrusted with plumbic chloride, and the liquid in the enveloping cyst also contained lead. The body of the lung and the muscle of the diaphragm were found to contain lead.]

1858. Action of Hot Muriatic Acid upon some Metallic Nitrates. *Proc. Am. Ass. Advt. Sci.* (Baltimore, 1858), 181.

1859. On the Occurrence of Cobalt and Nickel in Gaston County, North Carolina. *Am. Journ. Sci.*, xxvii. 24, April, 1858.

1859. Modes of Increasing the Heat of the Mouth Blowpipe, with some blowpipe manipulations. *Ibid.*, xxvii. 24. [Paraffine candles proposed. Blowpipe with tube filled with potassic hydrate. Powdered silica may be fused or semi-fused into transparent globules. Borax beads, so highly supersaturated with oxides as to become opaque on cooling, found to remain transparent, if plunged while hot into cold water, and colored reactions thus brought out. New facts and experiments on interference of colors in blowpipe beads. Decolorization of ferriferous glass by manganese, shown to be due, in part at least, to such neutralization of colors.]

1866. Sodium Amalgam. *Ibid.* [2], li. 216.
1866. On Grahamite. *Ibid.*, lii. 420.
1869. Atmospheric Air mixed with Gas. *Ibid.*, lviii. 40.
1870. Gas Well in New York. *Ibid.*, lix. 336.
1870. On Flame Temperatures. *Ibid.*, lix. 339.

Samuel W. Johnson, Professor of Theoretical and Agricultural Chemistry in Yale College, has made the following contributions to chemistry :—

*Memoirs and Lectures.*

On the Houghite of Prof. Shepard. *Am. Journ. Sci.*, xii. (1851), pp. 361–365.

Chemische Notizen: 1. Chromsaures Kali-ammoniak; 2. Chromsaures Natron, Leichte Bereitungsweise desselben; 3. Ueber Kartoffel-fuselöl, Vorkommen von Propylalkahol und Caprinsäure in demselben; 4. Verbindung von Amylalkohol mit Chlorcalcium. *Journ. für Prakt. Chemie*, lxii. (1854), pp. 261–264.

Ueber das zweifach schleimsaure amyloxyd. *Journ. für Prakt. Chemie*, lxiv. (1855), pp. 107–9.

Ueber die schleimsauren Salze der Alkalien. *Liebig's Annalen*, xciv. (1855), pp. 224–230.

Chemische Untersuchung verschiedener Pflanzenaschen, Bodenarten, und Gewässer. *Liebig's Annalen*, xcv. (1855), pp. 226–242, von Prof. O. Sendtner und S. W. Johnson.

Essay on the Physical Properties of Soils as affecting Fertility. *Trans. N. Y. State Ag. Soc.*, 1856, pp. 101–124.

Examination of two Sugars (Panoche and Pinite) from California. *Am. Journ. Sci.*, xxii. (1856), pp. 6–8.

Lecture on the Relations that exist between Science and Agriculture. *Trans. N. Y. State Ag. Soc.*, 1857, pp. 73–95.

Lectures on Agricultural Chemistry. *Report of Smithsonian Institution*, 1859, pp. 78.

On Some Points of Agricultural Science. *Am. Journ. Sci.*, xxvii. (1859), pp. 71–85.

Soil Analysis. Notice of the Agricultural Chemistry of the Geological Surveys of Kentucky and Arkansas. *Am. Journ. Sci.*, xxxii., 1861, pp. 20.

With joint authorship of O. D. Allen.

On the Equivalent and Spectrum of Cæsium. *Am. Journ. Sci.*, xxxv. (1863), pp. 7.

The Assimilation of Complex Nitrogenous Bodies by Vegetation. *Am. Journ. Sci.*, xli. (1866), pp. 4.

With joint authorship of JOHN M. BLAKE.

On Kaolinite and Pholerite. *Am. Journ. Sci.*, xliii. (1867), pp. 13.

Sources and Supply of Nitrogen to Crops. *Lecture to Conn. Board of Agriculture*, 1867, pp. 25.

On Native Crystallized Terpin. *Am. Journ. Sci.*, xliii. (1867), pp. 2.

On the Estimation of Carbonic Acid, and on Construction of Bunsen's Air-pump. *Am. Journ. Sci.*, xlviii. (1869), pp. 111–114.

On Nitrification. *Am. Journ. Sci.*, xlvii. (1869), pp. 234–242.

Soil Exhaustion and Rotation of Crops. Two Lectures. *Report of the Conn. State Board of Agriculture*, 1871, pp. 47.

On the Estimation of Nitrogen. *Am. Chemist*, iii. (1872), pp. 161–2.

On the Use of Potassium Dichromate in Ultimate Organic Analysis. *Am. Journ. Sci.* [3], vii. (1874), pp. 465–8.

*Reports.*

Reports to the Connecticut State Agricultural Society, Hartford, Ct.

For 1857. General Considerations on Manures; Examination of forty-three fertilizers, pp. 58.

For 1858. Essay on the Nature and Agricultural Uses of Peat and Swamp Muck, and Analyses of thirty-two samples; Examination of twelve fertilizers, pp. 174.

For 1859. Examinations of twenty fertilizers, pp. 67.

Reports to the Connecticut State Board of Agriculture.

For 1868. Examinations of sixteen fertilizers, pp. 18.

For 1869. Valuation of Commercial Fertilizers, pp. 18.

For 1872. Composition of the Ash of Connecticut Tobacco leaf, etc., pp. 40.

For 1873. Analyses of thirty-one Commercial Fertilizers, pp. 21.

*Systematic Treatises.*

Peat and its uses as a Fertilizer and Fuel. N. Y., O. Judd & Co., 1866, pp. 168, 12mo.

How Crops Grow. N. Y., 1868, pp. 394.

The same, edited by Church and Dyer, London. 1869.

The same in German, translation by Baron H. v. Liebig. Braunschweig, 1871.

The same in Russian, translation by N. R. Temashev. St. Petersburg, 1873.

How Crops Feed. N. Y., 1870, pp. 375.

The same in German, translation by Baron H. v. Liebig. Braunschweig, 1872.

Any notice of Prof. Johnson's contributions to chemistry would be extremely deficient, should it fail to mention his well-known edition of Fresenius' Manual of Qualitative and Quantitative Analysis, in two volumes, 1869–1870. A new edition of this work by Prof. Johnson is now in preparation.

John Leconte, Oakland, California. — Dr. Leconte's contributions to science are all from the physical side, and how important they are is too well known to require comment. He is now the Professor of Physics and Mechanics in the University of California. The following physico-chemical papers by Dr. Leconte fall properly within our scope.

1. "Observations on a Remarkable Exudation of Ice from the Stems of Vegetables, and on a Singular Protrusion of Icy Columns from Certain Kinds of Earth during Frosty Weather." *Proceedings of American Association for Adv. of Sci.*, 3d Meeting, at Charleston, S. C., March, 1850, pp. 20–34.—*Lond.*, *Edin.*, *Dub.*, *Phil. Mag.*, 3d S., vol. xxxvi. pp. 329–342, May, 1850.

2. "Observations on the Freezing of Vegetables, and on the Causes which enable some Plants to endure the action of Extreme Cold." *Proceedings of Am. Assoc. for Adv. of Sci.*, 6th Meeting, at Albany, N. Y., August, 1851, pp. 338–359.—*Am. Journ. of Sci. and Arts*, 2d S. vol. xiii. pp. 84–92 and 196–206, Jan. and March, 1852.

3. "Preliminary Researches on the alleged Influence of Solar Light on the Process of Combustion." *Proceedings of Am. Assoc. for Adv. of Sci.*, 11th Meeting, at Montreal, C. E., Aug. 1857, Part I., pp. 93–109.—*Am. Journ. Sci. and Arts*, 2d S. vol. xxiv. pp. 317–330, Nov. 1857. Also, *Lond.*, *Edin.*, *Dub.*, *Phil. Mag.*, 4th S. vol. xvi. pp. 182–197, Sept. 1858.

4. "On the Influence of Musical Sounds on the Flame of a Jet of Coal-Gas." *Am. Journ. Sci. and Arts*, 2d S. vol. xxv. pp. 62–65, Jan. 1858. Also,

*Lond., Edin., Dub., Phil. Mag.* 4th S. vol. xv. pp. 235–239, March, 1858.

5. "On the Adequacy of Laplace's Explanation to Account for the Discrepancy between the Computed and the Observed Velocity of Sound in Air and Gases." —*Lond., Edin., Dub., Phil. Mag.*, 4th S. vol. xxvii. pp. 1–33, Jan. 1864. The latter part of No. 5 touches upon the question whether the atmosphere is a *Mechanical Mixture* or a Chemical Compound.

James Schiel, Ph.D., St. Louis, Mo.—Dr. Schiel's chemical contributions in the *American Journal of Science* are—

1853. On the Separation of Manganese from Iron and Nickel [2], xv. 275.

1855. On the identity of Sanguinarine and Chelerithene, and on the direct determination of Nitrogen [2], xx. 220–222. Compare *Ann. de Chem. und Pharm.*, Liebig and Wöhler, B. xliii. 233.

[See entry under Dr. James F. Dana.]

1860. On the Products of the Distillation of Common Rosin [2], xxx. 100–102.

Dr. Schiel is also the author of a systematic treatise on Analysis, entitled "*Anleitung zur Organischen und Gasanalyse,*" Erlangen, 1860. 8vo. pp. 200.

Charles A. Joy, Ph.D., Professor of Chemistry, Columbia College, New York. Professor Joy has published—

1852. Analyse des Narwall-zahns und des Gehaüses von Helix Pomatia. *Ann. der Ch. und Pharm.*, lxxxii., Bd. 3, Heft 365.

1853. Uber das Selenäthyl. *Ibid.*, lxxxii. 35.

1853. Analyse des Meteoreisens von Cosbys Creek. *Ibid.*, 39.

The chemical papers by Dr. Joy, published in the *Am. Journ. of Sci.*, are as follows:—

1863. On Glucinum and its Compounds. [2], xxxvi. 83–91.

1864. Analysis of a Meteorite from Chili. *Ibid.*, xxxvii. 243–248.

Prof. Joy has been a constant contributor to the current literature of science in various publications not available for our present purpose.

Besides the papers enumerated, Prof. Joy has contributed to Dana's Mineralogy the chemical analyses of several minerals. The research on selenäthyl cited above, is among the earliest contributions to a class of alcohol radicals combined with a metallic base which appeared in chemical literature.

Charles A. Goessmann, Ph.D., of Amherst, is now the chemist of the Massachusetts Agricultural College located at Amherst. During his residence at the salines of Syracuse Dr. Goessmann made himself well known by his able discussion of the chemistry of brines. But Dr. G.'s contributions to chemistry cover a wide range, and prior to his coming to this country he was a frequent contributor (1854–58) to the *Annalen von Wöhler, Liebig, and Kopp*, as will be seen by the following list of chemical papers:—

| | | |
|---|---|---|
| In 1854. | *Annalen der Chemie u. Pharmacie, von Wöhler, Liebig, u. Kopp* | |
| | On Palmitic Acid | Bd. 89—H. 123 |
| | On Arachidic Acid—a new fatty acid | 89—i.–11 |
| | On the Composition of the Cocoa-Oil | 90—126 |
| | On Benzoglycolic Acid from Hippuric Acid | 90—181 |
| | On a New Mode of Procuring Ethylamin | 90—122 |
| | On the Constitution, etc., of Leucine | 91—129 |
| In 1856. | A New Mode of Procuring Amarine u. Lophine | 93—329 |
| | On Hypogaeic Acid—a new acid in Peanut Oil | 94—230 |
| | On the Combinations of Arachidic Acid | 97—257 |
| | On the Constitution of the Lophine | 97—283 |
| | On the Separation of Coumarin | 98— 86 |
| | On the Separation of Styracin | |
| | On Certain Products from Hypogaeic Acid, Gaidic Acid, etc. (This paper was published by C. A. G. and G. C. Caldwell, of Cornell University) | 99—305 |
| | On Manganate of Potassium as a Suitable Substance to Decolorize Uric Acid, Hippuric Acid, etc. | 99—373 |

In 1856. On a New Mode of Procuring Triphenylamine 100— 57

On the Action of Zinc Chloride on Hippuric Acid 100— 69

On the Crystallization of Sulphocyanide of Silver 100— 76

In 1857. On the Action of Iodide of Ethyl on Tungstate of Silver 101—218

On a New Mode of Producing Tricapronylamine 101— 31

On the Transformation of Nitrobenzol into Aniline by Means of Arsenious Acid and Caustic Potassa 102—127

On a New Sugar Plant, Sorghum Saccharatum 104—335

In 1858. Contribution to the Knowledge of the Nature of the Chinese Sugar-cane, Sorghum Saccharatum; see Transactions of the New York State Agricultural Society, of 1861, 785.

In 1862. Report on the Chemical Composition of the Brines of Onondaga, New York: Syracuse, December, 1862.

In 1862-63. Report on the Brines of Michigan; see Senate Report. New York: 1862—63. (House Documents); also,

House Committee of the Legislature of Michigan. No. 37. 1865.

In 1863. Report on the Best Mode of Manufacturing Coarse or Solar Salt from the Brines of Onondaga. Syracuse: December. 1863.

In 1864. Contribution to the Manufacture and Refining of Sugar; or the Application of Caustic Magnesia for Sugar Refining. Syracuse. Reprinted, *Chemical News*, London, etc., 1864-65.

In 1865. Notes and Criticism on the Manufacture of Sugar upon the Island of Cuba. Syracuse. Reprinted, *Chemical News*, London, etc., 1865.

In 1866. Contribution to the Chemistry of the Mineral Springs of Onondaga. Syracuse: February, 1866. Also *Amer. Journ. of Sci.*, September and October, 1866.

In 1867. Report on the Salt Deposit of Petite Anse, Louisiana. Published by the American Bureau of Mines. New York: January, 1867.

Contribution to the Chemistry of Brines. *Amer. Journ. of Sci.*, July and November, 1867.

In 1868. Report on the Salt Resources of Goderich, Canada. Syracuse.

In 1869. On the Chemistry of Common Salt with Reference to our Home Resources. Read before the National Academy at the Northampton Meeting; see *Amer. Journ. of Sci.*, January, 1870.

On Salt and its Uses in Agriculture; see Report of Massachusetts State Board of Agriculture. Boston: 1870.

In 1870. On the Cultivation of the Sugar Beet-Root as an Agricultural Enterprise. College Report of the Trustees of the Massachusetts Agricultural College. December, 1870; see also *Amer. Chem.*, 1871.

On Cheese as Food; see Report of American Dairymen's Association, Utica, New York, January, 1870.

In 1871. Report on the Chemical Composition of some Dairy Products; see Annual Report of the Massachusetts State Board of Agriculture, 1871–72, pp. 305.

In 1872. On the Stassfurt Potash Compounds, and their Present Reputation in the Agricultural Industry of Europe; See *Amer. Chem.*, 1872. July.

Report on the Quality of Sugar Beet-Roots raised upon the Farm of the Massachusetts Agricultural College, with regard to their Fitness for Sugar Manufacture; see *Amer. Chem.*, 1872.

Contribution to the History of the Beet Sugar Manufacture within the United States; See *Amer. Chem.*, 1872, July.

Contributions to the Requirements for a Successful Home Beet Sugar Industry; see *Amer. Chem.*, 1872, August and November.

In 1873. On the Fertilization of our Farm Lands with Reference to the Judicious Application of Mineral Fertilizers; see Journal of New York State Agricultural Society of January and February, 1873.

In 1873. Report on Commercial Fertilizers, and their Importance in our Present Condition of Agricultural Industry; see Tenth Annual College Report of the Massachusetts Agricultural College, 1873.

On Nitrogen and the Extent of its Natural Resources for Agricultural Purposes; see Report of Massachusetts State Board of Agriculture of 1873–74.

In 1874. Results of Experiments with the Cultivation of the Sugar Beet-Roots throughout the State of New York, Eastern Canada, and upon the College Farm during the year 1873; see College Report for 1873–74.

Report on the Present Condition of our Resources of Commercial Concentrated Fertilizers; see First Official Report of the State Inspector, C. A. G., Amherst, Mass., July 8, 1874.

Eugene W. Hilgard, Ann Arbor, Mich.—Prof. Hilgard, long of the University of Mississippi, and attached to the Geological Survey of that State, is now the Professor of Chemistry at the University of Michigan.

His chemical papers are as follows:—

1. Beitrag zur Kenntniss der Lichtflamme (Inaug. Diss.). *Ann. Chemie und Pharm.*, vol. xcii. p. 129, 1854. (Fifteen analyses of the gases from the "dark cone" of the tallow and wax flames; demonstrating the presence of N and H in the lowest parts of the flame, the absence of free O, and *the combustion of C prior to H*, contrary to the statement in most text-books.)

2. On the Quantitative Assay of Chromium by blowpipe processes. In *Proc. A. A. Sc.*, 1857; abstract *Am. Journ. Sci.*, 1857.

3. On the Condition of our Knowledge of the Chemical Processes in Luminous Hydrocarbon Flames. *Proc. Am. A. Sc.*, 1868.

4. On the Geology of the Delta, and the Mudlumps of the Passes of the Mississippi. *Am. Journ. Sci.*, vol. I., 1871, with analyses of the waters and gases, and a discussion.)

5. On Soil Analyses and their Utility. *Am. Journ. Sci.*, Dec. 1872.

6. On the Silt Analysis of Soils and Clays. *Am. Journ. Sci.*, Oct. and Nov. 1873.

7. Silt Analyses of Mississippi Soils and Sub-soils. *Am. Journ. Sci.*, Jan. 1874.

Analyses of soils and rocks published in various Geological Reports.

John M. Maisch, Philadelphia, Pennsylvania.—Mr. Maisch has been editor of the *American Journal of Pharmacy* since the death of Mr. Procter, whose labors have been before mentioned. His chemical researches have been chiefly in pharmaceutical chemistry, and have been published in the *American Journal of Pharmacy* and in *Proceedings of the American Pharmaceutical Association*, as follows:—

*Proximate Analysis.*

Notes on the Alkaloids of Menispermum Canadense. *Am. Journ. Pharm.*, 1863, p. 301.

Berberina in Podophyllum Peltatum. *Ibid.*, 1863, p. 303.

On Resin of Podophyllum, Solubility in Boiling Water. *Ibid.*, 1874, p. 231.

Absence of Alkaloids in the Dead Stalks of Veratrum Viride. *Ibid.*, 1864, p. 98.

Alkaloid in Solanum Pseudo-Capsicum. *Ibid.*, 1864, p. 99.

Active Principle of Rhus Toxicodendron (Toxicodendric Acid). *Proc. Am. Pharm. Assn.*, 1865, p. 166.

Balsams of Liquidambar styraciflua and Orientale. *Am. Journ. Pharm.*, 1874, p. 163.

Chinese Blistering Bugs (Amount of Cantharidin in). *Proc. Am. Pharm. Assn.*, 1872, p. 246.

Chemical Examination of Coca Leaves. *Am. Journ. Pharm.*, 1861, p. 496.

*Adulteration Notes, Assays, etc.*

Carbonate of Lime substituted by Sulphate of Lime. *Am. Journ. Pharm.*, 1854, p. 210.

Examination of Bitartrate of Potassa. *Ibid.*, 1855, p. 204.

A New Falsification (Nitrobenzole) of Oil of Bitter Almonds. *Ibid.*, 1857, p. 544.

Examination of Adulterated Oil of Peppermint. *Ibid.*, 1860, p. 105.

Analysis of Commercial Glacial Phosphoric Acid. *Ibid.*, 1860, p. 193.

On the Detection of Croton Oil in Mixtures. *Ibid.*, 1860, p. 306.

Assay of Milk. *Ibid.*, 1860, p. 431.

Adulteration of Carmine. *Ibid.*, 1861, p. 17.

Assay of Commercial Iron by Hydrogen. *Ibid.*, 1861, p. 20.

Tests for the Purity of Glycerin. *Ibid.*, 1867, p. 117.

Note on Cheap Glycerin. *Ibid.*, 1867, p. 309.

Detection of Turmeric in Powdered Rhubarb and Mustard. *Ibid.*, 1871, p. 259.

On Volatile Oils (Detection of Adulterations). *Proc. Am. Pharm. Assn.*, 1858, p. 344.

Behavior of Essential Oils to Iodine and Bromine. *Ibid.*, 1859, p. 338.

Occasional Occurrence of Arsenic in American Sulphuric Acid. *Ibid.*, 1863, p. 255.

Assay of French Brandy and Whiskey. *Ibid.*, 1864, p. 291, and 1866, p. 267.

Quality and Assay of Sherry Wine. *Ibid.*, 1863, p. 296, and 1866, p. 269.

Analysis of a Chalybeate Water from Sharon Spring, New York. *Am. Journ. Pharm.*, 1861, p. 105.

*Inorganic Chemistry.*

Effects of Sunlight upon Solution of Ferrous Iodide. *Am. Journ. Pharm.*, 1854, p. 408, and 1855, p. 218.

Solubility of Iodides in Syrup of Ferrous Iodide. *Ibid.*, 1857, p. 210.

Protiodide of Mercury (Processes for obtaining it). *Ibid.*, 1857, p. 11.

Alumen Exsiccatum (Heat required for preparing it). *Ibid.*, 1860, p. 16.

Crystalline Forms of the Chlorides of Potassium and Ammonium. *Ibid.*, 1860, p. 521.

Conversion of Monohydrated into Common Phosphoric Acid. *Ibid.*, 1861, p. 385.

Pyrophosphate of Soda and Iron. *Ibid.*, 1867, p. 388.

Hydrobromic Acid (Preparation of). *Proc. Am. Pharm. Assn.*, 1860, p. 220.

*Organic Chemistry.*

On the Strength of Diluted Acetic Acid. *Am. Journ. Pharm.*, 1858, p. 306.

Notes on Benzoic Acid and some Benzoates. *Ibid.*, 1860, p. 204.

Specific Gravity of Aqueous Solutions of Tartaric Acid. *Proc. Am. Pharm. Assn.*, 1863, p. 204.

Acid Reaction of Chloral Hydrate. *Ibid.*, 1873, p. 621.

Chloride of Mercurethyl (Review of Literature). *Am. Journ. Pharm.*, 1873, p. 9.

Citrate of Ammonia a Solvent for Phosphate of Iron. *Ibid.*, 1859, p. 410.

Solution of Citrate of Magnesia. *Ibid.*, 1867, p. 1.

Solution of Acetate of Iron. *Ibid.*, 1867, p. 7.

Preparation of Heavy Oil of Wine. *Ibid.*, 1865, p. 100.

Decomposition of Pure Chloroform. *Proc. Am. Pharm. Assn.*, 1866, p. 264, and *Am. Journ. Pharm.*, 1868, p. 289.

On Amylo-Nitrous Ether (Preparation of Nitrate of Amyl). *Am. Journ. Pharm.*, 1871, p. 146.

Monobromated Camphor (New Process, Properties, Analysis). *Ibid.*, 1872, p. 337.

On Colchicia. *Ibid.*, 1867, p. 97.

Decomposition of Acetate of Morphia in Aqueous Solutions. *Ibid.*, 1871, p. 49.

Precipitation of Morphia Salts by Alkaline Cyanides. *Ibid.*, 1871, p. 258.

Decomposition of Sulphate of Quinia by Acetates. *Ibid.*, 1855, p. 97, and 1858, p. 385.

Precipitation of Quinia by Iodide of Potassium from Acid Solutions. *Ibid.*, 1871, p. 51.

Solubility of Glue in Glycerin. *Ibid.*, 1870, p. 515.

Theo. G. Wormley, M. D., Professor of Chemistry and Toxicology at Starling Medical College, Columbus, Ohio, is widely known to chemists by his beautiful work, "The Micro-Chemistry of Poisons," which, as an original contribution to the special department of chemistry which it covers, has no equal in any language. This work is unrivalled in its exquisite plates, drawn and engraved by the graceful hand of Mrs. Wormley. Besides this standard work, Dr. Wormley has contributed the following original papers:—

"Systematic Quantitative Analysis of Urine," *Ohio Med. and Surg. Journ.*, vol. vii. July, 1855.

"Chemical Reactions of Strychnine," *Amer. Journ. Sci. and Arts*, 2d series, xxviii. Sept. 1859.

"Chemical Reactions of Atropine," *Chemical News* (London), vol. ii. June, 1860.

"Chemical Reactions of Brucine," *Ibid.*, ii. July, 1860.

"Chemical Reactions of Morphia," *Ibid.*, ii. Sept. 1860.

"Chemical Reactions of Narcotine and Meconic Acid," *Ibid.*, ii. Sept. 1860.

"Chemical Reactions of Corrosive Sublimate," *Ibid.*, ii. No. 43.

"Chemical Reactions of Veratrine," *Ohio Med. and Surg. Journ.*, xii. No. 6, 1860.

"Chemical Reactions of Nicotine and Daturine," *Ibid.*, vol. xiii. No. 1.

"Chemical Reactions of Solanine," *Ibid.*, vol. xiii. No. 2.

"Chemical Reactions of Codeine, Meconine, Narceine, and of Aconitine." *Ibid.*, xiii. No. 4, 1861.

"Chemical Reactions of Conine," *Ibid.*, xiv. No. 1, 1862.

"Chemical Reactions of Oxalic Acid," *Ibid.*, xiv. No. 5.

"Contribution to our Knowledge of the Chemical Composition of Gelseminum Sempervirens," *Amer. Journ. Pharmacy*, 3d series, xviii. No. 1, 1870.

The last-named paper contains an account of the mode of preparation and the chemical and physiological properties of a new alkaloid (gelseminine), and of a new organic acid (gelseminic acid).

"Methods of Analysis of Coals, Iron Ores, Furnace Slags, Fire Clays, Limestones, and of Soils," *Report of Progress of Geological Survey of Ohio for* 1870.

Dr. John C. Draper, of the College of the City of New York, has made the following contributions:—

1. "Origin of Urea in the Body," *N. Y. Journ. of Med.*, Feb. 1856.

2. "Products of Respiration," *N. Y. Med. Times*, July, 1856.

3. "Determination of the Diurnal Amount of Sunshine by the Precipitation of Gold," *Lond. Phil. Mag.*, Aug. 1859.

4. "Insensible Perspiration," *Proceedings of N. Y. Academy of Medicine*, 1864.

5. "Adulterations in Coffee," *Lond. Phil. Mag.*, Aug. 1867.

6. "Improvement in Filtration," *Ibid.*, May, 1870.

7. "New Light Unit," *Scientific American*, Oct. 21, 1871.

8. "Causes of Decay in Brick and Stone," *Ibid.*, Nov. 25 and Dec. 2, 1871.

9. "New Process for the Quantitative Determination of Arsenic," *American Chemist*, June, 1872.

10. "Growth of Seedling Plants," *Amer. Journ. of Science and Arts*, Nov. 1872.

11. "Influence of Cold on the Temperature of the Body," *Ibid.*, Dec. 1872.

James Schiel, St. Louis, Mo.—In addition to the titles given on page 111, we note as follows:—

On the Classification of Organic Substances by series, *Am. Journ. Sci.* [2], xxxii. 48, 1861. This author had previously, as early as 1842, enunciated already the principle of progressive series, afterwards adopted by Gerhardt, unchanged, save only in name, under the title of Chemical Homology. Dr. Schiel's original paper was entitled—

"Bemerkungen über die Organischen Radikale," *Liebig & Wöhler's Annalen der Ch., etc.*, xliii. 107. July, 1842.

Dr. Schiel's paper, in 1861, is certainly one of the most important contributions made in America to chemical theory.

*Einleitung in das Studium der Organischen Chemie.* Erlangen, 1860, 8vo. This excellent treatise followed close upon the author's work on Organic and Gas Analysis, noticed on page 111. It contains a chapter on the classification of organic bodies by series, which fully sets forth the author's original views on this subject.

"On the Presence of Phosphoric Acid in Igneous Rocks." *Am. Journ. Sci.* [2], xxxi. 383, 1861.

The following additional titles of papers by Dr. Schiel are found in *Liebig und Kopp's Annalen, etc.*, Ueber die Angebliche Eigenschaft der Galle, den Zucker in Fett überzuführen, lviii. 96, 1846.

Beiträge zur Kenntniss des Krapps, lx. 74, 1846.

Annalyse der Krappsamenasche, lxix. 143.

Alex. Means, LL.D., Prof. Natural Philosophy, Emory College, Oxford, Ga.—Dr. Means has published the following essays and contributions falling within our plan:—

1. A treatise upon "Electro-physiology," published by request of the Class of the Medical College of the State of Georgia, in the year 1840, in which institution the author was for nineteen years Professor of Chemistry and Pharmacy. It was subsequently republished in the *Medical and Surgical Journal*, issued by that college.

2. An article upon "The Dichloride of Mercury (Calomel)," published afterwards in the same Journal, for March, 1845.

3. An essay on "Alcohol—its *History*, *Pharma*

*ceutical Origin* and *Uses, Chemical Constitution, Medical Claims* and '*Modus operandi;*' together with the *Physiological* and *Pathological Phenomena* consequent upon its administration, and the *Antidotal Treatment* required." Published in the *Augusta Med. and Surg. Journal*, Feb. 1847.

4. An article entitled "The Philosophical Construction of Chemicals," adapted to practical use, and the chemical laws involved explained and illustrated by appropriate diagrams. Published in the *Educational Repository and Family Monthly*, the organ of the "Educational Institute of the Methodist Episcopal Church South," July, 1860.

5. An essay on "Electricity," embracing its history as a science, and its phenomenal manifestation in the organic and inorganic kingdoms of nature. Published serially in *Scott's Monthly Magazine*, Atlanta, Ga., in 1867.

6. An article on "The Poison of Venomous Reptiles." Published in the *Medical and Surgical Journal* of Augusta, Ga., Jan. 1846.

7. Analysis of the Atlanta Mineral Springs, and of the Warm Springs of Merewether County, Ga. Carbonated chalybeate waters; together with the Cold Spring. Acidulo-carbonated chalybeate waters in the same locality. These were published by Mr. George White, formerly of Savannah, in his volume entitled "Statistics of the State of Georgia," in 1849.

Dr. Means has invented several new forms of apparatus for chemical and physical illustration, for which he has received premiums of silver plate. These pieces of apparatus are all to be found in the catalogue of Mr. E. S. Retchie, 1855.

P. D. Keyser, M.D., Philadelphia, Pa.—Dr. Keyser, while a student in Dr. F. A. Genth's laboratory, published the following analyses, which are all to be found in the fifth edition of Dana's Mineralogy.

1853. Owenite from Harper's Ferry. *Am. Journ. Sci.* [2], xvi. 168.

1854. Thalite of Owen. *Ibid.* [2], xvii. 131.

1855. Allanite from Reading and Bethlehem, Pa., and from Orange County, N. Y. *Ibid.* [2], xix. 20.

1857. Barnhardite, a new mineral. *Ibid.*, 17.

Josiah P. Cooke, Jr., of Harvard University, has been an assiduous and successful laborer, both in the field of authorship, teaching, and research, alike in pure chemistry, molecular physics, and theoretical chemistry.

His "Chemical Physics," published in 1860, is an elaborate treatise, in advance of anything before attempted in this country, or in fact in our language; and in his "First Principles of Chemical Philosophy" (1868), we have the matured development of an earlier book, "Chemical Problems and Reactions" (1857). These works mark an important advance in the methods of chemical instruction in this country. In the Chemical Philosophy the subject is developed according to the modern theories of the science. In Part First the fundamental principles of the science are discussed, and in the Second Part a brief summary of the more important elements and compounds is given, illustrated and enforced by means of familiar reactions and problems. As is well known, Prof. Cooke had been largely instrumental in changing the older didactic methods of chemical instruction formerly in use, rendering them more exact and searching by a free use of the blackboard in the recitation room and laboratory.

In 1854, Prof. Cooke communicated to the American Academy, at Boston, a memoir on "The numerical relation between the atomic weights, with some thoughts on the classification of the chemical elements." This paper is also found in the *American Jour. of Science* ([2], xvii. pp. 387–407), accompanied by a table of the "Isomorphs," "Homologues," and "Atomic weights" of the several series, or groups of elements, with their "affiliations." This memoir received the highest encomiums of Sir John Herschel in his remarks on chemical science, at the Leeds meeting of the British Association for Advancement of Science, in 1858. Its principles are embodied in the author's Chemical Philosophy.

In 1855, Prof. Cooke published a memoir "On an apparent Perturbation of the Law of Definite Proportions observed in the compounds of Zinc and Antimony" and this paper was in September, 1860, followed by a second on the same subject entitled "Crystalline Form not necessarily an indication of Definite Chemical Composition; or on the possible variation of constitution in a mineral species independent of the phenomena of isomorphism." These papers are both founded on the careful study of the compounds of zinc and antimony, the nature of which was first set forth by the same author in his memoir "On Stibiotrizincite and Stibiobizincite, two new compounds of Zinc and Antimony, with some remarks on the decomposition of water by the alloys of these metals" (*American Journ. of Science*, [2] xvii., pp. 229–237); this whole research is a fine model of a chemical investigation. It is noteworthy that two of the gentlemen who were at the time of these investigations students in Prof. Cooke's laboratory, and whose work in this investigation the author gratefully recognizes, are Messrs. Eliot and Storer, names since, and now, so honorably associated in higher, and the highest duties, in Harvard University, and in joint authorship of books on our science of wide use in our best colleges and schools.

Another paper on theoretical chemistry by Prof. Cooke is that "On Atomic Ratio in Mineral Formulæ," published in 1869 (*Am. Journ. of Sci.*, [2] xlvii. pp. 386–390.)

"Chemistry and Religion" is the title of a series of Sunday evening lectures, delivered upon the Graham foundation in Brooklyn in 1861. It is an American Bridgewater Treatise, and considers in an able and attractive manner the proofs of God's plan in the atmosphere and its elements (8vo. pp. 348, N. Y., Chas. Scribner, 1864).

Prof. Cooke's paper "On Danalite, a new mineral species from the Granite of Rockport, Mass." (*Am. Jour. Sci.* [2], xlii. 73, 1866), is a fine example of chemical research, and of the value of accurate observation for the discovery of new and interesting facts in old fields supposed to have been long since gleaned.

Prof. Cooke has lately published "The New Chemistry," a volume of 326 pages in *The International Scientific Series*, which is a lucid and logical discussion of the principles of chemical philosophy in a series of thirteen lectures, which were delivered before the Lowell Institute in Boston, in the autumn of 1872. Of this volume it is remarked by the *Am. Journ. of Sci.* (April, 1874), "Prof. Cooke's style is always attractive for its clearness, precision, and polish, and any cultivated person, whether previously acquainted with chemistry or not, can read this discussion of chemical philosophy with both pleasure and profit. It is needless to add that the subject is discussed, as its title demands, in the terms of the new chemistry."

Of special researches in mineralogical and general chemistry, Prof. Cooke has published many valuable papers, chiefly in the *American Journal of Science*, and in the *Proceedings of the American Academy*, at Boston, special mention of which it is needless to make at this time. His last memoir, "On the Vermiculites," is certainly one of the most important contributions to mineralogical chemistry which has been made by any chemist, at home or abroad, in some years, whether we regard it from its chemical, physical, or mineralogical aspects. It forms part of the ninth volume of the *Proceedings of the American Academy of Arts*, etc., at Boston, and a full abstract of it will be found in the seventh volume of the 3d series of *Am. Journ. of Sci.*, pp. 420–437.

Prof. Cooke has also made many and important contributions to the apparatus for chemical and physical demonstration and research, with the cunning hand of a skilful experimentalist and manipulator.

Under the voluntary or elective system now in vogue at Harvard, and of which Prof. Cooke has been an earnest and successful advocate, that University has now the largest number of under-graduates devoted to chemical studies in their well-appointed chemical laboratories which have been assembled at any academical institution in this country.

JOHN ADDISON PORTER.—The late Prof. Porter, who died in 1866, was a graduate of Yale College in 1842, studied chemistry with Liebig at Giessen after a brief term of service as Professor of Rhetoric and Reub Languages in Newark College, Delaware; was appointed to the chair of Technical Chemistry at Breren University, when in 1853 he was transferred to the chair of Agricultural Chemistry, and then of Organic Chemistry, in the Scientific School at Yale College, afterwards to the Sheffield Scientific School. Prof. Porter was distinguished for his scholarly accomplishments. His published papers in Chemistry are—

1849. "Unterschung der Asche Menschlicher Excremente." *Ann. d. Ch. u. Pharm.*, lxxi. 109.

1849. "Ueber ein Product der Einwirkung der Salpeter säure auf Holzfaser." *Ibid.*, 115.

1850. "Aschenanalyse vol Hafer, Herr und dern Rückstand von der Destillation des Kartoffelbranntweins." *Ibid.*, lxxvi. 382.

1849. "Ash analysis: Potato refuse; Oats; Hay." *Amer. Journ. Sci.* [2], ix. 20.

1849. "A Product of the Action of Nitric Acid on Woody Fibre." *Ibid.*, 20.

Prof. Porter was the author of a Chemical Textbook for Schools, which has passed through many editions. A notice of his life will be found in the *Amer. Journ. Sci.* [2], xlii. 290, 1866.

NEWTON SPALDING MAUROSS, Ph.D.—The late Prof. Mauross, who fell while gallantly leading a charge at the head of his company in the sixteenth Connecticut Volunteers at the battle of Antietam, September 17, 1862, was then acting Professor of Chemistry at Amherst, Mass. Dr. Mauross was a graduate at Yale College in 1849, and took the Degree of Doctor of Philosophy, at Göttingen, in 1852. Dr. Mauross published :—

1852. "Artificial Formation of Minerals," an inaugural dissertation at Göttingen. The mineral species found and described, with analyses, were Heavy Spar; Celestine; Archydrite; Apatite; Pyromerphite; Wolfram; Tungsten; Scheeletine; Wolfenite; Crocoirite; and Anglesite. *Amer. Journ. Sci.* [2], xvi. 186, and *Ann. d. Chem. u. Pharm.*, lxxxii. 348.

"Ueber die Künstlicher Darsteltung von Krystaltisirtem Wolframsaurem Kalk." *Ann. d. Chem. u. Pharm.*, lxxxi. 243.

1855. Dr. Mauross also published an interesting "Notice of the Pitch Lake, Lake of Trinidad." *Amer. Journ. Sci.* [2], xx. 153.

Dr. Mauross was chiefly chosen to the work of an explorer and engineer of mines. He made extensive journeys in Mexico, Central America, and Venezuela, and was the first to bring to our notice the Auriferous deposits of the Oronoco.

JOHN DEAN, Ph.D., of Boston, Mass.—1. Value of Different Kinds of Prepared Vegetable Food. Communicated to the *Am. Acad. of Arts and Sci.*, April 25, 1844.

2. The Organic Compounds of Tellurium and Selenium belonging to the Alcohol Series. Göttingen, 1855.

HENRY DRAPER, of the University of New York, has made the following contributions upon subjects allied to chemistry :—

1. "On the Functions of the Spleen," in 1857.

2. "On the Use of Protochloride of Palladium," read before the British Association in 1857.

3. "On the use of a Silvered Glass Mirror 15½ inches in Aperture in Photographing Celestial Bodies," published in the *Smithsonian Contributions*, 1860.

4. A paper on "Astronomical Photography," in the *London, Edin., and Dub. Phil. Mag.*, 1864.

5. Memoirs on "The Determination of the Wave-lengths of the Ultra-violet Spectrum Lines and Diffrac-

tion Spectrum Photography," published in the *American Journal of Science*, 1873; the *Philosophical Magazine*, 1873; *Memoire Degli Spettroscopisti Italiani*, 1873; "*Nature*," 1873; *Poggendorf's Annalen*, 1874; and read before the French Academy, and published in the *Comptes Rendus* in full in 1874.

He also revised and republished in 1866 "Draper's Text-Book of Chemistry."

MATTHEW CAREY LEA, Philadelphia, Pennsylvania.—Mr. Lea has been an industrious worker in chemical research as well as in photographic chemistry. His chemical papers are as follows:—

1858. On Picric Acid and its Salts. *Sill. Journ.* [2], xxvi. 379.

1860. Numerical Relations of the Equivalent Numbers of Elementary Bodies. *Ibid.*, xxix. 98, 349; xxx. 399; [3], iv. 387.

1860. Production of Ethylamine. *Ibid.* [2], xxxi. 401.

1860. Optical Properties of Picrate of Manganese. *Ibid.* [2], xxx. 3, 99.

1861. On a Series of New Combinations of Ammonia, Picric Acid, and Metallic Bases. *Ibid.* [2], xxxi. 78.

1861. Sources of Error in the Employment of Picric Acid to Detect the Presence of Potash. *Ibid.* [2], xxxi. 75.

1861. Effects of Reducing Agents upon Nitrate of Ethyl. *Chem. News*, iv. 230.

1861. Estimation of Nitrogen, and on an Acidimetric Process. *Sill. Journ.* [2], xxxi. 189; *Chem. News*, iv. 195.

1861. Exact Separation of the Ethyl Bases. *Sill. Journ.* [2], xxxii. 26; *Chem. News*, iv. 71.

1861. Formation of Picramic Acid. *Sill. Journ.* [2], xxxii. 188; *Chem. News*, iv. 193.

1861. Preparation of Nitrate and Nitrite of Ethyl. *Sill. Journ.* [2], xxxii. 77, xxxiii. 86; *Chem. News*, iv. 219.

1861. Preparation of Urea from Ferrocyanide of Potassium. *Sill. Journ.* [2], xxxii. 179.

1861. Production of Ethyl Bases. *Sill. Journ.* [2], xxxii. 25; *Chem. News*, iv. 88.

1862. Action of Nitric Acid on Picramic Acid. *Sill. Journ.* [2], xxxii. 210; *Chem. News*, v. 18.

1862. Contributions to History of Picric Acid. *Sill. Journ.* [2], xxxii. 180; *Chem. News*, v. 5.

1862. Further Remarks on the Preparation of the Ethyl Bases by means of Nitrate of Ethyl, and their Separation. *Chem. News*, v. 211.

1862. Estimation of Nitrogen. *Ibid.*, v. 28.

1862. Nitrate of Ethyl. *Ibid.*, v. 158.

1862, 1865. Production of New Coloring Matters by Decomposition of Nitronaphthaline and Dinitronaphthaline. *Sill. Journ.* [2], xxxii. 211, xxxiii. 229, xxxviii. 360; *Chem. News*, v. 73, xi. 230.

1862. Production of Nitrate of Methyl. *Sill. Journ.* [2], xxxiii. 227; *Chem. News*, v. 310.

1862. Reaction of Ethyl Bases with Dr. Knop's New Hydrofluosilicic Acid. *Chem. News*, v. 143.

1862. Reaction of Ethylamine and Diethylamine. *Sill. Journ.* [2], xxxiii. 80; *Chem. News*, v. 127.

1862. On Methylamine. *Sill. Journ.* [2], xxxiii. 366; *Chem. News*, vi. 46.

1862. On Triethylamine. *Sill. Journ.* [2], xxxiv. 66; *Chem. News*, vi. 97.

1863. Arithmetical Relations between Chemical Equivalents. *Chem. News*, vii. 63.

1863. On a Constant Aspirator and Blower. *Sill. Journ.* [2], xxxiv. 245; *Chem. News*, vii. 37.

1864. Notes on Platinum Metals and their separation from each other. *Sill. Journ.*, xxxviii. 81; *Chem. News*, ix. 279, 301.

1864. Remarks on the Distillation of Substances of different Volatilities. *Sill. Journ.* [2], xxxvii. 377; *Chem. News*.

1865. Influence of Ozone and some other Chemical Agents on Germination and Vegetation. *Sill. Journ.* [2], xxxvii. 373; *Chem. News*, xi. 229.

1865. On the Platinum Metals. *Sill. Journ.* [2] xxxviii. 248; *Chem. News*, xi. 3, 13.

1865. On the Nature of the Invisible Photographic Image. *Sill. Journ.*, xl. 109; *Chem. News*, xii. 101.

1865. Reaction of Gelatine. *Sill. Journ.* [2], xl 81; *Chem. News*, xii. 73.

1866. Detection of Iodine. *Sill. Journ.* [2], xlii. 109; *Chem. News*, xiv.

1867. A New Test for Hyposulphites. *Sill. Journ.* [2], lxiv. 222; *Chem. News*, xvi.

1868. On Nitroglucose. *Sill. Journ.* [2], lxv. 381; *Chem. News*, xviii.

1864. Coloration of Faded Photographs. *Sill. Journ.* [2], xxxvii. 438.

1865. Ozone on Insensitive Iodide and Bromide of Silver. *Ibid.* [2], xxxix. 210.

1867. A Theory of Photo-Chemistry. *Ibid.* [2], xliv. 71.

1867. Germination. *Ibid.* [2], xliii. 197.

1867. Light on Iodide of Silver. *Ibid.* [2], xlii. 198.

1869. Transmitted and Diffused Light. *Ibid.* [2], xlii. 364.

1872. Method of Estimating Ethylic Alcohol when present in Mythylic Alcohol. *Ibid.* [3], iii. 365.

1874. A Combination of Silver Chloride with Mercuric Iodide. *Ibid.* [3], vii. 34.

1874. Color and Reduction by Light. *Ibid.* [3], vii. 200.

1874. Laboratory Notes. *Ibid.* [3], vii. 376.

1874. Action of Light on Silver Bromides. *Ibid.* [3], vii. 483.

In addition to the foregoing Mr. Lea has published over one hundred papers on photo-chemical and photographic subjects which have appeared in the British Journal of Photography and other photographic journals. He is also the author of a Manual of Photography, the first edition of which appeared in 1868 and the second in 1871.

Chas. F. Chandler, Ph.D., New York, Professor of Chemistry in the Columbia College School of Mines, etc., has been an industrious working chemist, and charged with numerous responsible duties of administration in the School of Mines and in other educational and public institutions in New York.

He has made the following contributions:—

1. Miscellaneous Chemical Researches.

Inaugural Dissertation for the Degree of Doctor of Philosophy. Göttingen, 1856.

I. Zircon from Buncombe County (North Carolina).
II. Saussurite from Zobten.
III. Stassfurthite from Stassfurth.
IV. Analysis of a rock resembling Talcose Slate, from Zipser.
V. Columbite from Middletown.
VI. Columbite from Bodenmais.
VII. Tantalite from Chanteloube.
VIII. Yttrotantalite from Ytterby.
IX. Samarskite from the Ural.
X. Experiments on the Cerium Metals.
XI. Artificial Heavy Spar.

2. An Investigation on the formation of Alcohol

during fermentation. Published in "Biblical Temperance," by E. C. Delavan, Esq.

3. Analysis of Dolomite. In the Report of the Geological Survey of Iowa, by James Hall and J. D. Whitney. Albany, 1858.

4. Examination of Interesting Urinary Calculi, included in a report of Dr. Alden March. Printed in the Annual Report of the N. Y. State Medical Society for 1858.

5. Analysis of Datolith. *Am. Journ. Sci.*, 1859, xxviii. p. 13.

6. A new Metal in the Native Platinum of Rogue River, Oregon. *Ibid.*, May, 1862. p. 351.

7. Analysis of 1 Blende, 2 Smithsonites, 1 Cerusite; and with J. P. Kimball, analyses of 9 Shales, 5 Galenas, 1 Dolomite.

In the Report of the Geological Survey of the Upper Mississippi Lead Region, by Prof. J. D. Whitney. Albany, 1862.

8. Report on Water for Locomotives and Boiler Incrustations, made to the President and Directors of the N. Y. Central R. R., including analyses of Waters between Albany and Niagara Falls, and Analyses of Incrustations. Pamphlet, 8vo. 35 pp. New York, 1865.

9. Report on the Petroleum of the Taro, Italy. 8vo. 8pp. New York, 1866.

10. Sanitary Qualities of the Water Supplies of New York and Brooklyn. Report to the Metropolitan Board of Health. 8vo. 9 pp. New York, 1868.

11. Analysis of the Ballston Artesian Spring. By C. F. Chandler and E. Root. *American Supplement to the Chemical News*, July, 1869, p. 54.

12. A New System of Assay Weights. *Ibid.*, August, 1869, p. 113.

13. Analyses of six New Mineral Springs at Saratoga. *Ibid.*, Sept. 1869, p. 194.

14. Analysis of the Saratoga Seltzer Spring. By C. F. Chandler and Paul Schweitzer. *Ibid.*, Dec. 1869, p. 395.

15. Report on the Quality of the Milk Supply of the Metropolitan District; made to the Metropolitan Board of Health. 8vo. 13 pp. New York, 1870. Also in the *Am. Chemist*, August, 1870, p. 41.

16. Report on the Water Supply of New York and Brooklyn; made to the Metropolitan Board of Health. 8vo. 9 pp. New York, 1870.

17. Report on the Quality of the Kerosene Oil sold in the Metropolitan District; made to the Metropolitan Board of Health. 8vo. 23 pp. New York, 1870.

18. Report on the Gas Nuisance in New York; made to the Metropolitan Board of Health. Including a special discussion of the different methods of purification. 8vo. 109 pp. New York, 1870.

19. Report on Dangerous Cosmetics; made to the Metropolitan Board of Health. 8vo. 7 pp. New York, 1870. Also in *American Supplement to the Chemical News*, May, 1870, p. 293.

20. The Purification of Coal Gas, and the Gas Nuisance in New York. *Ibid.*, February, 1870, p. 117; March, 1870, p. 177.

21. Analyses of the Chittenango Sulphur Springs, Madison Co., N. Y. *Ibid.*, April, 1870, p. 221.

22. Saltness of the Waters around the Island of New York. *Ibid.*, April. 1870, p. 225.

23. A Simple Lecture Experiment to show the Solubility of Carbonate of Lime in Carbonic Acid. *Ibid.*, April, 1870, p. 228.

24. Analysis of the Geyser Spring of Saratoga. By C. F. Chandler and F. A. Cairns. *Ibid.*, June, 1870, p. 373.

25. Lecture on Water; delivered befere the American Institute. 8vo. 49 pp. Albany, 1871.

26. Lecture on Water. (Revised and Elaborated.) *Am. Chemist.*

1. General. November, 1871, p. 161.
2. Mineral Waters. December, 1871, 201.
3. Water for Manufacturing and Domestic Purposes.
   January, 1872, p. 259.
   February, 1872, p. 281.
4. The Croton. March, 1872, p. 321.

27. Report on Petroleum as an Illuminator, and the Advantages and Perils which attend its Use, with Special Reference to the Prevention of the Traffic in Dangerous Kerosene and Naphtha; made to the Health Department of the City of New York. 8vo. 110 pp. New York, 1871.

28. Analysis of the Florida Sulphur Spring. *Am. Chem.*, February, 1871, p. 300.

29. Reduction of Nitrate of Silver by Charcoal. *Ibid.*, March, 1871, p. 346.

30. Analyses of Staten Island Waters. By C. F. Chandler and F. A. Cairns. *Ibid.*, March, 1871, p. 347.

31. Composition of Commercial Zinc. *Ibid.*, May, 1871, p. 420.

32. Condensed Milk; its Manufacture and Composition. *Ibid.*, July, 1871, p. 25.

33. Report on the Water of the Hudson River; made to the Water Commissioners of the City of Albany. A special discussion of the destruction of the sewage contamination of large rivers, caused by the dissolved oxygen. 8vo. 25 pp. Albany, 1872.

34. Report on Petroleum Oil, its Advantages and Disadvantages; made to the Department of Health, (Revised and Elaborated.) *Am. Chem.*, May, 1872, p. 409; June, 1872, p. 446; July, 1872, p. 20; August, 1872, p. 41.

35. Analysis of the Empire Spring at Saratoga. By C. F. Chandler and F. A. Cairns. *Ibid.*, Sept., 1872, p. 93.

36. Analysis of the Glacier Spouting Spring at Saratoga. By C. F. Chandler and F. A. Cairns. *Ibid.*, November, 1872, p. 165.

H. B. Nason, Ph.D., Professor of Chemistry, Rensselaer Institute, Troy, N. Y.—Prof. Nason has published in the German journals some time since papers of which he has supplied only the titles, as follows:—

On the Formation of Ether.

On the Analysis of Meteoric Masses.

On some Minerals of Iceland named by Waltershausen.

On the Mineral called Skeroklas by Sartorius v. Waltershausen.

And subsequently:—

Table for Qualitative Analysis, indicating color of precipitates with diagrams.

Translation, with many additions, of Wöhler's Mineral Analysis.

1873. Elderhorst's Manual of Blowpipe Analysis. Edited with C. F. Chandler.

Frank H. Storer, Bussey Agricultural College, Harvard University, Jamaica Plain, Mass.—Prof. Storer's "Dictionary of Chemical Solubilities," and his "Cyclopedia of Quantitative Analysis," are the constant companions of every American chemist. He has also published the following papers:—

1858. "Behavior of $\dot{Ca}\ddot{C}$ and $\dot{Ba}\ddot{C}$ with various Saline Solutions; on the Determination of Carbonic Acid." *Sill. Journ.* [2], xxv. 41.

1858. On Larves of Flies resisting Arsenic. *Ibid.* [2], xxviii. 166.

1860. On Loss of Light by Glass Shades. *Ibid.* [2], xxx. 420, xxxi. 284.

1860. Review of Antisell on Photogenic Oils. *Ibid.*, xxx. 112, 254.

1861. On Impurities of Zinc. *Ibid.* [2], xxxi. 142, xxxii. 380.

1861. Alloys of Copper and Zinc. *Ibid.* [2], xxx. 286, 423.

1861. Lead in Silver Coins. *Ibid.* [2], xxxi. 430.

1861. Keroselene. *Ibid.* [2], xxxii. 276.

1862. American Process of Working Platinum. *Ibid.* [2], xxxiii. 124.

1862. Arsenic Eating in Styria. *Ibid.* [2], xxxiii. 126.

1867. Hydrocarbons from Animal Fats. *Ibid.* [2], xxxiii. 250.

1867. Naphtha from Rangoon Petroleum. *Ibid.* [2], xliii. 251.

1869. On Nitric Acid and Chlorate of Potassium as an Oxidizing Mixture. *Ibid.*, xlviii. 190.

1859. Dépòt de soufre dans les tuyaux à gaz. *Rept. de Ch. App.*, 495.

1860. Influence de l'argent sur la durée des doublages. *Ibid.*, 82.

1861. Sur l'extrême difficulté qu'on éprouve à enlever les dernieres traces d'acide carbonique d'une volume considerable d' air atmospherique. *Rept. de Ch. App.*, 205.

1861. La question du pain aéré, description du procédé Horsford. *Ibid.*, 347.

1861. Sur le chromate de chrome et les chromates analogues. *Ibid.*, 390.

1861. Recherche du chrome en présence du fer. *Ibid.*, 58.

1863. Substitution du verre soluble au savon resineux dans la fabrication des savons. *Ibid.*, 5.

1863. Sur les cartouches imperméables de M. Dornbach. *Ibid.*, 91.

1863. Sur la contrafaçon des billets de banque. *Ibid.*, 109.

1865. Hydrocarbon Naphtha obtained from Product of Destructive Distillation of Lime Soap. Jointly with C. M. Warren. *Am. Acad. Bost.*, vii. 1.

1863–64. First Outlines of a Dictionary of Solubilities of Chemical Substances. 1 vol., 8vo., pp. 713.

1863-64. Memoir on the Alloys of Copper and Zinc, 4to., pp. 29.

1866. Ethics of Adulteration. *Harper's Magazine*, xxxii. 635.

1870. Soluble lead-salt and free S̈ in sherry wine. *Chemical News*, xxi. 17.

1870. Assay of Galena. *Ibid.*, xxi. 137.

1870. Examples for Practice in Quantitative Analysis. *Ibid.*, xxii. 89, 187.

1870-73. Cyclopædia of Quantitative Analysis. 8vo., 2 parts, pp. 112 and 113-224.

1874. Bulletin of the Bussey Institution [Jamaica Plain (Boston)]. 8vo., 2 parts, pp. 80 and 81-184. Cambridge.

*With Charles W. Eliot.*

1874. A Manual of Inorganic Chemistry, arranged to facilitate the Experimental Demonstration of the Facts and Principles of the Science. 1 vol., 8vo.

1874. A Compendious Manual of Qualitative Chemical Analysis. 1 vol., 8vo.

1874. Memoir on the Impurities of Commercial Zinc. 4to., pp. 39.

James P. Kimball, PhD., F.G.S., Professor of Geology in Lehigh University.

On Sodalite and Elaeolite from Salem, Mass. *Am. Jour. of Arts and Sciences*, 1859.

A series of analyses of bituminous shales in connection with Prof. C. F. Chandler. Geology of Wisconsin. Vol. I., by Prof. J. D. Whitney.

On Aluminous Magnetite (Emery) and its uses in Iron Metallurgy. *Am. Chemist*, Vol. IV., p. 321.

Dr. Kimball's contributions to science have been mainly geological.

C. Gilbert Wheeler, Prof. of Chemistry in the University of Chicago, Illinois, has made the following contributions to our chemical literature:—

1859. Analysis of various Missouri Coals. *Report of Missouri Geological Survey.*

1865. The Inorganic Constituents of Bavarian Hops and Analyses of the Leading Soils on which they are cultivated. *Journal für Praktische Chemie*, vol. xciv.

1865. A Method of Determining Carbon, Hydrogen, Nitrogen, and Oxygen at one Operation. *Ibid.*, vol. xcv.

1867. On the Action of Zinc and Sulphuric Acid

upon Cyanacetic Acid. *Ann. Chem. and Phar.*, vol. cxliii. *Bull. Soc. Chem.* [2], viii. 116.

1867. On the Bisulphide of Phenyl, and the Bisulphide of Brom-phenyl. *Zeitsch. für Chem.*, 1867, pp. 436.

1867. Action of Hypochlorous Acid on Oil of Turpentine. *Bull. Soc. Chim.* [2], x. 288.

1867. Action of Hypochlorous Acid on Camphor. *Zeitsch. Chem.*, 1868, 122.

1866. On a Method of Determining C.H.N+O at one operation. *Am. Jour. Sci. and Arts*, 1866, January number.

1868. Action of Binoxide of Manganese on Uric Acid. *Am. Jour. Sci. and Arts* [2], vol. xliv. p. 218.

1871. Recent Progress in Chemistry in the United States. Read before the British Association at Edinburgh, 1873.

1872. On the Polyscope, a new Optical Instrument. Read before the American Association at Dubuque.

1873. Analysis of Spring Lake and Frankfort Mineral Waters. Published in Dr. Watson's "Mineral Springs of the United States."

1874. Analysis of the Mineral Water of Grand Haven. Completed and about to be published in *Am. Jour. of Sci. and Arts.*

Note.—Many of the above were copied into other journals of England, France, and Germany.

C. M. Warren, Brookline, Massachusetts.—Prof. Warren, formerly of the Massachusetts Institute of Technology, whose researches upon the volatile hydrocarbons are so well known, has made the following contributions to chemistry.

1860. On some Compounds of Zirconia and Titanic Acid.

1. A New Sulphate of Zirconia, containing some Potassa.

2. A Double Sulphate of Zirconia and Potassa.

3. A Double Sulphate of Titanic Acid and Potassa. *Pogg. Ann.*, cii. 449.

1862. On a Safety Heating Lamp for use in Laboratories. *Am. Journ. Sci. and Arts*, [2], xxxiii. 275.

On a Process of Organic Elementary Analysis, by Combustion in a Stream of Oxygen Gas. *Proc. Am. Acad.*, vi. 251.

On a Process of Fractional Condensation Applicable to the Separation of Bodies, having small differences between their boiling-points. *Mem. Am. Acad.*, N. S., ix. 121.

Researches on the Volatile Hydrocarbons:—

1. On the Volatile Hydrocarbons from Coal-tar Naphtha.

2. On the Volatile Hydrocarbons from Oil of Cumin and Cuminic Acid. *Mem. Am. Acad.*, N. S., ix. 135.

On the Influence of $CH_2$ upon the Boiling-points in Homologous Series of Hydrocarbons, and in some Series of their Derivatives; with critical observations on methods of taking boiling-points. *Loc. cit.*, p. 156.

On a New Process for the Determination of Sulphur in Organic Compounds, by Combustion with Oxygen gas and Peroxide of Lead. *Proc. Am. Acad.*, vi. 472.

On a New Process of Organic Elementary Analysis for substances containing chlorine. *Proc. Am. Acad.*, vii. 84.

Note on an Improved Apparatus for the Determination of Vapor Densities, by Gay-Lussac's Method; being a modification of Bunsen's apparatus for measuring aqueous vapor. *Proc. Am. Acad.*, vii. 99.

In joint authorship with F. H. Storer.

Researches on the Volatile Hydrocarbons:—

Examination of a Hydrocarbon Naphtha, obtained from the Products of the Destructive Distillation of Lime Soap. *Mem. Am. Acad.*, N. S., ix. 177.

Examination of Naphtha, obtained from Rangoon Petroleum. *Loc. cit.*, p. 208.

Frederick Hoffmann, Ph.D., New York.—Dr. Hoffmann's chemical papers and publications are as follows:—

Untersuchungen der Bleiweiss Sorten des Handels. *Hirzel's Zeitschrift für Pharmacie*, 1852–1853.

Untersuchungen der Weinstein Sorten des Handels. *Hirzel's Zeitschrift für Pharmacie*, 1852–3.

Ueber die Ermittlung des Phosphor in der gerichtlich-chemischen Analyse. *Berliner Allgemeine Medicinischs Central Zeitung*, 1859, *Kopp & Will Jahresberichte*, 1859, p. 663.

A Critical Review of the History of Anilin and the Anilin Colors. Sacket & Cobb, New York, 1863.

Die Steinkohlen und deren Destillations Producte. A course of lectures delivered before the New York Gewerbe Verein. *Sonntagsblatt N. Y. Statts Zeitung*, 1863.

Die Chemie und das Leben. A popular lecture.

*Butz, Deutsch-Amerikanische Monatshefte*, Chicago, 1864.

Arabesken, am der Geschichte der Chemie. *Butz, Deutsch-Amerikanische Monatshefte*, Chicago, 1864.

Annual Report on the Progress of Pharmacy and Pharmaceutical Chemistry. Philadelphia, 1868.

On the Preparation of Zinc Sulpho-phenate. *Amer. Journ. of Pharmacy*, 1870.

Manual of Chemical Analysis, as applied to the Examination of Medicinal Chemicals. New York, 1873.

Dr. Hoffmann's "Manual," last named, is a work of very high character, and has received well-deserved commendation wherever it is known.

Maurice Perkins, Prof. of Chemistry Union College, Schenectady, N. Y.—Prof. Perkins has published An Analysis of the Parotid Saliva, in Dalton's Physiology.

P. B. Wilson, Baltimore, Md.—Mr. Wilson has contributed the following papers:—

1859. 1. On Wax obtained from Myrica cerifera (in Genth's Laboratory).

2. Electro-metallurgical Preparation of Chemically pure Metals, prepared for Bunsen and Kirchhoff, for their Spectroscopic Investigation (in Bunsen's Laboratory).

3. Improvement in the Clark Method for Determining the Hardness of Waters (in Baron Liebig's Laboratory while acting assistant there).

4. Cause of Mono-calcic Phosphate losing its Solubility.

5. On a Meteorite from Hartford County, Maryland (The above were published in *Ann. de Chem. und Pharm*).

S. Dana Hayes, Ph. D., State Assayer of Massachusetts, Boston.—Dr. Hayes is a working chemist, most of whose labors are necessarily hidden in cases in the United States courts, or remain unpublished as the property of those for whom they are made.

But he has found time to make the following contributions.

"A new Lead Salt corresponding to Cobalt Yellow." *Quar. Journ. Chem. Soc.*, and *Am. Journ. Sci. and Arts*, 1861.

"Ueber den Feldspath im geschmolzenen Zustande." *Pogg. Ann.*, Bd. III. S. 351.

"Influence of the Oxides of Chromium and Titanium

on the Composition of Pig-Iron." *Lond. Chem. News*, June, 1869.

"Adulterated Aniline Dyes." *Am. Suppl. to Chem. News*, May, 1870.

"Destructive Distillation of Light Petroleum Naphthas at comparatively Low Temperatures." *Am. Journ. Sci. and Arts*, 3, II. Sept. 1871.

| | |
|---|---|
| "A common Source of Lead in Drinking Water."<br>"Assaying One Hundred and Thirty Years ago."<br>"Some New England Waters."<br>"Substitution of Soda for Potash in Plants." | *Am. Chem.*, vol. i. |
| "History and Manufacture of Petroleum Products."<br>"Peculiar Conditions of Waters." | *Am. Chem.*, vol. ii. |

"Miscellaneous Chemical Notes," generally appertaining to industrial chemistry. *Am. Chem.*, vols. iii., iv., and v.

James M. Crafts, Professor of Chemistry in the Massachusetts Institute of Technology, Boston, Mass.—Mr. Crafts has made numerous researches, chiefly in organic chemistry. His published papers are as follows:—

1861. On the Action of Sulphite of Ammonium on Nitro-benzole (contributed in the name of Professor Carius).

In joint authorship with C. Friedel, Mr. Crafts made in the laboratory of Mr. Wurtz, in Paris, an elaborate investigation on new compounds of silicon with compound radicals, and on the atomic weight of silicon. Notices of these researches were published from time to time in the *Comptes Rendus* and elsewhere, but the final results were given in two memoirs in the *Ann. de Ch. et Phys.*, Paris, as follows:—

1866. Recherches sur les Éthers Siliciques et sur le Poids Atomique du Silicium. *Op. cit.*, 4me série, t. ix. pp. 5–51.

1870. Recherches sur les Combinaisons du Silicium avec les Radicaux Alcoholiques. *Op. cit.*, 4me série, t. xix. 334–367.

[These two memoirs are reproduced in the *Am. Journ. Sci.* [2], xliii. 155–171 and 331–344; xlix. 307–330.]

Mr. Crafts has also published separately in *Comptes Rendus*:—

Sur les Éthers des Acides de l'Arsenic.

Sur les Produits d'Oxydation du Sulfure d'Éthylène.

Sur le Sulfure d'Éthylène et sur une Combinaison qu'il forme avec le Brome.

In the *Am. Journ. Sci.* Prof. Crafts has published as follows:—

1863. Action of Bromine and of Bromhydric Acid on the Acetate of Ethyl, [2] xxxvi. 42.

1864. Note on the Product of the Reaction between the Monosulphide of Potassium and the Bromide of Ethylene, and on the several compounds derived from it, [2] xxxvii. 390.

1865. On the Replacement of one Alcohol Radical by another in Compounds of the Ether class (by C. Friedel and J. M. Crafts), [2] xl. 34.

1865. On Etherification (the same), p. 40.

1869. A Short Course of Qualitative Analysis, with the New Notation, with five Tables. New York. 12mo. 133 pages.

1873. The Estimation of Iron with Hyposulphite of Sodium. *Am. Chem.*, iii. July.

Henry M. Seely, Middlebury College, Vermont.—Professor Seely's papers have mostly been on topics not properly chemical, or have been in connection with some other person. We find, however, in the *Berkshire Medical Journal*, 1861, Art. XXXVI., entitled—

Report of a Chemical Analysis of Specimens of Hydrargyrum cum Creta, by Professor Seely, in which he notes the passage of finely-divided mercury, first into black and finally into red oxide of mercury.

John W. Langley, M.D., Professor of Chemistry, W. University of Pennsylvania, Pittsburgh, has published a paper entitled—

1862. On the Detection of Picrotoxine. *Am. Journ. Sci.*, xxxiv., 109, also in *London Medical News.*

B. F. Craig, M.D., Washington, D. C.—Dr. Craig has for some years been in charge of the laboratory of Army Medical Museum at Washington.

1861. On the Products from the Combustion of Gunpowder under different pressures. *Am. Journ. Sci.* [2], xxxi. 429.

1861. Report on Nitrification (presented to the Smithsonian Institution in 1858). *Smithsonian Report*, 1861, pp. 305–318.

1864. Remarks on the Production of the Combustion of Gun-Cotton and Gunpowder. *Ibid.*, 1864, pp. 232–234.

1871. Experiments on Ventilation and Composition of Air in Military Barracks. Appended to Surgeon-General Barnes's Report in "Circular No. 4," Washington, 1870. Noticed in *Am. Journ. Sci.* [3], i. 475.

1871. Variations in the Temperature of the Human Body. *Am. Journ. Sci.* [3], ii. 330.

SAMUEL P. DUFFIELD, M.D., Ph.D., Dearbornville, Michigan.—Dr. Duffield's contributions are chiefly in the department of pharmaceutical chemistry, and are as follows:—

Remarks on Analysis of Brandy. *Am. Journ. Pharm.*, March, 1862.

Hypodermic Injections in their Relation to Toxicology. *Proc. Am. Pharm. Ass.*, 1866.

Report on New Remedies. *Detroit Review of Medicine*, 1866.

On Preparation of Pyrophosphate of Iron.

On Proportion of Digitalin in Digitalis grown in different Countries.

On Properties of the Leaves of Podophyllum Peltatum. *Proc. Am. Pharm. Ass.*, 1868.

Emanations from Sewers a Secret Cause of Disease. *Detroit Review of Medicine*, 1869.

On Medicinal Fluid Extracts. *Ibid.*, Nov. 1866.

On a Case of Aconite Poisoning. *Proc. Am. Pharm. Ass.*, 1870.

On the Geological Relation of the Mineral Waters of Michigan. *Detroit Review of Medicine*, 1871.

O. D. ALLEN, Professor of Metallurgy in the Sheffield Scientific School, New Haven, Connecticut.—Prof. Allen's researches on Cæsium and Rubidium, and the determination of the atomic weight of cæsium, are well known to all chemists. These memoirs are entitled:—

1862. Observations on Cæsium and Rubidium [in Contributions from the Sheffield Scientific Laboratory, Yale College, iv.]. *Am. Journ. Sci.*, xxxiv. 367–373.

1863. On the Equivalent and Spectrum of Cæsium [in Contributions from the Sheffield Scientific Laboratory, Yale College, v.]. Jointly with Prof. S. W. Johnson (q. v.). *Am. Journ. Sci.* [2], xxxv. 94–98.

GIDEON E. MOORE, Ph.D., Jersey City, New Jersey. —Dr. Moore has published the following original papers:—

1. On the Chemical Constitution of the Wax of the *Myrica cerifera. American Journal of Science* [2], xxxiii. 313, May, 1862.

2. On Brushite, a new Mineral occurring in Phosphatic Guano. *Proceedings* of the California Academy of Sciences, September 5, 1864. *American Journal of Science* [2], xxxix. 43.

3. On the Occurrence in Nature of Amorphous Mercuric Sulphide. *Journal für prakt. Chemie*, 1870: *American Journal of Science* [3], ii., January, 1872.

4. On the Electrolysis of the substituted Derivatives of Acetic Acid. *Ber. d. Deutschen chem. Gesellschaft*, May 22, 1871. *American Journal of Science* [3], iii., March, 1872.

P. Collier, A.M., Ph.D., Burlington, Vermont., Professor of Chemistry in the University of Vermont, has written chiefly on agricultural chemistry in the daily journals and for the State Agricultural Society, to which he is chemist.

1864. Indirect Determination of Potash and Soda. *Sill. Journ.* [2], xxxvii. 344.

J. M. Merrick, Boston, 59 Broad Street.—Mr. Merrick's papers are as follows:—

Inhalation of Vapor of Nitroglycerine. *Am. Journ. Sci.*, 1863.

Assay of Gold and Silver. *American Chemist*, vol. i., 1871.

Testing Cochineal. *American Chemist*, vol. i., 1871.

" Indigo. " " " "

Zinc Poisoning. " " " "

Assay of Pyrites for Gold. *American Chemist*, vol. ii., 1872.

Electrolytic Deposition of Nickel. *American Chemist*, vol. ii., 1872.

Separation of Nickel and Copper. *American Chemist*, vol. ii., 1872.

On the Double Chloride of Nickel and Ammonia. (Jointly with Isaac Adams, Jr.) *American Chemist*, vol. ii., 1872.

Electrolytic Determination of Copper. *American Chemist*, vol. iii., 1873.

Estimation of Tannin. *American Chemist*, vol. iii., 1873.

Note on Geissler Bulbs, etc. *American Chemist*, vol. iii., 1873.

Luckow's Method for Determining Copper. *American Chemist*, vol. iii., 1873.

Chemical Experts. *American Chemist*, vol. iv., 1873.
Analysis Crude Sugar. " " " "
Various Chemical Notes. *American Chemist*, vol. iv., 1874.
Estimation of Tannic Acid. *American Chemist*, vol. iv., 1874.
Numerous translations in *American Chemist*.
Analysis of Manures. *Chemical News*, xxiv.
Determination of Copper, Nickel, and Zinc. *Chemical News*, xxiv.
On a New Dye-stuff. *Chemical News*, xxv.
On Testing Cochineal. " " "
Various minor notes.

CHARLES PIERCE, Cambridge.—Mr. Pierce's scientific memoirs are mostly mathematical or physical; but the following important paper falls within our scope:—

1863. The Chemical Theory of Interpretation. *Am. Journ. Sci.* [2], xxxv. 78.

ALEXIS A. JULIEN, School of Mines, Columbia College.

1864. On Metabrushite and other Guano Minerals, from Sombrero, W. I. *Am. Journ. Sci.* [2], xl. 367.

1870. On Examples for Practice in Quantitative Analysis. *Am. Chemist*, i. 256, 280, 322, 412.

On a supposed New Mineral from Chesterfield, Mass. *Am. Chemist*, i. 300.

1871. On the Proximate Analysis of Coals. *Am. Chem.*, i. 460.

JOSEPH WHARTON, Philadelphia.—Mr. Wharton does not claim to be distinctly a chemist, but his contributions to the metallurgical arts closely related to chemistry demand respectful mention here, as well as one or two of his papers on other chemical and physical subjects. Mr. Wharton's principal labors have been the establishment in this country of the manufacture of metallic zinc or spelter, and of nickel and cobalt with their immediate products, though he has been largely engaged in lead, copper, iron, and steel.

That he has written little concerning nickel will not surprise those who consider that each of the very few nickel works in the world has to some extent its peculiar processes which cannot prudently be imparted to its rivals. Mr. W.'s nickel is remarkable for purity and uniformity, and comprises about one-sixth of the entire product of the world.

The following papers appear in the *Am. Journ. Sci.*, viz.:—

1865. xc. p. 190. Speculations upon a possible Method of determining the Distance of Certain Variably Colored Stars.

The diverse sensations caused by the several colors being due to the diverse numbers of light-wave impulses therefrom falling upon the retina, and those wave impulses being presumably longitudinal as well as lateral, rapid removal of the retina from the source of light should, by diminishing the number of wave impulses received (as rapid approach should by increasing the same) produce a corresponding change in the color perceived. Supposing the velocities of light answering to certain colors to have been ascertained by experiment, and a variably colored star with a determinable alternation of position to have been sought out—or, better, a pair of binary stars alternately eclipsing each other and of alternating colors—then measure the angle of greatest elongation of the line connecting those stars, and observe the time occupied by them in effecting a reversal of their positions—that is, in traversing a semicircumference of their orbit: equal to $\frac{t}{2}$.

Assume the extreme colors to indicate a difference in the rate of arrival of light impulses, or, in other words, a difference in the velocity of light arriving from the stars when their entire orbital speed is of approach or recession to the spectator equal to $2\,v$.

Then their actual orbital speed $= v$, and, as the orbital period has been found $= t$, it follows that $\frac{v \times t}{3{\cdot}1416}$ is the real length of that diameter, which is the measured angular distance between the extreme positions of the stars. Knowing the angle and the length of the subtending base, we have the distance of the stars.

1869. xcvii. p. 251. Observations upon Autumnal Foliage. Conceiving that the autumnal change from green to red might be due to the acidifying influence of atmospheric oxygen upon the leaf sap after the vitality of the leaf is lost or is destroyed by frost, thus enabling the thin acid sap to redden the vegetable blue element of the chlorophyl, Mr. W. undertook as a test of this supposition to reverse the process by immersing red autumn leaves in an alkaline atmosphere. The red leaves of sassafras, blackberry, maple, oak, etc., were restored to a green color, by leaving them under a bell-glass wherein ammonia was evaporating for periods of a few minutes, varying with the impermeability of the cuticle of the leaf.

1870. xcix. p. 365. On two Peculiar Products in the Nickel Manufacture. One of those products being basic crystals of iron, nickel, and cobalt sulphide, found in the matte furnaces of Gap Mine, having the unusual formula $R_6S$. The other being metallic bubbles or hollow spheroids formed on pouring melted nickel-copper alloy into water, the gases contained in a drop of metal sufficing to distend it into a bubble while cooling.

1871. cii. p. 168. Memoranda concerning the Introduction of the Manufacture of Spelter into the United States. This paper gives a detailed account of the establishment of this manufacture, with statements of materials consumed, cost, and product. After some preliminary experiments, Mr. W. erected at Bethlehem, Pa., in the year 1860, a spelter works of sixteen Belgian furnaces with all appurtenances, stipulated to produce 3,000,000 lbs. yearly, but which exceeded that quantity in 1861, and produced in 1862 over 3,700,000 lbs.

The zinc or spelter was of most excellent quality, and was made so cheaply as to afford a reliable profit, and to plant this industry firmly in this country.

The original features of the enterprise were: 1. The reduction to metal, on a large scale, of silicate of zinc, which had theretofore not been effected. 2. The successful application of anthracite to the manufacture of spelter, instead of the bituminous coal or wood which European practice had apparently shown to be indispensable. 3. The use of American clays for the making of zinc retorts.

Samuel D. Tillman, New York, 11 Cooper Union.—Mr. Tillman's contributions to chemical literature have been mainly in the department of chemical philosophy. His published papers are as follows:—

A New Chemical Nomenclature. See *Transactions of American Institute* for 1865–6, pp. 670–692. Applicable to more than 7000 bodies, each name indicating the exact composition of the body designated.

Chemical Diagrams and Derivative Symbols, illustrating the Prominent Characteristics of Chemical Elements. *Proceedings of the American Association for the Advancement of Science*, for 1867.

Atoms and Molecules. *Am. Chem.* for April, 1872, and *Nature* (London) for June, 1872.

CHARLES U. SHEPARD, Jr., M.D., Charleston, S. C —Dr. Shepard has published the following memoirs:—

1866. On the Origin of Hippuric Acid in the Animal Organism. This is a small volume published in joint authorship with Prof. George Meissner, of Göttingen, Hanover, 1866.

1867. On the Change of Benzoic Acid in the Organism of Birds. *Zeitschrift der Ration. Medicin.*

1869. Notes on the Occurrence and Composition of Nodular Phosphates of South Carolina. *Am. Journ. Sci.* [2], xlvii. 354–364.

Dr. Shepard has published some other communications, the titles to which I have not been able to obtain.

JAMES F. BABCOCK, Boston, Mass. (No. 8 Boylston St.), Boston University.—Prof. Babcock has published as follows:—

1866. On the Preparation of Sulphocyanide of Potassium. *Lond. Chem. News*, vol. xiv., 1866.

1866. On the Preparation of Iodide of Ammonium. *Proc. Am. Pharm. As.*, Philadelphia, 1866.

1867. On Beeswax. *Proc. Am. Pharm. As.*, Philadelphia, 1867.

1872. Reports on the Adulteration of Milk. *City of Boston*, 1870, 1871, 1872.

1873. On the Adulteration of Milk. *Report of the State Board of Health*, State of Massachusetts, 1873.

1874. On the Impurities of Commercial Iodide of Potassium. *The Laboratory*, Sept. 1874.

Report on the Preservation of Wood Pavements. *City of Boston*, 1873.

H. CARRINGTON BOLTON, Ph.D., School of Mines, Columbia College, New York.—All Dr. Bolton's contributions to chemistry fall within the last eight years. The following list does not embrace Dr. Bolton's latest contribution, for which he has placed us all under lasting obligations. I allude to his happy thought of memorializing the day we celebrate, for it is to him we owe the pleasure of this gathering at the grave of Priestley to-day.

1866. On the Fluorine Compounds of Uranium. Monatsb. der Berlin. Academie, 1866, p. 299. Also as pamphlet 40 pp.

1869. On the Action of Sunlight on Uranium. *Am. Journ. of Sci.*, Sept. 1869.

1870. Index to Literature of Uranium. Annals New York Lyc. Nat. Hist., vol. ix., p. 362.

1870. History of the Defunct Elements. *Am. Chemist*, vol. i., p. 1.

Extraction of Uranium. *Ibid.*, vol. i., No. 2. August, 1870.

1872. Observations on the Platino-Cyanide of Magnesium. *Ibid.*, vol. ii., No. 10.

On Galvanic Action in the Mouth. *Dental Cosmos*, vol. xiv., p. 298.

1873. Washing Bottles a Cause of Fire. *Am. Chemist*, vol. iii., p. 286.

Views of the Founders of the Atomic Philosophy. *Ibid.*, vol. iii., p. 326.

With Prof. Henry Morton: Investigation of Fluorescent and Absorption Spectra of Uranium Salts. *Ibid.*, vol. iii., p. 361, *et seq.*

Zettnow's Scheme for Qualitative Analysis. *Ibid.*, vol. iii., p. 452.

Notes on the Early Literature of Chemistry. Four papers. *Ibid.*, vol. iv.

1874. Chemical Paradoxes. *Journ. of Appl. Chem.*, June, 1874.

Le Roy C. Cooley, Ph.D., Albany, New York — Prof. Cooley, of the State Normal School, has published the following:—

On Teaching Advanced Classes in Chemistry. Read at "University Convocation," etc., published in *Proc. of Third Anniv.*, 1866.

On Elementary Chemistry in Preparation for College. Read at "University Convocation," published in *Proc. of Fifth Anniv.*, 1868.

On a Steady Air-Blast for Laboratory Purposes. *Journ. Frank. Inst.*, vol. lxv., 1870.

On a Blowpipe Assay with the Automatic Air-Blast. *Ibid.*, vol. lxi., 1871.

On the Effect of the Action of Water on Gypsum. *Proc. Albany Inst.*, vol. i., Part I., 1870.

Report on the Progress of Chemistry, 1871. *Trans. of Albany Institute*, vol. vii.

"From Newton to Kirchoff" (sketch of spectrum analysis), 1872. *Ibid.*, vol. vii.

John M. Blake, New Haven, Connecticut.—Mr. Blake's contributions are chiefly mineralogical and physical. We note the following:—

1866. On Measuring Angles of Crystals.

1866. Gaylussite from Nevada.

1867. Natural Terpin.

1867. On Kaolinite and Pholerite.

1869. On Hortonolite.

All in the 2d series of the *Am. Journ. Sci.*

H. Endemann, Ph.D., New York. Dr. Endemann has contributed the following papers:—

1866. Die neutralen und sauren Aether der schwefligen Säure. *Annalen der Chemie und Pharmacie.*

1872. Meat and the Methods of Preserving it. *Am. Chemist*, January.

1869 to 1872. Disinfectants and Disinfection. Reports of the Health Department of the City of New York.

1872. Confectionery sold in the City of New York. Report of the Health Department of the City of New York.

1872. Examination of the Air in Schools, Manufactories, Tenements, Cellar Lodgings, Prisons, Theatres, and Public Halls in the City of New York. Report of the Health Department of the City of New York.

1873. Also another series. *New York World*, Dec. 27.

1872. Chemical and Mycological Examination of the Blood, Bile, and Urine of Horses sick with the Epizootic Influenza. Report of the Health Department of the City of New York.

1874. Warming and Ventilation. *Sanitarian*, April.

North Carolina Prisons. *Annals of the Lyceum of Natural History*, N. Y. vol. ix.

1874. Criticisms of Prof. Wurtz's Test for Free Oxygen in Water. *Am. Chemist*, July.

S. P. Sharples, Boston (114 State Street).—Mr. Sharples has published:—

1866. Chemical Tables. 8vo. pp. 192.

Papers in the *American Journal of Science*—

1868. On some Minerals from Chester County, Pennsylvania.

1869. On a New Salt, containing Tin, Calcium, and Chlorine (March).

1871. On some Dredgings from the Gulf Stream (February).

1871. On some Forms of the Galvanic Battery (April).

1874. Crystals of Zinc (March).

Papers in the *American Chemist*—

1872. The Waters of Eastern Massachusetts (November).

1873. The Disposal of Animal Refuse: and several shorter articles.

Papers in *Journal of Applied Chemistry*—

1873. On the Preservation of Food (August).

1874. On Common Salt (September).

Mr. Sharples has also, since 1871, been a constant contributor to the *Boston Journal of Chemistry*, of which journal he is assistant editor, having been previously (1866) a graduate of the Lawrence Scientific School, Cambridge; assistant (1867–8) at Lehigh University; assistant (1868–71) at Lawrence Scientific School; and (1872) State Assayer of Massachusetts. Dr. Sharples's Chemical Tables are in the hands of all American chemists.

George F. Barker, Professor of Physics in the University of Pennsylvania, Philadelphia, has published the following chemical and physical papers:—

*Theoretical Chemistry.*

On Normal and Derived Acids. *Am. Journ. Sci.*, Nov. 1867.

Formic *versus* Carbonous Acid. *Ibid.*, Sept. 1867.

On the Rational Formulas of the Oxides of Chlorine and of Oxides analogously constituted. *Am. Chem.*, July, 1871.

On Molecular Classification. *Ibid.*, April, 1871.

*Physics.*

Note on the Spectrum of the Aurora. *Am. Journ. Sci.*, Dec. 1871.

On the Aurora of October 14th, 1872. *Ibid.*, Feb. 1873.

*Toxicology.*

Report of a Trial for Poisoning by Strychnia. *Am. Journ. Med. Sci.*, Oct. 1864.

Testimony in the Sherman Poisoning Case. *Am. Chem.*, June, 1872.

Dr. Barker has also contributed valuable abstracts of chemical researches, chiefly from European journals, in the *Am. Journ. Sci.*, since volume xlv. of the second series (1868). Also, a series of "Notices of papers in Physiological Chemistry." *Am. Journ. Sci.* [2], xlvi. 233–379; xlvii. 20, 258, 393; xlvii. 49.

"A Text-Book of Elementary Chemistry, Theoretical and Practical," 12mo., which has met deservedly with great favor as a clear exposition of the "New Chemistry."

The *Journal of the Franklin Institute* is now under the editorial care of Dr. Barker.

EDWARD W. ROOT.—The late Prof. Root, of Hamilton College, has published the following chemical papers:—

1867. "On Wilsonite from St. Lawrence County, N. Y." *Am. Journ. Sci.* [2], xlix. 47.

1868. "On Enargite from Mercury Star Mine, California." *Ibid.*, xlvi. 201.

Prof. Root died, in his 30th year, in November, 1871, highly esteemed for his scientific and literary attainments, integrity of character, and tested ability.

BEVERLY S. BURTON, Ph.B., has published ("Contributions from the Sheffield Laboratory of Yale College, No. xvi.")—

1867. "Contributions to Mineralogy" with Analyses of: i. Enorgite from Colorado; ii. Argentiferous Jamesenite from the Sheba Mine, Star City, Nevada; iii. Argentiferous Tetrahedrite from the De Soto Mine, Nevada (the 2d and 3d collected in 1864 by B. Silliman). *Am. Journ. Sci.* [2], xlv. 34.

U. J. KNOWLTON, Rockport, Mass.—"On a New Mineral from Rockport, Mass." An altered zinc ore. *Am. Journ. Sci.* [2], lxix. 224. 1867.

S. F. PECKHAM, Minneapolis, Minnesota, University of Minnesota.—Professor Peckham's papers are:—

1867. On the Supposed Falsification of Samples of California Petroleum. *American Journal of Science*, May, 1867.

1867. On a New Apparatus for Technical Analysis of Petroleum; together with Experiments upon the Formation of Asphaltum. *American Journal of Science*, September, 1867.

1868. Notes on the Origin of Bitumens. Read before the Natural Academy of Sciences, August, 1868. Published in the *Proceedings* of the American Philosophical Society, x., 441.

1869. On the Distillation of Dense Hydrocarbons at High Temperatures, technically termed "Cracking." *American Journal of Science*, January, 1869.

1869. On the Probable Origin of Albertite and Allied Minerals. *American Journal of Science*, November, 1869.

1871. Evaporating Niches at the Laboratory of the Maine State College of Agriculture and the Mechanic Arts. *American Chemist*, August, 1871. *Proceed-*

*ings* of the American Association for Advancement of Science, 1871.

1873. American Asphalts. *American Chemist*, July, 1873.

Four reports to the State Geologist of California, which have been printed, but not yet published:—

1st. 1866. On the Oil Interests of Southern California.

2d. 1867. On the Results of a Technical Examination of California Bitumens.

3d. 1871. On the Results of an Examination of California and other Petroleums in Reference to their Ultimate Chemical Composition. Made at Cambridge in 1869.

4th. 1872. On the Results of Proximate Analyses of California and other Coals, and a Quantitative Determination of the Sulphur contained in them. Made in Providence in July, 1872. Also—

1873. Report to State Geologist of Minnesota in Report of Board of Regents of the State University of Minnesota.

1874. Peat for Domestic Fuel. Report to Geological Secretary of Minnesota, July, 1874.

P. Casamajor, Williamsburg, New York.—Mr. Casamajor's papers, partly physical, partly chemical, are as follows:—

1867. On the Method of Measuring the Angles of Crystals by Reflection without the Use of a Goniometer. *American Journal of Science*, September.

1870. Action of Water on Lead. *American Chemist*, July.

1871. On the Purification of Sugar Solutions for the Optical Saccharometer. *American Chemist*, November.

1872. Researches on Voltaic Batteries. *American Chemist*, May, June, and July.

1873. Testing Sugar Solutions by Means of Areometers and the Optical Saccharometer. *American Chemist*, October and November.

1874. On the Formula of Francoeur for Correcting the Indications of Beaumé's Areometer into Corresponding Specific Gravities. *American Chemist*, February.

1874. New Portable Apparatus which may be used as a Filter Pump or Laboratory Bellows. *American Chemist*, April.

1874. On the Expansion of Sugar Solutions by Heat. *American Chemist*, June, 1874.

W. Goold Levison, Brooklyn, New York.—Mr. Levison has contributed the following papers:—

Letters on the Properties of Sodium Amalgam. Dated New York, June 11, 1867. Published in the *American Journal of Mining*, June 15, 1867, vol. iii., No. 12.

Letter on the Action of Sodium in the Pan. Dated New York, July 16, 1867. Published in the *American Journal of Mining*, July 20, 1867, vol. iv., new series, No. 3.

Paper on the Peat Deposits of Prospect Park. Read before the Natural History Department of the Long Island Historical Society, February 28, 1867.

Letter on an Improvement in Galvanic Batteries. Dated Cambridge, Massachusetts, May 1, 1870. Published in the *Journal of the Franklin Institute*, June, 1870, vol. lix., No. 6.

Paper on the Precipitation and Determination of the Metals of the Magnesian Group in the Form of Oxalates. Lawrence Scientific School Contributions, No. 12. *American Journal of Sciences*, September, 1870, vol. l., No. 149.

Note on an Improved Screw Cup and a New Connector for Volta-Electric Instruments. Read before the Lyceum of Natural History in the city of New York, November 11, 1872.

Note on the Production of Ammonia in Nitric Acid Batteries. Read before the Lyceum of Natural History in the city of New York, March 10, 1873. Published in the *Journal of the Franklin Institute*, May, 1873, vol. xlv. No. 5. Republished, with corrections, in the *Proceedings* of the Lyceum of Natural History for 1873.

Note on a Simple Connector for Battery Carbons. Read before the Lyceum of Natural History in the city of New York, April 13, 1874.

O. Loew, Smithsonian Institution Laboratory, Washington, D. C.

Mr. Loew's contributions to chemistry are in the *Am. Journ. of Sci.*, as follows:—

1867. Action of Water on Carbo-Hydrates. [2], lxiii. 371.

1868. Ferrocyanide of Potassium on Monochloracetic Ether. [2], lxv. 383.

1868. Nitrate of Ammonia. [2], lxvi. 29.

1868. Bisulphid of Carbon in Sunlight. [2], lxvi. 363.

1869. Derivatives of tri-chlormethyl-sulphon-chlorid. lxvii. 350.

1870. Action of Sunlight on Sulphurous Acid. [2], lxix. 368.

1870. Ozone from Rapid Combustion. [2], lxix. 369.

1870. On Hydrogenium-amalgam. [2], l. 99.

1874. On Wheelerite, a New Fossil Resin. [3], vii. 571.

Isidor Walz, Ph.D., New York, has published the following chemical papers :—

1868. On the Oxidation of Diamylene by means of Chromic Acid. *Sill. Am. Journ. of Sci.*, 2, xlv. 57.

1870. A Modification of Bunsen's Filtering Pump. *Chem. News*, 22, 163.

Notes on the Extinctive and Reducing Powers of Mercury. *Ibid.*, 22, 217.

1870. On the Reduction of Sulphuric Acid by Zinc Amalgam. *Amer. Chemist*, i. 242.

1870. On the Reaction of Chloral Hydrate and Sulphide of Ammonium. *Ibid.*, i. 441.

1871. Determination of Moisture in Bone-black. *Ibid.*, ii. 169.

1872. On the Action of Chromium Trioxide on Iodine. *Ibid.*, iii. 84.

1873. On Antimony Terchloride as a Reagent for Oils. *Ibid.*, iv. 169.

A series of articles "On Chemistry applied to Textile Arts and Dyeing," of which eighteen chapters have appeared in *The Manufacturer's Review and Industrial Record* since 1872, and which, when finished, will be collected in a volume.

Frank W. Clarke, S.B., University of Cincinnati, O.—Prof. Clarke has made the following contributions to chemistry :—

1868. On New Processes in Chemical Analysis. *Am. Journ. Sci.*, xlv. 173.

1869. Upon the Atomic Volume of Liquids. *Am. Journ. Sci.*, xlvii. 180.

1869. Upon the Atomic Volume of the Elements. *Am. Journ. Sci.*, xlvii. 308.

1869. A Qualitative Separation of Cobalt and Nickel. *Am. Journ. Sci.*, xlviii. 67.

1870. On a New Method of Separating Tin from Arsenic, Antimony, and Molybdenum. *Am. Journ. Sci.*, xlix. 48.

1870. On the Atomic Volume of Solid Compounds. *Am. Journ. Sci.*, l. 174.

1870. An Examination of the Doctrine of Atomicity. *Am. Chem.*, November.

1873. Evolution and the Spectroscope. *Pop. Sci. Month.*, Jan.

1874. The Constants of Nature; Smithsonian Miscellaneous Contributions, Part I.; Specific Gravities; Boiling and Melting-points; and Chemical Formulæ, pp. 203. 8vo. *Smith. Inst.*

1874. On the Molecular Volume of Water of Crystallization, and—

1874. On the Molecular Heat of Similar Compounds. *Am. Jour. Sci.* [3], viii.

W. G. Mixter, Instructor in Chemistry, Sheffield Scientific School, Yale College.—Mr. Mixter's chemical papers are:—

1868. "On Nillemite and Tephroite" (from Mine Hill, Sussex, New Jersey, with Analyses). *Am. Journ. Sci.* [2], xlvi. 230.

1872. "On the Estimation of Sulphur in Coal and Organic Compounds." *Ibid.* [3], iv. 90.

1873. In connection with E. S. Dana, "On the Specific Heat of Zirconium, Silicon, and Boron." *Ann. Chem. u. Pharm.*, Bd. 195, 388, and *Am. Journ. Sci.* [3], 506, Abstract.

William H. Chandler, Professor of Chemistry in the Lehigh University, Bethlehem, Pennsylvania, has published the following chemical papers:—

The Economical Purification of Zinc, containing Iron. *American Supplement to American Reprint of Chemical News*, Sep. 1869, p. 193.

On the Determination of Sulphur Compounds in Mineral Waters. *Ibid.*, April, 1870, p. 221.

Production of Iodine and Bromine. *Am. Chem.*, vol. i. p. 47.

Carbon Photographs. *Ibid.*, vol. i. p. 94.

The Sherman Process for Refining Iron. *Ibid.*, vol. i. p. 366.

The Peruvian Guano Islands. *Ibid.*, vol. i. p. 439.

A Day in Dublin. *Ibid.*, vol. ii. p. 88.

Henry Morton, LL.D., President of Stevens Institute of Technology, Hoboken, New Jersey.—Most of Prof. Morton's papers are more properly physical than chemical, but the following fall within our scope.

1869. Research on the bright line beyond the Moon's Edge, in partial phase eclipse photographs. *Comptes Rendus, French Acad.*, V. lxix. p. 1234. Also *Journ. Frank. Inst.*, lviii. 373.

This research demonstrated that this phenomenon was a result of chemical reaction, a "local re-development" of the image, as Dr. Morton called it, and that consequently the views of Airy and Prest. Barnard, that it was either subjective or from diffraction, was no longer tenable.

1872. Researches on Anthracene and Chrysogen. *Am. Chemist*, Sept., and *Phil. Mag.*, Sept., p. 345.

1872. Research on Certain New Solid Hydrocarbons in Petroleum Distillates, "Thallene and Petrollucene." *Am. Chemist*, Nov., and *Phil. Mag.*, V. xlvi. p. 89, *Revue Scientifique*, *Chem. News*, etc.

1872–73. On Fluorescent and Absorption Spectra of Uranium Salts, a series of papers running through the *Am. Chemist*, vols. iii. and iv. In joint authorship with Dr. H. Carrington Bolton.

1873. On Basic Salts of Uranium. *Am. Chemist*, iv. 125; also *Revue Scientifique*, etc.

1874. On Pyrene and Chrysene. *Am. Chemist*, current Nos.

Rossiter W. Raymond, Ph.D., New York City.

1869. Dr. Raymond's Annual Reports as U. S. Commissioner of Mines since 1869 have been an important contribution to technical literature, and especially to metallurgists.

Dr. Raymond has also established the *Engineering and Mining Journal*, which for about ten years has been a principal authority in all chemical matters relating to the smelting and assay of ore, and has done a good work for practical science generally. One who is absorbed by such editorial labors finds little time for original research, but Dr. Raymond has contributed an important memoir upon the Tertiary and Cretaceous lignites of Western America, entitled—

1873. Calorific Value of the Lignites of Western America. *Engineering and Mining Journal*, and *Am. Journ. Sci.* [3], vi. 220.

Albert H. Gallatin, M.D., 10 E. 17th Street, New York.—The only original paper by Dr. Gallatin which I have seen is entitled—

On Hydrogenium Alloys. *Phil. Magazine*, London, July, 1869.

Paul Schweitzer, Ph.D., Professor of Chemistry, Columbia, Boone County, Missouri, has published the following chemical papers:—

I. On Tribasic Phosphoric Acid; its history, its modes of separation from sesquioxides, principally sesquioxide of iron, and its estimation. *Annals of the Lyceum of Natural History of New York*, vol. ix. Nos. 5 and 6, 1869.

II. On the Quantitative Separation and Determination of Iodine, Bromine, and Chlorine. *Chemical News*, American reprint, vol. v. p. 317, 1869.

III. The Various Methods for the Determination and Separation of Baryta, Strontia, and Lime; also, some Remarks on the Precipitation of Sulphuric Acid by Salts of Baryta (five papers). *Chemical News*, American reprint, vol. vi. pp. 119, 222, 295, 370, 1869; *Am. Chem.*, vol. i. p. 9, 1870.

IV. Analyses of Pure Lead. *Proceedings of the Lyceum of Natural History of New York*, p. 8, 1870.

V. Kresol and Phenol and their Homologues. *Am. Chem.*, vol. i. p. 239, 1871.

VI. Notice of a Curious Boiler Deposit. *Am. Chem.*, vol. i. p. 287, 1871.

VII. On the Action of Sulphurous Acid on Metals. *Am. Chem.*, vol. i. p. 296, 1871.

VIII. Notes on the Feldspathic Sandstones (Felsites) of the Palisade Range. *Am. Chem.*, vol. ii. p. 23, 1871.

IX. Contributions to the Mineralogy of Manhattan Island. *Am. Chem.*, vol. iv. p. 443, 1874.

X. Columbia Chalybeate Spring. *Report University of Missouri*, 1874, p. 160.

XI. On the Water Supply of the Town of Columbia. *Report University of Missouri*, 1874, p. 161.

XII. Action of Rain-Water on Lead Pipes. *Report University of Missouri*, 1874, p. 163.

Wm. Ripley Nichols, Professor of Chemistry at the Massachusetts Institute of Technology, Boston, has published:—

On the Chromites of Magnesium. *Am. Journ. Sci.*, xlvi. 16, 1869.

On the Composition of the Acid Oxalates of Potassium, Ammonium, and Sodium. *Proc. Am. Assoc.*, xviii. (1869), 159.

On the Solubility in Water of the Oxalates of Sodium, Potassium, and Ammonium. *Proc. Am. Assoc.*, xviii. (1869), 163.

Report on the Action of Cochituate Water on Lead Pipes. *Mass. State Board of Health*, 2d *Annual Report*, 1871, p. 32.

In connection with Geo. Derby, M.D.:—

Sewerage; Sewage; The Pollution of Streams; The Water Supply of Towns. A Report to the State Board of Health of Massachusetts. *Mass. State Board of Health. 4th Annual Report*, 1873, p. 12.

On the Present Condition of Certain Rivers of Massachusetts, together with considerations touching the water supply of towns. *Mass. State Board of Health, 5th Annual Report*, 1874, p. 61.

J. Blodgett Britton, Philadelphia.—In his capacity of Chemist to the "Iron Masters' Laboratory" 339 Walnut Street, Philadelphia, Mr. Britton has performed a great amount of technical work in the Analysis of Iron Ores, Furnace Products, etc. etc., which need not be given in detail here. But the following papers come properly in as contributions to chemistry.

1870. 1st. "A Method for determining quickly and accurately the Amount of Chromium and Iron in Chrome Iron Ores." *Journal Franklin Institute* for March, 1870.

2d. "Mounted Burettes for Volumetric Analysis." *Journal Franklin Institute* for May, 1870.

3d. "The Determination of Combined Carbon in Iron and Steel by the Colorimetric Process." *Journal Franklin Institute* for May, 1870.

Albert B. Prescott, Professor of Applied Chemistry, University of Michigan, Ann Arbor, Michigan, has contributed as follows to our chemical literature:—

Simple Apparatus for Rapid Vaporization at limited heat under reduced pressure without use of pump. *Chem. News*, xx. 222 (1870).

On Sulphophenic Acid. *Proc. Am. Pharm. As.*, xix. 550 (1871).

And in joint authorship with Prof. Silas H. Douglass, Prof. Prescott has published—

Qualitative Chemical Analysis, a guide in the practical study of chemistry, and in the work of analysis. 8vo. pp. 260. 1872.

Arnold D. Hague, New York.—Mr. Hague, who has long been connected with the United States Geological Exploration of the 40th Parallel, is the author of a paper—

1870. On the Chemistry of the Washoe Process of Amalgamation. This paper forms part of vol. iii. "Mining Industry" of the Reports of the United States Geological Exploration of the 40th Parallel, 4to. 1870.

Samuel P. Sadtler, Professor of General Chemistry in the University of Pennsylvania, Philadelphia, has published the following papers on chemistry:—

On Potassio-cobaltic Nitrites, with analogous and related compounds. *Am. Journ. Sci.*, March, 1870.

On some Iridium Salts. *Inaugural Dissertation*, Göttingen, April, 1871.

Abstract of the same Work. *Am. Journ. Sci.*, Nov. 1871.

Analytical Notices of New Processes. *Am. Journ. Sci.*, March, 1874.

J. M. SILLIMAN, Lafayette College, Easton, Pa.—Prof. Silliman has published—

1870. Examination of the Bessemer Flame with Colored Glasses, and Spectroscopic Examination of the Bessemer Flame. *Am. Journ. Sci.*, l. 297, and *Proc. Am. As.*, xix. 119.

SIDNEY A. NORTON, Columbus, Oh o, Ohio Agricultural and Mechanical College.

1870. "On a Bichloride of Platinum + $5H_2O$." This salt is less deliquescent than the ordinary salt, and is a new form. *Journ. fur Prakt. Chem.*, Bd. 2, S. 469.

1872. A second paper on the same. *Ibid.* Bd. 5. S. 365.

RICHARD H. LEE has published ("Contributions to Chemistry from the Laboratory of the Lawrence Scientific School, No. 16") an important paper, entitled—

1871. "On the Atomic Weights of Cobalt and Nickel." *Am. Journ. Sci.* [3], ii. 44.

THOMAS M. CHATARD has published ("Contributions to Chemistry from the Laboratory of the Lawrence Scientific School, No. 15") a valuable contribution—

1871. "On some New Analytical Methods: § 1. On the Determination of Molybdic Acid as Plumbic Molybdite. § 2. On the Evaporation to Dryness of Gelatinous Precipitates (a former paper of M. Chatard's on this subject is printed in *ibid.* i. 247). § 3. Tests for Nitrous Acid. § 4. On the Determination of Small Quantities of Manganese." *Am. Journ. Sci.* [3], i. 416.

CHARLES E. MUNROE, Professor of Chemistry, etc., U. S. Naval Academy, Annapolis, Md.—Prof. Munroe has published:—

"On the Estimation of Phosphoric Acid." *Am. Journ. Sci.* [2], i. 359. 1871.

"On the Use of a Porous Cone in Filtration." *Ibid.* 336. Also reproduced in Fresenius' *Zeitschrift.*

ELWYN WALLER, School of Mines, Columbia College, New York.—Mr. Waller has published:—

1872. Notes on the Petroleum of St. Domingo. *Am. Chem.*, ii. 220.

1872. Application of Osmose to Purification of Sugars. *Ibid.*, iii. 139.

1872. Coal Tar Colors. *Ibid.*, ii. 9.

Also, in the Report of the New York Board of Health for 1872:—

Report on the Croton Water, for the year 1872.

Report on Baking Powders, etc.

Report on Disinfection and Disinfectants. A paper read before the American Public Health Association, November, 1873.

Carbolic Acid, Tests of its Presence, and a New Method for its Quantitative Estimation. *Sanitarian*, November, 1874.

Mr. Waller, as one of the editors of the *American Chemist*, is a constant contributor, by his abstracts of chemical literature, foreign and domestic.

Edwin J. Houston, Philadelphia, Pennsylvania, has contributed the following original memoirs:—

On the Change of Color produced in Certain Chemical Compounds by Heat. *Journal of the Franklin Institute*, vol. lxii., No. 2, August, 1871.

Color Changes produced in Chemical Compounds by Solution. (Unpublished.) Read before the Optical Section of the Franklin Institute during the winter of 1872.

On the Nature of White Light. *Journal of the Franklin Institute*, 1873.

On the Artificial Production of Cold. *Journal of the Franklin Institute*, 1873.

On a Supposed Allotropic Modification of Phosphorus. *American Phil. Society Proceedings.* Read January, 1874.

Prof. Elihu Thomson, of Philadelphia, was jointly associated in the first and last of the above investigations.

Arthur W. Wright, New Haven.—Dr. Wright, Professor of Chemistry and Molecular Physics at Yale College, is the author of important researches in physics. The following are his chemical contributions:—

1. On a simple Apparatus for the Production of Ozone with Electricity of High Tension. *Am. Journ. Sci.*, iii. vol. iv., July, 1872.

2. On the Action of Ozone upon Vulcanized Caoutchouc. *Ibid.*

3. On the Oxidation of Alcohol and Ether by Ozone. *Ibid.*, vol. vii., March, 1872.

A. EMERSON DOLBEAR, Bethany, West Virginia.—Prof. Dolbear's contributions to chemistry are—

1872. A Method of obtaining Potassium. *American Chemist*, February, 1872.

1874. On the Use of Iron Sulphide as a Disinfectant and Deodorizer. *Scientific American.*

A. E. FOOTE, Professor of Chemistry in the Iowa State Agricultural College, Ames, Iowa, has published as follows:—

1872. Zeonochlorite, a new hydrous silicate from Nupigon Bay, north shore of Lake Superior. *Am. As. Proc.*, 1872; republished in *Am. Chem.*, vol. p.

1873. A Modification of the (Jagn) Vacuum or Filter Pump, that can be used with from three to five feet fall of water, and does not easily get out of repair. *Proc. Am. As.*, 1873, p. 141; also *Am. Journ. Sci.*, 3d ser., vi. 360; and likewise *Am. Chem.* and *Journ. Frank. Inst.*

E. S. DANA, Yale College, New Haven, Conn., has contributed as follows:—

"On the Composition of the Labradorite Rocks from Waterville, N. H." *Am. Journ. Sci.* [3], vol. iii. 48.

Also the following mineralogical and physical papers:—

"On Datolite from Bergen Hill." *Am. Journ. Sci.* [3], vol. iv. p. 16. 1872.

"On Datolite." *Tschermak's Mineralogische Mittheilungun*, i. 1874.

"On a Remarkable Crystal of Andalusite." *Am. Journ. Sci.* [3], vol. iv. p. 473.

"On Atacamite." *Tschermak's Mineralogische Mittheilungen*, i., 1874.

"On the Thermo-electrical Properties of some Minerals." *Am. Journ. Sci.* [3]. vol. viii. p. 255.

"On the Trap Rocks of the Connecticut Valley." *Am. Journ. Sci.* [3], vol. viii. p. 390.

And in company with W. G. MIXTER, of the Sheffield Scientific School—

"On the Specific Heat of Zirconium, Silicon, and Boron." *Ann. Chem. u. Pharm.*, vol. clix. p. 388.

ALBERT R. LEEDS, Professor of Chemistry, Stevens Institute of Technology, Hoboken, New Jersey, has contributed as follows:—

1873. Contributions to Mineralogy with analyses of: I. A Hydrous Unisilicate approaching Pyrosclerite.

II. Talc Pseudomorphous after Pectotile. III. Leucangite from Amity, N. Y. IV. Mineral associated with Corundum and approaching Ripidotile. V. Moonstone from Media, Delaware County, Pa. VI. Antholite from the "Star Rock," Concord, Delaware Co., Pa. VII. Wernerite from Van Arsdale's Quarry, Bucks Co., Pa. *Am. Journ. Sci.* [3], vi. 22.

Spectroscopic Examination of Silicates. *Am. Chem.*, vol. iii. 446.

Blake Crusher for Laboratory Use. *Ibid.* 453.

On the Volumetric Determination of Chlorine with Standard Silver Solution and Potassic Chromate. *Ibid.* 290.

1874. On the Dissociation of Certain Compounds at very low Temperature. *Am. Journ. Sci.* [3], vii. 197.

On the Purification of Mercury. *Am. Chemist*, vol. iv. 309.

Upon Alizarin as a Test. *Ibid.* 333.

Upon the Alteration of Albite and the Genesis of Deweylite. *Ibid.* 164.

The Student's Practical Chemistry. In connection with Prof. H. Morton. 1865.

Chemical Notes, Reviews, and Experiments. *Jour. Franklin Institute*, 1867–1871.

Gasometer for Accurate Measurements. *Jour. Franklin Institute*, 1868.

Chemical Tables according to the Theories of Modern Chemistry. *Jour. Franklin Institute*, 1870, and *Chemical News.*

Analysis of some hitherto Undetermined Minerals. *Jour. Franklin Institute*, 1870.

On the Spectra of Certain Metallic Compounds. *Jour. Franklin Institute*, 1870, and *Quarterly Journal of Science.*

On Aventurine Orthoclase. *Amer. Jour. Sci.*, 1872.

Ira Remsen, Professor of Chemistry, Williams College, Williamstown, Mass.—Prof. Remsen has contributed the following important papers:—

1870. "Uber die Homologen des Naphtalins." *Liebig's Annalen.*

"Investigations on Piperic Acid" (Dissertation for Degree of Ph.D. at the University of Göttingen).

1871. "Ueber eine neue Darstellungsmethode der Paraoxbenzœsäure." *Zeitschrift für Chemie.*

1871. "Ueber die Constitution der Protocatechusäure." *Ibid.*

"Ueber Parasulfobenzœsäure." *Ibid.*

1872. "Weitere Untersuchungen über die Constitution der Piperinsäure." *Liebig's Annalen.*

1873. "Investigation on Parasulphobenzoic Acid." *Am Journ. Sci.* [3], pp. 179–186; *Ibid.*, 274–282, and 354–362. Prof. Remsen has also published a translation. *Am. Journ. Sci.*

"On Isomeric Sulphosalycylic Acids." *Am. Journ. Sci.*

1874. "On the Formation of Paratoluic Acid from Parasulphotoluenic Acid." *Ibid.*

"On Nitroparasulphobenzoic Acid." *Ibid.*

"On the Action of Potassium upon Ethyl Succinate." *Ibid.*

In 1873 he edited Fittig's Wöhler's "Outlines of Organic Chemistry;" with additions. Prof. Remsen also furnishes abstracts and articles of the *Berichte der deutschen Chem. Gesellschaft* for each number of the *American Chemist.*

W. C. May has published ("Chemical Papers from the Massachusetts Institute of Technology, No. 11")—

1873. "On the Determination of Lead as Peroxide." *Ibid.* [3], vi. 255.

H. B. Cornwall, E.M., Professor of Mineralogy and Chemistry in the John C. Green Scientific School, College of New Jersey, Princeton, has contributed papers—

1873. On the Occurrence of Indium discovered in American Blendes. *Am. Chemist,* January.

A Quantitative Analysis of Roxbury Blende. *Am. Chemist,* October.

We are also indebted to Prof. Cornwall for his excellent translation of—

1872. Plattner's Manual of Qualitative and Quantitative Analysis with the Blowpipe. From the last German Edition, etc. N. Y.: D. Van Nostrand. 8vo. pp. 548. And—

1873. A second edition of the above.

F. M. F. Cazin, M.E., Denver, Colorado.—Mr. Cazin has published a paper entitled—

1873. Fluor Spar in its application in the Cupola Furnace, and in the Puddling and Bessemer Process. *Berg. und huetten Marnnsch. Zeit.*, xxxii. No. 15.

Regis Chauvenet and A. A. Blair, St. Louis, Mo., have published, in joint authorship—

Chemical Analyses of the Coals, Iron Ores, and Iron of Missouri. 8vo. pp. 1873, N. Y. Extracted from the Report of the Geological Survey of Missouri. 1873.

William J. Land, Atlanta, Georgia.—Mr. Land has published the following contributions in the *American Chemist*, vol. iii.:—

Determination of Hydrosulphuric Acid in Mineral Waters.

Improved Atmospheric Washing Bottle for the Use of Analytical Chemists.

Improved Apparatus for General Gasmetry (with a drawing).

He has also published in Georgia—

Analysis of the Ash of the Cotton Plant, etc.

Analysis of the Ash of the Cotton Seed.

A. P. S. Stuart, Professor of Chemistry, Illinois Industrial College, Champaign, Illinois, has published as follows:—

1. In the third and fourth *Reports of the Illinois Industrial University*—

On the Organic Matter of Soils.

On the Origin and the Physical and Chemical Properties of the Inorganic Matter of Soils.

2. In the *Prairie Farmer*—

On the Influence of Light in the Growth of Plants.

3. In the *Transactions of the Illinois State Horticultural Society*—

On the Distribution of Nitrous Acid in Plants.

On the Use of a Glazed Wrought-iron Tube for Nitrogen Determinations.

Wm. McMurtrie, Washington, D. C.—In his capacity of Chemist to the Department of Agriculture, Mr. McMurtrie has contributed a number of interesting researches, the results of which are embraced in the Monthly Reports of that Department for 1873–4. These are chiefly analyses of fertilizers, corn, wines, soils, etc., which are important additions to agricultural knowledge.

Charles A. Brinley, Midvale Steel Works, near Philadelphia.—Mr. Brinley's paper, "Notes on a Charcoal Furnace" (*Am. Chem.*, iii. No. 1), contains some analyses of iron and furnace products.

E. S. BREIDENBAUGH has published ("Contributions from the Sheffield Laboratory of Yale College, No. 27") a valuable research with numerous analyses—

1873. "On the Minerals found at the Tilly Foster Iron Mines, New York." *Am. Journ. Sci.* [3], vi. 207. This locality proves to be one of the most interesting chapters in American mineralogy, furnishing the material for Prof. Dana's paper, "On Serpentine Pseudomorphs and other Kinds" (Nov. 1874), and a wonderful development of new crystalline forms of Chendrodite now under examination by Mr. Edward S. Dana.

EDWARD W. MORLEY, Professor of Chemistry, Western Reserve College, Hudson, Ohio.—Professor Morley has described—

"An Apparatus for Rapid Filtration." *Am. Jour. Sci.* [3], vi. 214. 1873.

C. W. HINMAN, B.S., Boston, Mass.—Mr. Hinman has just published Description of a new Apparatus for Gas Analysis. *Sill. Journ.* [3], viii. 182. Sept., 1874.

---

HENRY WURTZ.—A considerable number of the contributions of this chemist we find have been overlooked in the former list (see pp. 109, 110). To some of these he has called our attention, as follows:—

1868. On Some New Chemical Relations of Metallic Aluminum. *Am. Association at Chicago, in* 1868, p. 196.

1869. Studies in Chemical Geogony. Three subjects: 1. On the Prozoic Atmosphere, and the Ocean of the Zoic Dawn. 2. Zoic History, from a Chemical View-Point. 3. Chemical Revelation of a Final Zoic Catastrophe. *Am. Association at Salem*, 1869, pp. 217, 223, 225.

1872. Lithology of the Rocks of the Palisade Range. *Am. Chemist*, Jan. 1872, p. 258.

1872. Some Chemi-Genetic Views regarding the Past and the Future. *Am. Chemist*, April, 1872, p. 385.

1873. Chemical and Sanitary Report upon the Passaic River. *Am. Chemist*, Sept. 1873, p. 99, and Oct. 1873, p. 133.

1874. Second Chemical and Sanitary Report upon the Water Supply of the Cities of Newark and Jersey City. *Am. Chemist*, March, 1874, p. 323.

1874. Subaerial Oxygenation of Waters. *Proceedings of N. Y. Lyceum of Natural History*, Feb. 1874.

1874. Discussion of the above Subject with Dr. H. Endemann. *Am. Chemist*, July, 1874, pp. 9, 10.

---

## ERRATA.

On p. 9, 18th line from top, *for* D. Wolcott Gibbs, *read* O. Wolcott Gibbs.

On p. 21, 5th line from bottom, *for* Vaquelin, *read* Vauquelin.

On p. 29, 22d line from top, *for* Sybert, *read* Seybert.

On p. 45, 2d line from bottom, *for* Brougniart, *read* Brogniart.

On p. 46, 6th line from top, for Brougniart, *read* Brogniart.

On p. 101, 24th line from bottom, *for* Gysolite, *read* Gyrolite.

On p. 102, 17th line from bottom, for New Precipitation, *read* Non-precipitation.

On p. 118, in each of the first five lines, the references li., lii., lviii., lix. should be xli., xlii., xlviii, xlix. There is no volume beyond l. The third series commences again vol. i., etc.

On p. 135, 1st, 2d, 6th, 8th, 19th and 22d line from top, *for* Mauross, *read* Manross.

On p. 131, 15th line from bottom, *for* Retchie, *read* Ritchie.

On p. 151, 17th line from top *for* Interpretation, *read* Interpenetration.

On p. 158, 8th line from top, *for* Mercury, *read* Morning.

On p. 158, 17th line from top, *for* Enorgite, *read* Enargite.

On p. 130, 14th line from bottom, *for* Natural Philosophy *read* Physical Science.

On p. 131, 8th line from top, *for* chemicals, *read* chimneys.

On p. 131, 22d line from top, in place of paragraph 7, *read* Analyses of the Atlanta Mineral Spring published and circulated throughout the State. Also, Analysis of the Mineral Springs of Meriwether County, viz.: the warm springs—carbonated chalybeate waters; and the cold spring—acidulo-carbonated chalybeate waters. Analyses of the two latter were published by Mr. George White, formerly of Savannah, Ga., in his volume entitled "Statistics of the State of Georgia."

# INDEX.

CPSIA information can be obtained
at www.ICGtesting.com
Printed in the USA
LVHW030141210323
742063LV00002B/711

9 783382 502065